CROOKS

works by Bill Reed
novels:
Dogod
The Pipwink Papers\
Me, the Old Man
Stigmata
Ihe
Crooks
Tusk
Throw her back
Are You Human?
Awash
Tasker Tusker Tasker
1001 Lankan Nights book 1
1001 Lankan Nights book 2

Nonfiction: Water Workout

professionally-staged/ published plays:
Burke's Company*
Truganinni*
The Pecking Order
Mr Siggie Morrison with his Comb and Paper*
Jack Charles is Up and Fighting
Just Out of Your Ground
You Want It, Don't You, Billy?*
I Don't Know What to Do with You*.
Paddlesteamer*
Cass Butcher Bunting*
Bullsh
More Bullsh
Talking to a Mirror*
Auntie and the Girl*
*Available in print and ebook formats

award-winning short stories (see title 'Passing Strange'):
Messman on the C.E. Altar
The 200-year Old Feet
The Case Inside
Blind Freddie Among the Pickle Jars
The Old Ex-serviceman
Mahood on the Thin Beach
The Shades of You my Dandenong

CROOKS

a novel by
BILL REED

First published by Hyland House Publishing Pty Limited, Melbourne, 1984, with the kind assistance of The Australia Council for the Arts.

This new edition is published independently by Reed Independent, Dandenong, Australia, in 2015

Printed by CreateSpace, an Amazon.com company

Available from Amazon.com, CreateSpace.com, and most international retail outlets. Ebook formats are available from all major online ebook retailers.
paperback: ISBN13-9780994280541
ebook: ISBN13-9780994280558

Cover: 'The Cloud Man', painting on oil on canvas by Charles Blackman (courtesy of Nadine Amadio)

National Library of Australia Cataloguing-in-Publication entry
Creator: Reed, Bill, 1939-author.
Title: Crooks/ Bill Reed.
ISBN: 9780994280541 (paperback)
Subjects: Australian fiction, crime, family illusions/disillusions.
Dewey Number: A823.3

National Library of Australia Cataloguing-in-Publication entry
Creator: Reed, Bill, 1939-author.
Title: Crooks/ Bill Reed.
ISBN: 9780994280558 (ebook)
Subjects: : Australian fiction, crime, family illusions/disillusions
Dewey Number: A823.3

To my dear Evangeline, who hadn't yet showed up, otherwise this would have come out much better.

PART 1

1

Prologue

If I'm going to write about my father, I'm not going to beat about the Timorese bush, no sir.

I can always look back with him on that day on Timor when he and his small band of seven commandos watched the 45th Division of Japan landing -- 15,000 of them -- and the most experienced of all the Jap Divisions. He turned to his men and all he said was:

'Bugger them. Let's get on with the job'.

That was my father. Captain Harry Stein, VC. That is my father. A VC, even more. He is as mute and as still and as alive as a Hindu statue in his wheelchair now, but that day and that statement will always stay typical of him. My father. That demiurge, yes!, of fittingness in whatever he did or would get on to do. Survived Timor, Changi Gaol, the Burma-Thailand railway and all to go on to be Commissioner of Police here.

That time in Timor they were all volunteers and specially trained to fight behind the lines in jungles that only a few of them had experienced before. There were only a few hundred of them, known as the Australian 2/2nd Independent Company. They had not surrendered to the enemy on the day of 23 February 1942, like the rest of the main force of Australians, Dutchmen and a few Portuguese. No, they stayed in the mountains that ran as a central spine alone the island and they set about establishing secret depots of food and ammunition to give them the means of mobility and surprise for their ambushers. That's what they had been trained for and, now with the surrender of the island to the Japanese, they waged guerilla warfare against overwhelming odds. My father had said:

1

'Bugger them. Let's get on with the job'.

They knew that the next Japanese step was to invade Australia itself. But even though it had come to that, my father had said that, and in the next nine months a few hundred of them had killed hundreds of crack Japanese regulars. The official Japanese records stated the number as 'over a thousand', but unofficially the head count was well over two thousand. Twenty-five /Australians were killed. My father was not one of them.

They ambushed; they sniped; often my father would go out alone with his 'Criado' Liyi -- his personal Timorese/Chinese guide; a type of Tonto -- literally to hunt down Japanese. Liyi was later shot by the Australians; they said he had been spying for the Japanese. Though my father was absent when Liyi was tried for his betrayal by something very much akin to a kangaroo court, he never forgave himself. Always mourned the futility of the death. Such was my father.

There was the time, too, when my father rode a bicycle into a Japanese camp firing an Owen gun as he went. Unharmed he went pedalling out of the camp. They found eleven Japanese dead in their huts there. He had pedalled towards a VC on their backs.

The Japs always believed there were more of then that there really were. The commandos used to fire at them from all directions to give this impression. They had to eat banana skins, roots, leaves, insects and, if they were lucky, bully beef rinsed down with water. My father had a pet monkey which used to sleep at the bottom of his sleeping bag. They used to delouse each other.

I once asked my father what was the longest range at which he had shot someone and he replied that he was alongside one of his men who had shot a Jap with his sights set on 1200 yards. The man had been standing on top of a cliff at sunset, stupidly silhouetted against the sky. He was seen to fall over the cliff. But he said the longest and the shortest, both, was the time, later, that he copped a sniper's bullet. The bullet lodged in his left lung. That was then he got captured. It was only last year, forty years after the event, that he coughed that bullet up.

I am here to tell you that really happened. That was my father. A VC, a Commissioner of Police (honourably retired), a survivor for three years of the worst of POW treatment, a Rhodes Scholar, a cougher-up of a forty-year-old Jap bullet.

He was born with a single mindedness that always drove him to the achievement of good works. My father has been an intensely moral man. Sometimes that fact has rained down hard on me. It has been hard to follow a man like my father. The ultimate achiever. Rhodes Scholar. More than that, he actually left Cambridge University to come home and be a guerilla in probably the worst arena of that war in the world. Of course, he returned to Cambridge after the war to do an unnecessary Masters degree of course, then Commissioner of Police in record time, of course. I don't know why I say 'of course' there. I said it three times. I don't know why I want to say that, of course, my father survived the war against all odds in the worst war arena in the world.

Of course he did. What else. He was my father. He is my father.

The only blemish on his life was that he once had an unhappy marriage. That was my mother.

My father and what was left of his fellow commandos eventually were able to steal parts of a radio from the Japs and succeeded in getting a very weak signal through to Darwin. Command in Australia had listed them as killed in action, so the message was initially thought of as a hoax. But names, serial numbers and then more detailed identifications convinced the Services Reconnaissance Department that my father had incredibly stayed alive against all odds and the rest of them were picked up by a submarine a month later.

This is the story I want to tell. It speaks of my father. It is what my father is. Through it, I am writing about my father. How he is, has

3

been. Is now, mute and silent as a Hindu statue; still, as though he had finally come to a deserved full stop, and is left as a sternish and monumental reminder to me that I am unworthy to tie his shoelaces, kiss his feet, lick between his toes, get callouses on my knees before him...'

This is as far as Frank Stein ever gets with writing a book about his father which he so badly wants to lay at the feet of that old man, that fix'd sentinel, as a small measure of acknowledging that he did not measure up. He has had to write it: He cannot say it, because he does not know how much his father can hear him. Besides, he could not have said it out loud anyway. It has had to be written down. It is the only way, and he knows it. The trouble is that Frank Stein has taken eighteen months to write those few hundred words. And he a journalist turned publisher of a book himself...

But the real problem has been that after the words '... get callouses on my knees before him' he has never been able to overcome an absolute compulsion to insert a new paragraph right there that would have run:

'My name is Frank E.R. Stein. My father foisted that name on me at birth as a poor phonetic riddle and large joke. He had called it his "monstrous joke" for a poor joke of a baby son who was some error, a grotesque, a creature spawned not by love's brightest cuddle of all, but by whipping it out and wiping it. That is me. Frankerrstein, sometimes Frank N. Stein. Take your laughing pick.'

And no matter how often he tries to approach it, or however much he has tried to rephrase it, that paragraph clogs the draining of any further literary release about the life of his father.

Frank Stein falls back into the hole of the never-ending beginning.

Frank Stein will come to decide to kill his father.

Stein, Frank, sits at the table he has called a desk in the house (his father's) and has been working away at his biography of his father.

In the hour he has been hard at the task, he has not added one word to the original Prologue. He has re-punctuated the first three-and-a-half paragraphs, but that is nothing unusual, for he has done as much at least forty times in the eighteen months he has been trying to finish the Prologue. And those have been the explosively creative times which in summary have driven him to the necessity of having to retype the whole of the first page of the intended four hundred or so a number of times uncounted.

Now a drowsiness flutters upon him as soon as it would take a fine gossamer net to drop upon him from the ceiling. His arms feel as heavy and as unable to move to the keys of his typewriter as if they can only move by the whims or whirly wishes of an absent controller of pulleys connected to the contraptions that were otherwise his arms by invisible piano (he dozily muses) wires.

In truth Frank Stein is nodding off under the exertion of having thought that he might finally get re-started with an opening viz: 'Chapter 1: My father was...' Its ring of possibility sent him reeling to the couch behind him, where he lies somnolent as a stranded fish with the enormity of the tasks of tide ahead. He lies in a side-shoot of a room of the Victorian mansion ('fourteen rooms full of piss') that his father has acquired for a song and for a shockingly sumptuous renovation some thirty years before.

Frank Stein has come to bunk, back home. Father's home. Sent skidding from his own home-come-flophouse by his own suddenly concupiscent wife whom he can still often remember, and often not, is called Lorna through the use of a worthy personal relevance of the mnemone of sex raising its ugly head. Not that that matters very much, and certainly less so than the equally sudden expressions of contempt quaffingly coined, albeit after many years on the smoulder, of his twin prodigal son and daughter. Look alike look alike. He bears them through the dozy hum in his ears, like.

'Dads, it may be simply a case of teaching laughter and grief like the classical crab, but our heads together have come to the inexorable conclusion that thou art too fucking dumb for us kids.' Erika, daughter, blood curls to match what Stein wishfully fancies as shelling up ashen wrinkles. And followed upon by her frater Jude:

'Your lacking of the old Intelligence Quotient, Dads. A mite too embarrassingly uggers, too. Boo hoo, but...'

'...we're sure you appreciate honesty, even though you have never practised it on us. In consequence of these two unfortunate realities, we have...' Erika.

'...petitioned Mother, who, if it's any consolation to you, would pretty well fail dismally on both counts as well if she mattered,' Jude.

'... petitioned Mother to evict you, not evince you.'

Oh, very witty, very toothsome, Erika, you bucktoothed of the two of you dopeforms.

'Chapter 1: My father was...' Behind the swim of that phrase as it could have been said to be floundering in his mind, Frank Stein recognises he has been fantasising again. Cracking up. As though it matters. But it ought to, especially on this day, a day of inspiration, of a family achievement that must, surely, make his father as proud of him, his genetic son and the elder to boot (ain't that been the living truth? Metaphors in them there metaphoric hobnails, crackings in them there fatherly faulty-Jewish brogues) as his father has always been augustly proud of Costas, that adoptee and younger by all that's holy. That Costas that I love like a brother. All these years together, moving our bodies towards the boxes of two-by-fours together... this day finally come together hapfully by pursuit on the ole rosary bead trail of sucker existence. Costas and

Heinz-Steiny, that's me. 'Chapter 1: My father was....' This is the day of our book. Launching. Lynching? Cracking up. Bottles of champagne. Bitters of the ovarian campaign trail. The one human being I really love. Costas. That eyetite fart of a half-brother of mine. Our book.

Not precisely, though, *their* book. Stein has put up the twenty-five thousand dollars for the book that his half and worthier brother has written and published himself. Not that that brushes the flaps of Stein's mind, daydreaming: Let's hear it for Frank Err Stein, hotshot publishing financier and his eyetite greaseball adoptee half-brother lovely-effer Costas, the author and publisher with their acts together finally. Bros. Costas'n'me. Put that in your pipe, Father. I came through out of all the living up to nothing and paid for the publishing of some one thing today of our family that must make your old freckled concavitied stroke-bestricken chest puff up in the jingle-jangle metaphorical sense, cause I made Costas's book happen and it's about big-time crime in this town and its low-time gamble, make that gambol, of money-moolah and it's called *Australian Crime Bosses*, but the point is I paid for it and my brother didst do the writ of it and its launching was today upon which I didn't really attend because of being a bit worse for wear, I admit, but I know all the media did. Hopefully, since I was paying. Coverage, Father! Coverage. Said the vicar's daughter to a reticent sinner. Coverage is what we would have got. Sell two thousand of the ten and I'm home and hosed. Coverage, Father dear, because your adopted son and my step-brother is the best crime reporter in this sin-baked country and you know it and I know it and *they* know it now and I suspect through that quiet demeanour and that wife and kid of his that damn beautiful grafted sibling of mine knows it even himself. On this day.

Father.

So I really should be able to restart my own book about magnificent you what I started eighteen months ago, ought to be able to, nearly did, quite well might. 'Chapter 1: My Father was...' Got that spurt on eighteen months ago, no reason why not now too. 'My Father was…' I am Frankerrstein. Among the creatures of ugh.

Stein jolts awake to find his own finger in his own ear, and finding that immensely annoying tries to get up from the couch to start work again and also to remove the self same finger from the self same ear. And does not somehow succeed in either. Before the task, torpor has mounted him, again. His body he suddenly imagines gargantuan fat continues to lie sedentarily out before him. His marriage continued to lie in ruins about him. He continues to lie in the house of his father, finally the only retreat despite years off and running by himself. His father would continue to be sitting dry-shelled in his wheelchair by the window in the front room of the building called house or home or refuge or retreat or seat, depending, solidly muffed by a stroke and ruggled by that blanket across the knees and looking for all the world sightlessly senatorial upon everything that passes by, beyond there, the front manorial fence.

'Chapter 1: My father was…'

Nothing ever kindles or kindly changes. Frank Stein, fly watching. He hears the water hiccough in the house's old pipes and tries to clear his own throat. It comes out as a fart. Very satisfying. Must be the literary assertion. Same as whenever I had to sit down and write sports copy for a bastard of a paper. My literary talents have always been ventose when it comes to laying down the lore. The daily sporting columns I have writ have always been sent to bed upon the gusty breezes of farts of unbearable foul play, sphincter speaking. Not like Costas, out of the loins of father's once-friend and childhood oppo, one Mario Flocco (the name fluffed itself into Stein's mind and he even still amazes on its actuality). Step-brother Costas. Seriously Italianate, with much to make for in the world and a quiet disposition to go about it as quiet superbly as he does it quite self-effacingly. Costas just seems to know it all.

Yep and yeah, my brother Costas just seems to know it all. Maybe he's stupid and courageous and maybe has the hubrises and the egotistics and the particles of self-destroying martyrdom and maybe is dumb not to think of his wife and rottenly autistic kid vulnerable as all get out, but he still does care. Emotes terms still of A Clean-up and social deep-rooted corruption and crime commissions like they still had something other than catch-as-catch-can going for them.

He still believes. Beyond the bullshit of loving to be centre stage, my brother is finally good, and therefore maybe finally intolerable.

Here's Flash Gurton. Stein now remembers floatingly how, at the launching of the book that day, Flash Gurton buttonholes him as Stein scrambles for the door as much as if oxygen was elsewhere. The black sportswriter swims into his path, swaying on his heels to a drunken ringcraft that he knew how to make newsworthy without ever being very much sober. A longstanding relationship, much of it horizontally pissed, and very passing. He was once a flyweight that now-tipped the scales middleweight, aptly anatomical, and he gave a playful straight left at Stein's shirtfront beneath a grin that was as passably a Moorish leer as it was a genuine Australian Aboriginal in-smirk. One trouble is that he still has his glass of beer still clutched in that hand. But Frank Err Stein the munificent. He merely wipes down the front of his beer-swilled shirt with the back of a hand that would have preferred going for the throat and dispenses a host's dutiful gleety greeting.

'Ugh and how?'

'Remember the big game last Saturday, ole whitey you?' Again the left hand goes out, but this time it is a mere slurp upon the Stein personage. If a toothy grin could kill drunken bums... 'Old son,' Stein catching hold of the wrist as though they were going through a few preliminary rounds to a Strauss waltz, 'course I remember'.

'You even wrote up the fucking losers fucking won.'

'Could have happened to anybody. Typographical error.'

'Not when you leave ten minutes before the fucking end.'

'Anybody can make a mistake. Watch must have been fast.'

'Stein, you old Jew bastard you, you're a disgrace to the profession.'

'What profession?'

'The halfcut members of the Guild of the Great Sportswriter in the Sky, that's what fucking profession.'

Flash Gurton steps back and onto the instep of a lady journalist who threatens to destroy whatever looks he has left even as she moves him back to upset the last of the beer in his glass upon the two earlier layers (where it meets the shirtfront) upon Frank Stein and attends upon that a burp of Polynesian proportions with undesirable garlic Aboriginal undertones.

The thought occurs to Stein that if this is being a publishing financier it is an affront fronted up. He goes to push past black fat stuff but the stuff of black history stands his ground before him:

'Want land rights, whitey.'

'Have another glug.'

'They're going to have your guts for a Woomera thrower. You reckon the mob's going to let that whitey do-goodie brother of yours get away with putting that crapuloso down in print and you paying for it? I wouldn't give your chances a banjo's bum, or whatever I mean. What do I mean? You know what I mean, mug.'

'Don't get punchy, Flash.'

Stein managed to force himself through the gap with a desperate lunge, spurred by hearing his brother call his name from the back of the convention room. It mingled with Gurton's grunt in his ear of, 'You're gonna be out on your feet, whitey. Judges've got you trailing.' Nor does he even hesitate on his flight to freedom to tell the other sportswriter to go boot a dungbeetle's ball, when this is added by Flash in flash-harry style:

'Hey, can you throw an old mate a free copy, Steiny?'

I am Frank Err Stein. Thirty-three years as a wanderer with the natives, it being my fate to inhabit dwellings of a very different description, having for their roofs only the wide spread of heaven. It would have been well had I continued in the line of rectitude, but my imperfect education, and early feeling of discontent returning upon me, I unfortunately became associated with several men of bad character, which very soon led me into scenes of irregularity and riotous dissipation.

And Stein now returns mentally to the room of his father, to the front room of the family seat he had escaped to from: out of the masticating jaws of a monster called marriage, of the beast with two backs -- one of them fortuitously not his but belonging to A. N. Other -- of the living daylights of being a father in his own twin rot. Where he sits across from his own father and stares at the profile of that taxidermied pelt that used to be recognisable as ibis poppa bold and big and knockabout. No more. My Aged P. 'Chapter 1: My father was...' That's how I can start it. If I get to start it.

Needless to say, there has not been a Costas-for squeal of delight when Stein has entered upon his father. There has not been even an Aged P's grunt. There has been the shifting of the old man's eyes by way of a mere summary of presence, which makes it even worse for Stein because he knows his father knows he's there. The old man sits immobile, a throbbing culture beneath a sculptured blanket and a picture of a wheelchair. Continues to look out over the landscape of front lawn to the wall, the earthworks beyond. And there's Stein, having wanted to burst in and yell that he has done it, because this day I come to tell you I have paid for the publishing of a book for the People, even if I, had to cadge the coin from a bank manager who had piles. On his arse. Stand up the People. Meet on the comers, buy lots of books called Australian Crime Bosses and make me a fucking fortune. Stein studies the grey wisps of hair that made

11

a strewn patch around the old man's ear. Pink yet grey. Callowed. Cold when it was warm outside. In frieze in the shadows of a living sun. In freeze about the shallows of the living son. And he wonders momentarily about what the, that, ear could hear now and what the, that, eye could see now, and he knows the answer was most probably zilch and that the image his father had of him was almost certainly locked away in there and not to be changed, an image immutable, exposed, developed and fixed. And, like an embarrassing photograph that cannot be laid hands upon to change or turf out, fading surely but far too slowly.

So Stein sighs an average sigh and rings no bell of sympathy in the world with the self-pity contained in it. Does Frank Err Stein. I have not even said out aloud about the book. I was going to bullock my way in and shout it into the old cove's pinky if need be that I've laid the ghost that I am a useless and monstrous-joke member of this family. And, if he is real to himself, he would admit this was why he had fair raced back and away from the launching. But instead he is tippytoeing out of his own father's room now, blunted by the sound of salience. Dad done-down again.

I am a deaf, blind and dumb monstrous joke in my father's world. The fortress. 'My father was Police Commissioner. If I say he was a boss all his life and an important man...' No; right, but wrong to start with. Sometimes, often, their voices inside would be lowered and the boy Stein would strain against the door to hear. But only the whispers and he did not know why the tears came and he did not know that why the whispers made him so uncomfortable was that he really thought they were whispering against him and also he did not realise, know or even guess that sometimes the whispers were because his father inside was about to mount that dry crust of a nanny, that motherless substitute for a nomination of a human being reputed to have once been part and vital to my youthful existence. Young Stein would only know that he would hear his father bellow and that dry crust of a woman would somehow crackle, alarmingly, incongruously, hatefully, so that he didn't know why he hated her then and hated the whispers. But did that at those times the chairs could be heard springing. As unceremonial as was his father's bellow so was the short time in which the woman would come out, close the door, walk past little wide-eyed Stein and would not speak to him for two days, often more. Silent and empty house.

Frank Stein turns and leaves. But has only taken a few steps down the hallway when he hears something shift in the parlour of the father. He stops. What passes? Incredibly, incredulously, he hears the wheels of the wheelchair squelch slightly across the floor in there. Such awe of his father that he might be moving towards me. Some last mad dash of destruction against me. A final curse in my face and the unspeakable throes. Deuteronomy and fiery horsemen. A plague on the runt of the house. But nothing comes more. But he cannot move more. I am Frankerrstein, the monstrous joke, and his cry out for the male nurse Cowcher now suddenly no verbal joke:

'*Cowcher!*'

Reflective of his silent master's will, as it seems sounding egg-shellwise to Stein, Cowcher comes running so promptly past him that, if Stein could ever be foolish to even imagine that Cowcher has not been in waiting lurk somewhere around close during his possibly-upsetting visit to his father, then the personification of another think coming just sprinted by him. Not by way of beg your pudding either. Cowcher, familiar to the inner sanctum.

Cowcher. Old Cowcher, not so old at the age of the mid-fifties with his sad and almond eyes and his tight mouth and his silver mop atop heightful hunched protective shoulders, fitted the bill of both at all times observable. Tendrils of service. Had come over from the Service of constabularies when the old man had retired early, first as assistant and now a true-made nurse.

Frank Stein could remember once upon a time that the nanny had not lasted long after Cowcher had come.

Now, having given Cowcher at least two minutes' start he moves back over the eggshells beneath his feet to the doorway of the parlour. From in there, there are two people surprisingly looking his way, naturally, but not naturally, at him. He expects Cowcher to be, as he leans expectedly cluckishly across the old man putting the finishing touches to the immaculate restoration of the blanket across the knees and baldly throwing a 'What have you done with him?' look the way of the door to the Stein presence. He does not however expect that Stein senior to have his vibrating head turned to the door as well and looking with wide-eyed urgency at Stein junior that there could almost be an X-marks-the-spot laser-beaming right in the middle of his -- junior's -- forehead. There is spittle running down his chin and grey suds of froth at the lower corner of his mouth and he is actually making sounds in Stein junior's direction.

'What did he say?'

'He said,' Cowcher accusingly at the son with a blunt despise, 'he said, "Criado!"'

That is the time that Frank Stein decides to kill his father.

2.

'Chapter 1: My father was …

But Stein has bumbled his way back to his room and past the table on which his stricken manuscript lay. Back to the bloozy couch. That he is to kill his father. 'Criado'. He tries to think why that one word from his father's reservoir of a mouth has brought him to the realisation that he is to kill his father.

But all he can think of is the book of today and his half-baked manuscript of all those unstarting yesterdays and how he must make a killing. Out of killing his father. To make a killing; the thing is not to kill Father, but assassinate an ex-VC, an ex-Rhodes Scholar, an ex-Commissioner of Police:

'Chapter 1: I assassinated the ideal farm that was my father was...'

A million bucks from the sells-out of at least five printings stashed away for when they release you out on parole, psychiatrically adjusted. The trouble is it takes at least a year to write the book and get it published after I've done the dirty deed, and who'll care by then anyway. No million bucks, only the pay-out of Life in the slammer. Fug. I am Frank Err Stein, the monstrous joke. Joker. Yes.

Frank Stein sees what the final and monstrous joke must be. He must assassinate his father but write about his father before he assassinates his father so is a hot cookie worth a sensational million bucks timed around the time he assassinates his father. Laugh that one off, Pops. He mulls over that with growing excitement. It is not an excitement of the final ineluctability of killing his father but a thrilling surge that his manuscript can (could only have) go (gone) on in that way.

Stein flings himself at the table to begin the work properly at least. He writes:

'Chapter 1: My father was assassinated by myself one day after I had finished this book about having assassinated my father. Don't think of the unleaven nature of it; think of the bread in it...'

He stops, know truly that he has started and will start again soon. No sweat. 'Criado', Cowcher has said that his father had said, Criado Liyi. It mounts an instant fury with Frank Stein almost obscenely. He remembers he has written about Criado Liyi already in the Prologue. He who was like his father's local guide, interpreter, spy, fellow guerilla in Timor. His Tonto, yes. Hatred, too, for the Japs slanting from his eyes, hard and dark. Who got executed for alleged treason against the Allies, but his father absent at the time and not able, so he has so recently in years and roundly remorsefully stated in public, to stop that Australian firing squad from committing a terrible injustice upon Criado Liyi. Five years ago, his father had tried to have a court of inquiry re-open the case of that little Chinese Timorese having his heart burst open with .303s. He had stood up at the press conference of his retirement and stunned the news gatherers by declaring he had just coughed up the bullet that he had got in an ambush in Timor and wanted to redress, now that it seemed the time to do so a miscarriage of military justice which had been on his conscience for forty years. While he had lain unconscious, his Criado had been accused of betrayal to the enemy by his Sergeant who had escaped the ambush but who had been killed four years after the war in a gangland kidnapping in Sydney. That sergeant had been Mario Flocco and those of the news hounds in the longer-toothed know remembered the Flocco case. Crime Head Victim of Gang War: Throat Cut in Rubbish Tip. He now believed, my father said, that the trial of Criado Liyi should have been delayed until he himself could give evidence, but being captured you know, being captured... Terrible things were done, best left at the time unfurled. Unfurled, flag, duty to the standard; my father had a politician's knack of the apt metaphor, however inapt. There had been interviews on many branches of the media; my father in the public eye. The bullet he had mounted. It is still there on that fusty mantlepiece like an ossified gob of a righteous coughing-up. There were brief spasms of demands for a re-opening of the Liyi slaying, until, a week later, Stein senior concurred with the plaint of a harassed Department of Defense Press Officer that the family of the said Criado Liyi could never be traced and all the other witnesses, save my father, dead. Nothing lost, nothing gained, except for one thing: my adopted brother Costas went on a bash that lasted for three weeks before Cowcher tracked him down. It was the first he had heard of being born with the surname Flocco, of being adopted by the Stein senior, not from a divine fingering in the confines of the orphanage but because his real father had served with his foster father... and, adding to this, of being the son of Mario Flocco, a Mob man famed among other things for cutting the little fingers off his enemies with a bolt cutter.

Poor Costas. My father had told him all with a gentle shrug. I am Frank Err Stein, the monstrous joke and I never had a gentle shrug like that and Costas, kid-gloved, had never had a knee in the cods like that. A verbal crunch to the konkers. Frank Stein remembers himself sympathetically wincing for the hardness that was his father. Is. 'Chapter 1: My father was assassinated by myself one day after I had finished this book about having assassinated my father...' Alas poor Costas, I nubbed him, Horatio. Say this for him. He came back even holier than thou after his binge and his clean-air wife had scrubbed the booze out of him. With their autistic, nephew-by-adoption, godson-in-a-fit-of-awful-sentiment brat screaming around them. Local Mr Big's Boy Makes Good. Crusader of the Press. Author of *Australian Crime Bosses*. .

There had been the three of them. The Stein senior, Captain, already nominated for the Victoria Cross for riding into a pigshit village on a bicycle and bren gunning the Japanese living daylights out of it. The Criado Liyi, bandy and dirty and only twenty and half Chow and half Timorese and hating the stench of his two eeeee-smelling round-eyed companions but not half as much as he hated those urine-swilling Nipponese and leading the way as usual. And trailing the two of them was Mario Flocco, said to have been even then weasel-sharp on a lookout for a make. The three were bruised and doggo tired. There had been too many months living in the mud, hunting and being hunted. Sliding along the natives' trails, sure that one day the betrayal would come or tiredness make them walk right between the eyes of the waiting gun sight.

Frank Stein eagerly pulled the typewriter towards himself. He could start again, having restarted. 'Chapter 1: My father will be assassinated by myself one day after He writes without the jerks:

'Along the native half-trail, my father, his Criado Liyi and Sergeant Flocco, ankle deep in mud. My father and Flocco were struggling with a makeshift bamboo and matting stretcher on which was Lieutenant J. F. Lang, now unconscious and not even moaning, his leg gone gangrenous from what had only been a bullet graze a week before. Even when one of them stumbled and lost control of the stretcher, Lang merely rolled like a stuffed toy and moaned as lowly as a cow in labour. They knew he was dying, but that was no longer the thing. In the drizzle and the sludge, within the jaggings of the torturous mountain path, in their sodden clothes heavy and gravitous on their weakened bodies, it did not matter whether Lang was dead or dying or with a chance. They had started out four hours ago for the next established post, and they now had to get their comrade to that next post. For the six months that they had been hitting at the Japanese using guerilla tactics and living off the land, this single-mindedness of original purpose had become engrained in them. It replaced duty. It almost replaced the war. It was how they had survived thus far; it was therefore the only automatic thing to do.

They did not try to beat the jungle back as they went. Criado Liyi led them as silently as he could. When they stumbled he was smartly there to help right poor Lang, right the stretcher while they slipped and slid for renewed purchase, right their bren gun back onto the stretcher with the dying man. In all those months with them, Liyi had hardly slipped once. He had never once showed hunger or illness of discomfort from the huge ulcers on his feet. Had remained silently apart whenever they camped. Would often slip off into the jungle to recce if he heard any unusual sound at night. If the Japs were close, he would unceremoniously hurry back into camp and start gathering up their things. They understood and just as silently followed him. If he found nothing out there he would slip

18

back into his spot; just as often as not they wouldn't have known he had left. He accepted food without thanks or a smile. My father believed they could have eaten in front of him when he was half-starved and he wouldn't have complained, nor let any disappointment show. Liyi endured the mud, the heat, the sores, the leeches, the fleas, the thirsts, the fear of all, and the every days without so much as a grimace and, even that, quickly displayed only on the askance. My father came to know what inscrutability was. It was not a fatal acceptance, but a mute confidence of being able to out-endure. Nor passive. Criado Liyi fought the Japanese with a near mania. As tiny as an orangotan, he rushed his enemies like one and one enraged. My father came to realise that it was not so much a charge as the only way to get within hand-to-hand combat with those he could only understand killing personally. The only way. Gutturally Chinese as the Nips were all screams. And on those days and nights when they were to rest, Liyi would see them safely settled, would draw a crude map in the soil or mud and handsign their position to my father, then slip away. He would be back well before they were to Start again. They did not worry, and certainly never about betrayal. They knew he had slipped back to his village and his family and would be \working in the fields while they rested exhaustedly and remembered times when they weren't brutish.

My father has one photograph of his Criado Liyi. It had gone stiff as a relic even when I first saw it. Age and the wet and the mildew had made it erupt upon its surface and had jaundiced its very image as much as if its image itself was subject to the same ageing processes as he and my father. Standing outside my father's tent in better, near-bad days. I can hardly read my father's caption on the board-stiff back as I remember it now; the ink lines faded now to rusty water markings. 6 March 1942. My Criado Liyi and self outside tent in camp near Sukabumi. Over-run two days later by the Nips. Five of the platoon killed, 2 wounded. The top of his shaven head only reaching to about my father's left shoulder. The only thing he was wearing was a pair of oversized Army shorts that were half as wide around the waist again as his waist would have measured, so that the line of its fly cut across his pelvis like a grotesque appendix scar. Liyi. Even then solemn for the modern moment and as thin as a

19

monkey god should forever be. There was no expression to be seen, even though the image of my father's amused smile has not yet faded. So bandy were Liyi's legs that their lines with the stiffness of his skinny little upright torso tended to form the shape of an inverted goblet. It was that that my father's mates dubbed him. Goblet. Little gob, big gorby. My father never called him this, nor would have it mentioned in his presence. It didn't matter. Most assumed that Criado Liyi possessed not a word of English. They were wrong, but it didn't matter. And my father there. Stripped too but for shorts, pistol at side with lanyard, boots without socks. He must have been called outside for the photograph to have been without socks, but he could not remember, except to look at me oddly when I ask it of him. He was forty, a month away from exploiting his way to a Victoria Cross and still thriving muscularly on rice, bully beef, biscuits and tinned milk. He could have been of any war, any guerilla. There was no doubt that he would be winning.

The jungle was dense and fading to chemical yellow behind them. And my father had his hand on the right shoulder of Criado Liyi.

When the three of them, and the injured Lang, came to the plateau and near the village, they started across the open paddy fields where there was no cover. They had not gone more than twenty metres when they came under fire from mortars and machine guns. The first burst ripped through the stretcher and the body of Lang with such suddenness that my father, for all his nerve and training, could only turn and stare in wonder at the frightful lightening of his load. It was only a fraction of a second. But it was enough. It was enough for him to hear the guttural cry of alarm from his beloving Criado and, at the instant, feel the thump on the back that, as he related to me one weirdly-unique time he did not laugh at me, felt as though Liyi or Flocco had gone obscenely music-hall on him all of a sudden with an almighty slap on the back.

From then there was only a series of inverberations in my father's ears. Voices came and hummed off. Voices hummed in and cut off. There were moments when he could suddenly see everything clearly

20

but not at factually all; and other times he could not see anything except as a blur but knew he was reasonably dry and reasonably content and reasonably safe for the time being. But he did feel he knew this: that in his last blanking moment, he could smell arid could feel the unmistakably sinewy strength of Liyi bearing him away. He could feel himself skimming across the top of the water of the paddy field. I am a skiff. I am being borne by the wind. The wind is dying. It was two weeks before my father regained consciousness to get up to become a prisoner of war in Changi, in the most atrocious place of all; before he could begin the next forty years before he would cough that bullet up finally as much as a curtain would come down.

In the meantime, my father's own people had executed his Criado Liyi for betrayal to the enemy. It made no difference, they said. They had Sergeant Mario Flocco to corroborate the evidential circumstantial evidence. On the face of it, in Changi when he first heard the telltale of it, my father agreed. Rip Van Winkle in a Dutch colonial hangover. He never did wake up to thank his Criado Liyi.

He said, too, that he never did learn if Liyi was Liyi's surname or given name or his only name. Or what his real name was, if Liyi wasn't.'

'Criado!'

On his way well and truly, Frank Stein stops there. Criado. His father's and Cowcher's spoken word leaps between him and the typewriter. I am Frank Err Stein, the monstrous joke. His father had stood up on his retirement and said look here this is on my conscience; this happened while I was unconscious; this happened during war; I want us all to say we're sorry. My fucking father had never stood up and said look here I want to redress making a monstrous joke out of the only true loin-shot son of my sperm; I must have been unconscious when I walked out of the premature ward after he was born and named him Frank Err Stein, a maker's monstrous withered little giggle of a pretty poor and desperate fuck y'know. No, his first word to me for years is about his Criado Liyi.

Fuck. Allasame fucking Costas, too. That golden burning bush of an adopted son, boy of his ex-Sergeant and the boy of an old now-dead bolt-cutting mauler of an old con. Pluckit.

It is thought with a smile. Now he knows the why and the wherefore of him going to kill his father and make a million bucks out of it. Not filial loyalty, but royalty. Not monstrous joke, but monetary joke.

Frank Stein goes on typing happily with a spring and a zing all over.

When it first happens, Frank Stein is at work. It is 11.30 at night and he still hasn't started his report on that night's rugby game under lights, even though the Man will be screaming for it in a half hour's time. The pity of it is Stein doesn't know how this game finished either. Perhaps it hasn't. Perhaps they're locked in mortal combat until as forever long as it takes to have one last survivor to crawl bloodily with the ball over his fallen mates and opponents to the line for the winning try before internally hemorrhaging. Around next Christmas.

The more's the pity of it is that he couldn't stop himself from reeling out of the sports ground when the closed-circuit television showing the game went on the blink in the bar under the members' area, about as far away from the press box as a circular arena could take you. He has not thought to put on the radio as he was driving away. He has not thought that the newsroom could be so empty of those so devoid of culture that they could dare imply how dare he ask what the final scoreline was. The copyboy he couldn't bring himself to ask, because he knew plugged-in Arnie, with wires from his headset running down beneath his shirt and undoubtedly curling around his body like an anaconda before undoubtedly disappearing up his arse where undoubtedly was permanently sutured the necessary transistor of a cat's-whisker, would know and would know that Frank Stein would not know and that is undoubtedly why the little Heeplike-in-licking little Polish bastard leers each time he

22

goes past me. Shades of my own two self-mounting geniuses they used to laughingly refer to as children. Have them all practise parallel bars on overhead cables. Who would have thought that Dial-a-Sports-Result could be engaged for so long this time of night? His very VDU stares at him in grey shuteye like the blinked television in the members' bar; I may be Frank Err Stein, the monstrous joke, but this fucking screening contraption in front of me is a monstrous joke too. How can I concentrate on the broken bones on the playing field? By the time the bloody reader gets to the end he will have forgotten he wanted to know what's with the score maybe. Take a punt on there being broken bones; if necessary, fall back tomorrow on the X-rays showing negative. Oh God, I'm the only human being left in the world.

It happens just after Stein has the brainwave to ring up Flash Gurton who might be still at his desk in the opposition's building across town. He might be sober enough to remember what passed on two hours ago at the sports ground, where he was snoring loud, but at least in the press box, last seen and heard.

'Yeah?'

'Kind and gentle tribal-Abo mate, that really you?''

'You wanna know the score. You white darkie, you.'

'Flash, old pal, old buddy, did Mick Davis go over for that disputed last try? You know the one.'

'Yeah, I know the one. He wasn't playing. Suck this one.'

'I see.'

'Well, suck it and see.'

The newsroom is, save Stein, deserted. It is midnight. Piteously, the copyboy Arnie appears at the doorway and rolls an eraser down the aisle to near perfect pitch of Stein's feet, some way below his gnashing teeth. Stein bends in that first minute of that new day and barely has time to read permanent-marker'd on it: '13-12 the Swan's way. PTO. Trick or Treat?' when the phone rings on his direct line, and thus it, as suggested, happens. Wife?, with some slug in the bath rather than flaccid in her bed?, the twins can't sleep until they've posted an obscene phone call to Pops, like, 'Father, are you really a melodrama or just a pale thing?'? Stein sighs, is not keen to answer it until he sees the angry Chief of Subs torpedoing into the newsroom with a tube of a hand outstretched for overdue copy. At the same time as he punches out 'Eagles Erased 13-12' by way of smokescreen, he lifts the receiver. It must be female because the voice has no balls:

'Uh, Mr Frank Stein?'

'Him.'

'Mr Frank Err Stein?' And for the time it takes for hackles to rise, there is a giggle on the other end of the line before: 'Aw, is that a joke?'

'Monstrous.' Stein, but really hackled.

'Sorry, Steiny-weiny. Didn't mean to... you know. Are you a Jewish person? It doesn't look like a Jewish wallet, not that I know what a Jewish wallet looks like, sort of.'

'Who's speaking? What wallet?'

'Aw, I'm just somebody. I thought I'd ring you up and tell you I've found your wallet right out here in Liverpool.'

'What wallet?' Stein auto-reacting to pat his wallet-full back pocket, even his fingers feeling relief.

'Your wallet, Steiny-weiny. I just thought I'd tell you that we found a wallet laying out beside one of those great big cement mixers in the cement works out here. You have to be careful of cement mixers.'

'I've got my wallet. It's not my wallet.'

'It's your wallet all right. It must be your wallet, Steiny love. Otherwise how would we know your direct line at work and your mobile right now and your home phone number that's ex-directory and your car reggo and where you work and what you do when you do it? You also make books, don't you?'

Frank Stein's blood begins to chill.

'Mr Stein?'

'Yes.'

'Funny this is not your wallet. I'll have to throw it in a cement mixer. Beware of those cement mixers, lovey.'

Jesus Christ. Not even a call from my wife sends me as shitless as that. Not even she is as sick as the innuendo in that. He is sweating and suddenly afraid. It is no joy to Frank Stein to have experienced his first threatening phone call. He can only look up with struck-out eyes to the Chief of Subs patiently standing over him with his hand still out, mindless of the look of distress below him. No Florence Nightingale in male garb, he. Stein can only helplessly shake his head at the plucky palm of the outstretched hand. It closes. For the moment it resembles a fist making a right fist, and:

'Okay, Stein, we'll write it our bloody selves.'

'You weren't there!' Stein, half-outrageously, half in hope.

'So?'

25

At 12.35, Stein is already sitting in the Journalists' Club, hunched over a deserted bar like it was a lost bit of copy that he might never get to write again. At that hour only the lost journalistic souls were there, but even Stein can tell he is the only truly perverted soul present amongst the word-walking dead because the whole three walls of poker machines behind him are crashing with lights and groans and gagglings of the lost but still expectant. If you play the pokies with your grog on one side and your fag on the other and your deadbeat mates draped over your shoulder miles away from the gropings of the cuntish gyrations of the halfhearted overheated quasi-disco upstairs, then there ain't much of a promise of tomorrow but at least there's a promise of tomorrow.

Stein sits over his double scotch, his third about to be polished off like the first two like there was no tomorrow, and ruminates on an ice cube that this day of a family (his) righteous and good publishing ought not really to have been the day he finally dried up as a sports scrivener, but opened out as an author-assassinator of his own father. What flesh travails? This is a poor venue for such seethings, he reflects.

My father had to fight malaria B plus, dysentery and perhaps a touch of the frights before he was able to come out of his coma. The bullet had entered through his right side and slanted towards his left clavicle. Somewhere between it gave up the ghost and snuggled within, as it were, the wheeze. The medico of the sorry remnants of the guerillas had no training or materials or, thank God, sense of divinity within him to perform an extraction. It was a case of block up the old bung hole and hope for the best. With the dysentery, it became a legendary saying within the near-future POW circles, that the young man stepped back from the wound, looked at my father's pants and said, 'With all that too, let's hope he shits it out'. He coughed it up forty years later. By the time he regained conscious, my father was on a filthy Japanese merchant tub crossing the Java Sea bound for Changi. They had surrendered and former Dutch and former Portuguese Timor was lost to the Rising Sun dawning over the Australian horizon and Criado Liyi summarily executed a week before...

Something like that, when I get home, if 'home' is what I can call my father's house where I'm still as unwelcome a guest as I was when I became christened as the monstrous fucking joke. Gut out a bit of the schmaltz and write in a fictional report on tonight's game where The Rams at gridiron beat the shit out of The Swans at rugby computed simultaneously over satellite according to soccer equivalents of scoring and call it 'Red Gills All over the Park'. What am I saving? What am I doing here? I am so full of piss I must be self-mending the leak hole in my head. Oh, my flagging Christ.

Frank Err Stein hears, but does not direction-find, at first:

'My name's Milly Hunt, not silly cunt.'

He expresses his humanoid residue by swinging bloody eyes around the bar area behind him. There are only, at this hour the baggy, strides brigade rooting the pokies because that's all there's left in the whole whirly-gig to root. Old journos beached on the night like rejected whales, wide awake because a decade ago each one of them decided it was more edifying to all and sundry, including mostly themselves, if they cultivated a full blown sleep during the hours of the day called working. Sleepless and lonely nights burning at their pensions, playing poker not with the boys but with the shit machines.

Stein sees Flash Gurton over there with a bottle of wine swinging sloppily from one mitt and the other arm punching the play lever with a cross-the-body flourish and a loud coding to the machine of 'You wanna date with a nice lady computer?' each time. He pauses only to guzzle at the vino, followed by a buddy-buddy pouring down the money slot. The machine doesn't care; the manager doesn't care. At this time of night, who wants to own up to being the manager? Flash Gurton has one leg wrapped lewdly around the machine. He is having intercourse with technology. He has refused intercourse with Frank Stein, except for the initial:

'Don't tell me, you white Abo. The subs had to knock your piece up. Fucking disgrace. Go home.'

He oughta fucking talk. Frank Stein is now in the burping stage. Frank Stein burps. He has forgotten why he turned around to feast his eyes on this enlightening sea of bladderless humanity, when he hears it again and has to turn back where he shouldn't have turned away from in the beginning -- before or beneath his very eyes:

'Name's Milly Hunt, not silly cunt, lovey.'

Lovey. Frank Stein thinks he hears the voice on the other end of the phone threatening him with cement mixers. But he sees there is no way of that. She must be a ring-in for the barman or tonight is Halloween. He presumes she is smiling at him, but the dark side of her mouth backing through at least four missing teeth makes it into a loutish leer. She is certainly leering at him. It is an odd plumpy and boozed face papier-mached around two thin lipstick gashes that presumably outline lips and it is a stout body. Legs of shapely oak. Breasts that are real tits. Broad a beam. A broad. It ain't no spring chicken and the flesh on its upper arm wobbles as it punches the air towards him with a half-swigged beer:

'Have I got something for you, Steiny-weiny.'

That gross familiarity of saying his name. The second time tonight he has heard it. Stein could almost have been hit between the disbelieving eyes.

'Who?'

'You, lovey. Where're you been?'

'Did you call me on the phone tonight, madam? Some rubbish about my wallet?'

'Don't call me silly cunt. Name's Milly Hunt. Nobody's gonna come on top of this old cunt. Waiting for you, lovey.' With that she cackles beneath a huge and wide wink and almost demolishes a whole trayful of glasses while fumbling with the video unit. This is no flick of the switch, but a ham of a fist, yet the pitch and roll of

28

her ample nates have all the attention that Stein is capable of giving the world these days anyway. The miracle is that she actually makes the television work, proving that it is an idiot's box, as it occurs to Stein. His mind, still trying to catch up with the voice on the telephone, this female, it knowing him and what's she doing behind the bar in his club and the sudden thought that she is going to replay the match he should have written up tonight courtesy of the Subs and Management.

It is not the game. As if to respond that it is not the game, Milly Hunt taps her nose with a yellow index finger at Stein. This is something in the know, lovey. Like.

As much, though, that the sound is up, Stein cannot hear the articulation of TV words over the gab of the pokies behind or the adulterated poundings of the disco upstairs. He tries enough to. What he can see though is that it is a taping of Costas being interviewed about the book and the infiltration of organised crime in the country. This is my brother, folks. This is the book that I went into the red for but, lo, this time it ain't Islamic State infiltration, no sirree. This be my book written by my brother and he's big, man. My brother's a big man and he has words to say that maybe I can't properly hear right now and I don't know why it's being flashed in front of me now but that there's me bro and those words are my brudder's words and they make sense. Like, sense. Oh God, I should've stayed till the end of the game. Whatever happened to me? I am Frank Err Stein. I am not just a joke. I be a monstrous joke. So .top that by my father if you piddling can. This is the Stein family charging crusade. We stand. We shimmy. We stand and we shimmy right down to when I assassinate my father. You think this book's right on. Wait until you see the next ball-tearer from elder brother, me. My father passed in and out of consciousness, drifting with the pain lodes and woke up really in the POW hospital in Changi. A Korean guard had just rifle-butted him in the groin for not attempting to sit up in bed as he went on through. He was in the B bed. There were four beds there -- D, C, B, and A. A was for the hopeless. B was for the likely-to-die. C was for the very ill.' D was for the bed-hedgers. After a week in B bed, he realised what the A bed was for and got so scared, he said that he frightened himself into getting well. That was my father. Even at that moment there was a Victoria Cross being processed for him...

Stein is fixed upon the television screen where his adopted brother Costas is in close-up. Stein hears the wind-swirls of phrases; 'Crime Commission has proved itself in the States to...', 'We should not pretend that any organised...', 'Sure, I'm worried about my own safety but someone has to...', 'We know who they are. Everybody really knows who they are. The police know.', 'I haven't tried to document corruption; I've tried to reiterate how much everybody already really knows...'

Costas in close-up. My brother is sandy Italianate and his blue eyes are honest. My brother's eyes have never wavered, funny that. Yet I know the wonder that is still in them. His eyes are still burning at the stake. Costas Stein is taken in middle view. He is wearing a grey suit and tie that are not so much ruffled as worn for too long. He stands, it seems, higher than his elder brother, even in a more sober moment, observed occasionally, would. His clothes, perhaps intended for stature, tend to hang upon a moderate frame. This is a knight with carapace cap-a-pie, rendered scholar and thereby all the more infuriating to those he hounds. But he has something a little indefinable if described as honour. He has something a little indefinable if described as handsome. He is Papal come up Jew. And I love the stupid bastard and I'm jealous of him. He is where the uphill gradient has always been beyond me. He has never been any sort of joke. He is my brother and, God, how I love him.

Stein turns full of fraternal pride and has asked the question even before he assimilates that it is only Flash Gurton leaning at the bar by him watching the box:

'Did you fucking know that my old man was Rhode Scholar, VC and Commissioner of Polfuckingice as well?'

Flash G., bored almost pure white: 'Write it on your headstone, bozo.'

'You the only prick left in the world for a man to speak to?'

'The Man's gonna speak to you all right, bozo, you like-I-said white Abo you.'

'Quote The Man unquote? Christ.'

'Okay, laugh. But they ain't gonna let you two get away with that junk in that book. Guts for garters, Steiny-weiny.'

Frank Stein's eyes narrow and are narked: 'Where were you when I got a certain phone call tonight?'

'Zzzzz.' Flash Gurton, dropping his head on the bar in pretence of slumber but still impressive the way he can still roll the whites of his Polynesians towards heaven and be shamelessly unmindful of the fact that he has peed his pants not inconsiderably.

'And how come you're calling me Steiny-weiny, fucking cheek, all of a sudden?'

'Zzzz.' But watching the video interview snap off unto an electronic snow storm.

'Up your cloaca, too, you poor excuse of an autochthon to end all autochthons.'

'Big words for a white dickhead what can't write one.'

'Listen,' this is Stein driven to antidote of the sting, 'you wiseacre, it so happens that I'm writing about my father at this...' Stein's attention is now wrung from Flash's crutch to the fact that the TV grab has finished, the woman behind the bar gone. He has to blink to register both behind the mounting whisky mist. The television set is a Sony; he doesn't know why that is momentarily of the utmost importance.

'Who was that sort?'

31

'What sheila?'

'The piece serving just then.' Stein tries to concentrate; the whole earth shifts.

'No female, whatcha on about? Fucking closed the bar one hour ago. You missing buses as well, Steiny-weiny?'

'No calling me that!'

Flash Gurton widens his thick features with a very puffy and dying-drunk smile of *knowledge*, finishes his bottle of wine by sucking very loudly through a battered barber's pole straw, burps in proud unison with one that Stein cannot hold back as he tries to stare concentratedly at the black other and lurches two steps to the left by way of warning here's momentum coming up that's gonna take me off right outa here. Whereupon Frank Stein panics and amazes even himself:

'Don't leave me!' It is a human cry that gets through both their mists, 'I mean, let's kick on, mate. I mean, I've got this fucking wife...'

'White man's burden, bozo.'

'I mean. I've got these two shouse kids.'

'I bet they're both under ten and still had to tellya you're too ugly and dumb for even white little shits like them.'

'Flash, old pal, old buddy, look at these tears in these very eyes.'

'Rather look at a side effect of VD. Okay, what dya want?'

'Dry your crutch and let's move on.'

I am Frank Eery Steiny-weiney. Forcing himself to get well, my father finally graduated back down through beds B and C to D by reading and complaining about the lack of hospital food, until he could leave blood-stained mattresses to the bare board communal platforms that served for beds in the stinking atap huts of Changi. For three months he walked stooped over like the old man he felt he was/. He relates how, on his first strolling day, he could not raise his arm to salute a Korean corporal and was punched to the ground and kicked. Which didn't help none. A complaint was filed. I object to this treatment. I'm sick. My name is...

Stein tries to mentally scribe in the taxi that is his own car driven with great flourishes approximating only to their side of the road by Flash Gurton who hasn't driven a car for ten years since they took his license away, not so booze-full anyway. White mongrels. He would have sued them for prejudice if he had remembered anything about that particular night. Most of the time spent in leering back at Stein in the back seat now, and 'Look, shitkicker, no hands.'

Stein's head lolls. He feels there is something he should be feeling sorrowful over and something he should express as scary. But no words come from that Stein cocoon. No words coming much at all lately. Have only to finish my clever masterpiece and then behind fucking bars. Not the drinking kind. Twenty years should go a good way towards lowering the alky level in the old bloodstream.

Sydney night lights flashing past in mad nightcap. He hears Flash yelling gleefully above other cars' horns. 'The Krondyke. Fifty short time. One fifty for an hour. Cheapest in town. For a good reason, Steiny-weiny. Most of 'em are dykes like you'd look like too if you worked there.'

Stein wonders after that last set of traffic lights whether he is going colour blind. Ninety-nine, a hundred, don't care if I do go blind...

Stein has sobered in The Krondyke. He knows not why.

33

The floss has come out of his head. It has been no ordinary man has been drinking. When he smacked his lips, the smack smacked back. The smidgeon smidgeons back. The fur on his tongue sways with the tide. He sits and he knows this much: that someone or thing has been churlish with de drinks, man. *The Man;* where been that phrase he bin heard of tonight? Fuzz of the duddy within his mind. He sits there. Frank Stein sits there on a stool at the corner of the bar. Now that his head is clearing, how did he get there, apart from the feeling he has just been on a trek from one waterhole to another with nomadic Aborigines. Tribal fellah. If I don't get some sports copy going, I ain't gonna be a tribal fellah for much longer, is for sure. Either some bugger's slipped me a mickey finn or somebody's slipped me a jag.

Existence in focus again, even if in wait. Another video unit mulching a television set. Some bad actress being ridden up a flight of stairs on her hands and knees by a skinny bad actor doing his best as a randy jock. The whole world's in mount. Two walls of mirrors make it three monstrous jokes in the corner of a bar stool. The short bar is three-tiered, crowded with guys in clusters of two and three around les girls in shirts and knickers and high heels. They must get the job by having their inner thighs measured. All of them keeping the dirty movie in their half sights. Off to his right and half behind, there is, incredibly, the parlour room, called Root Junction, lined with lounges around the walls, a few ladies of last year's girlhoods lounging, tuned to every coup d'oeil, all crossover gams, those classy knees of classy legs, waiting for the ultimate of a hard wallet and a kindly soft dick for a whole hour. This is warm in here? This is where I belong. I am a nice Jewish lad in the land of goyim gogetem.

'Stein, you cunt!'

Not even the renewed scuffle at the door makes Stein turn his head. He watches in the mirror behind the bar the reflection of Flash Gurton being bodily repelled by the cruel meat-maulers of a kindly bouncer and vaguely remembers, or thinks he remembers, that they didn't so much object to the colour of Flash, but simply to his being

34

bloody black. Well put, had said Stein. And zigzagged in without a backwards look at his companion's first ejection. The first of many. One thing that Abo has is bounce. All bum and bounce, the story of the race. Now take Flash G., old pal, old buddy; had to bounce back off the canvas so many times in the ring they should have changed his name from The Brown Bomber to The Brown Bomb. Always being dropped. Smart alec, still knocking over copy. Why is there a cleared area around me? What gives? He looks down. There is a quite full tumbler of near all gin in his hand which could only prove offensive to his own self. There are his legs still tacked on. There is a carpet around the bottom of the stool; nothing j|vey. There is the moll behind the bar staring at him.; She is magnificent, too young perhaps and too brunette perhaps for the mama-san perhaps, glasses and somehow masculine, but superb boobs under tight velvet, and she is arranging gladioli quite as though it was a perfectly natural thing to do in a bordello mooned over at two in the morning by a porn movie that now has the same female ridden neck and crop now down the stairs, each step a separate jump. But the real moll is saying to him:

'I could pull your stalk, too, hon.'

And Stein is about to quip that in his condition he might not flower like a gladdie because his tubers feel tied or somesuch when he hears in what is a sudden lull in the panting and grunting:

'Everybody knows that organised crime has really got a hold from top to bottom in this country. There are things being covered up that make Watergate look small. There's even a Mr Big. I know who he is. The police know who he is. You'd be surprised how many of our leaders are really his business associates...'

Frank Stein looks up from the carpet where he didn't realise he was looking from, for how long?, trying to compose a reply to the magnificent moll's challenge, how long ago?, because it is Costas's voice and it is electronic and how come the interview clip has suddenly come in on the dirty movie. But when Frank Stein really looks, Costas's face on the screen that he distinctly saw is not the face on the screen now, but the same actress is riding a forty-year-old delinquent right out of his school uniform on the parlour hatstand. Stein whips around to the magnificent moll, but she is still playing with the flowers in the vase and has not moved, nor is taking the slightest bit of low notice of him. Nor is anyone. Costas, he was there; I saw him, I heard him. I must get home. I have the fever. I am shaking and sweating with the fever; that's why they have cleared a space around me. But my father saw it in time, that he had 'graduated' to the B bed and saw the skeleton of just bones, the ecorche of a still-living human being, lying in his own seeping juices in bed A and knew they had cleared that space around him because they expected him to be next for bed A. He related to me some years ago that he had such a sudden rush of fear of death that he willed himself to get better. From the paddy field of Portuguese Timor he woke up scorching with fever with a bullet he would not cough up for forty years or suchlike, as a prisoner of war in Changi. He did not know his trials had only just begun. I wonder if Liyi, Flocco made it? But no one could help him. Nobody knew what the situation was in Timor and nobody knew anything about the incidents of Timor and not a body had heard of Sergeant Mario Flocco or Criado Liyi, let alone what had happened to them. You tell us. How's the Second World war going?

It was three years before my father found out about the execution of Liyi and that Sergeant Flocco had got away to fight another day and to be eventually picked up by a RAN submarine three months later and transported back to Darwin with twenty other survivors of the original company. During those three years, my father suffered such unbelievable hardships that it didn't seem to matter anymore anyway. So why, do you ask, am I going to, or, to put it more correctly, did I assassinate him so cold-bloodedly? You tell me.

Frank Stein registers now that the tumbler is only halffull of neat gin. Bugger, I hope I haven't swallowed a half slice of lemon and I'm going to choke. Peeling off, ha ha. He, too, now registers the woody tap on the point of his shoulder. He makes work his lamplighters; they roll up at the magnificent moll and at the object she has in her hand like they were a Greek film director's idea of a

36

funky Fury's gander in eye-sharp. Almost commiseratedly she holds the phone receiver against his ear. Stein has a mad moment of feeling that she too might reach over and wipe some dribble from the corner of his, a senile, mouth before he hears about five seconds before registering what it is he is hearing: 'Steiny-weiny, if I was you, lovey, I'd spring over to the Ravel car park. Fire stairs, level 3. That's the red one. On the fire stairs outside level 3, Costas needs you real bad, lovey. So scoot.'

'What?' Dumbly to the magnificent moll as though she was the now familiar digital voice on the other end of the phone now gone dead, am I suddenly one of the living dead?

'What are ya?' the same announces to him as she slams the receiver back onto the, yes, hook, 'One of the living dead? One-drink, no-broad screamer. Here...' and she shovels a piece of paper into his nongroping hand, 'they told me you'd have to need this. I'm a call girl not a calling-in service.'

'*Who?*'

But this lady has removed herself from his life for the short and sweet'n'bitter time she was in it, by replacing her presence with a brawn-made whole male who is staring at Stein from behind the bar as though he was distinctly low life even in a eat house like this. Stein wonders whether he has blinked and ten minutes has past. In fact it has. He tries to concentrate his mind and is apperceptive enough to feel very proud indeed that he actually manages to do so. The telephone, the note. Costas! The Ravel car park, level 3. Fire stairs? How did whoever know I was here. Steiny-weiny and lovey. What the furg's going on. I am Frank Err Stein and some joe has definitely slipped me a mickey.

Now panic enough grabs Stein literally by the throat. He swings bravely from the stool and heaves himself in a torturous path that manages well enough not to spill drinks or disrupt the human gestalt without too many passing waves. Costas. He moves, not well liked by the door people very much, on past the door people and out into that bitchy night of wind gusts. Memory, such as it ever is with me, a blank on the human blackboard, blows fairly back to him. At last. Oh God, at last. What's happening to me? He remembers the hair-raising trip there with Flash Gurton and promises himself to kick his arse when he next sees him; he remembers the Krondyke, even going in, even sitting there, even the phone call and the note, most of all Costas; he remembers even where they left the car. God make it that it's not parked in the middle of the road.

He has gone only half a block in the right direction (Stein feeling growingly confident because he can intellectualise that it is the right direction) when he stops not so much because of the crowd of people gathered up ahead but for the sensation of his hair beginning to stand on end. He fights back the panic that nothing is in control anymore and moves on.

For some reason, Frank Stein is not surprised to find it is his car that the crowd is gathered at. He can feel no immediate impact of shock either when, between heads, he spies that while it might be his car, it is not all his car. Not all of it is there to be wholly his car. The bomb that must have decimated it has left it only three parts his car. There is not a window left, except around the fagged edges. Oh God, oh fuck, that's unfair. The world hates me. I shouldnt've spoken so bad to the copyboy. Oh, no. The thousands chips of broken glass sparkle in the street light. It could have rained silicone shards. It could have poured silicone shards. Inside the exroadworthy vehicle there is so much broken silicone shards that it could have almost been that icing has been moulded to the interior contours. And so much about underfoot that each time someone moves from the spell of the forlorn sight, it sounds like it has positively pissed down, on this spot in this metropolis, silicone shards. Or else a meteorite of some fabulous intergalactial crystal has finally ended its three billion billion billion light years journey to the destination of my fucking car, now well and truly rooted.

In fact, Stein's car is such a sorry sight that the gathered are evincing loud mouthings of real sympathy for the car, a near-past living entity now made extinct, as though it could have been. What we are seeing are the remains, the bones. It looks so frail without windows (given a front, back and sides), with its top bashed in and its bonnet crunched upon that it's a wonder it could have ever survived for so long, really, in a highway world.

Stein wants to shriek or shrink, which? But while he makes up his mind, he takes in somewhat amazingly the verbal conjoining between a lady of the street in a smart ballet-type leotard number and high heels (stocking'd feet makes you climb the ballet wall, is all Stein can mentally punch up, not being able to take his eyes off them of her for all of his car, however shattered, and him too likewise) and a chubby-faced cop portentously arrived on the scene of Stein's near crying, such a crime:

'Somebody must have a real down on whoever owns this wreck.' This is Stein. Surprisingly other people's misfortunes bring eggs of different yokes to scramble together.

'How long ago?'

'Ten minutes ago, there was this bang bang bang. Far as I know, three of them hauled out of this thingummybob and took to it with them posts there. Ten seconds, demolish job and then off. I saw nothing.' She actually pouts and Stein watches her feet move likeasif her toes curl. Polished?

'Jesus, one Ford latest sports written off, suddenly jumped into the call-the-wrecker class.'

'Like on the beat but with fence posts, ha ha.' Her toes are curling.

'Ha ha.' Stein notices that cops actually do wear boots, two of, presumably for putting in such verbal boots. He finally hears himself shouting to nobody:

'What's a man gonna do, shrug shrug?'

And is already fleeing from the scene purely involuntarily.

He flees, yes, but for the soul of him he cannot flee far. Indeed, a few frisky paces has his eyes opened again to the world around. It is a concrete square he is beginning to escape route across and it is no great thing he has to do to notice, on a bench by that sycamore tree, Flash Gurton passing back a wine flagon to a figure huddled there. This is something *real*.

'You!' It comes out as a high-pitched battle-cry that only he and the neighbourhood dogs would recognise. Yet enough for Flash who doesn't need to look around before flashing off. It could be a relay race where he has thought he has taken the baton but miles too early. Besides, Stein has nothing left in his thumping heart to spurt on a pursual. He stymies to a halt by the bench and is still searching crazily into the light-glared night after Gurton even as he unloads himself onto the bench. I don't know what's happening and I don't know what to do about it. Costas. Costas. Then there is how to cope with the wine flagon, skirted with brown paper bag, passed and held under his nose. He has already taken hold of its neck automatically. Have I no control over events? What am I doing holding this wino's bottle apart from flirting with syphilis of the larynx?

'Help yourself, Steiny-weiny. Take a little weiny, Steiny, make you feel more human than you look, lovey.'

Stein is too metaphorically bruised around the solar plexus, wherever that is, to even look up at her. He merely slides his eyes from the flagon to the folds of the dirty raincoat the woman who said that is wearing and which is agape at the knees as much as her legs are vastly agape right up to a very unvirginal crutch. He merely shakes his head, oo la la. There is comfort in my squashed-down Jewishness.

'Drink. Suck of the old sav.'

Still he is, 'Why are you' too beat to, 'following me?' look up at her. Who needs a morbid verification?

'Who, me?'

40

'Why are you talking to me on the phone about wallets and cement mixers and saying "lovey" like that? What did you do to my car? Costas? What do you want?'

'I want to be a writer.'

This is said so disarmingly and so spittingly right to a spittle bullseye on his cheek and so miasmically that Stein rallies as a monumental wonder to human congress. He turns and sees. She is no better now than when he first saw her and, with her legs akimbo, her arms akimbo, her hair matted in mud-fight strains and her' puffy face all shot-to-pieces mascara intention and her breasts so drupaceous that they seem glued together along their two long inner lengths and her gumshoe raincoat so tatty that it could well have been cut up for soles. A person-female of much binding in any imagination's marsh. Her perfume is so stale it can only rank with her body odour. If she's fifty, she's a day, and she's more than a day or I'm no spring chicken by comparison. What's she trying to do to me?

'You what?''

'I want to be a writer. I know you, lovey. You do books. You'd do worse than doing me.'

I can't do my job. I've been threatened, I think, twice; I think, by this bint here. I've been slipped a mickey finn or some fucking thing. My vehicle's been pounded into the ground. I'm a freaking monstrous joke. There's no respect left in the world on a day that ought to have familial triumph by the leadership I have given into Literature, spell that with a capital Ell, spell that with one e and two ells. Something's up with my beloved brother. And I'm being propositioned by a three-part toothless paddle of a woman about being a writer and *doing* her book. I can't believe this.

'How old are you?', is all he can say.

41

'Fifty-two,' Quickly, as though she not only knew the answer but had answered the quiz about what's the funniest lie ever heard first. 'Now can I be a writer with you?'

'Lady....'

'Call me Milly. Name's Milly Hunt not silly...'

'Listen, stop! Listen; just... listen. You hear, World; you listen to me for a change.' Though saying it at her, this is cosmic; this is a hold-it-right-there. 'You can't be a writer if you're fifty-two and can't even keep a straight face about it. There's not a writer in history who's started out on a park bench at the age of fifty-two with very few teeth.'

'Who said?' There's go in the girl, I'll say that.

'Listen, do me a favour. What have you written?'

Poutingly, she: 'Yeah?, so what's that got to fucking do with anything?'

Stein now, Stein wants to get off. Not with her. He thrusts the flagon back into mitts that are only recognisable as hands beyond certain conjunctions of veins and bones by the nail polish being able to pass as congealed blood at the fingernails. This is all huff, too.

'Stop following me. Stop calling me up. *Stop* it.'

He is up on his feet. Stein is trying to walk away. But he has already stopped, much to his intense annoyance with himself, at what she is saying now:

'Steiny-weiny. That mean you're not taking me on just yet right away?'

For some reason, Stein finds himself down on his haunches. Squatting there like the ruin of the night has broken his standing.

Am I sinking or am I into it up to my neck? Where was I with my book? I am squatting by the campfire in the Dreamtime and some demmo's going to walk right over me. What passes, que passe, etcetera? He feels the arm not too ungently lift him to his feet. He smells the miasma of her breath; this ain't no honey anymore. She has the audacity to have kissed me sloppily on the fucking ear. What's she doing?

Milly Hunt is edging Stein towards a taxi on the other side of the square. The cabby has seen some strange sights, but... He shakes his head and is about to lie about being about to knock off for the night, when Old Lady Gabby shouts at him to shaddup and is opening the door and easing this sozzled Jew-looking hangdog sort of deadbeat of some closet sort into the back. Milly Hunt closes the door gently on Frank Err Stein, certainly a dummy of sorts, and sprays spittle in at him for him, Stein, and for him, the cabby, and for all to hear:

'Ravel car park. Level 3, fire stairs. Do I have to keep on helping you all the time. I got my best seller to work on, lovey. Now you,' enough to startle an innercity Sydney cab driver, 'piss on off there.'

Roll on Dearth.

Frank Stein is just about to hoick up his ring when the taxi pulls up opposite the fire stairs entrance to the car park of the Ravel. He registers strange that it has only been around the block, perhaps three hundred metres or three hundred yards, if there's any difference these days. What's happened to my sleuth's nose? my moth's antennae? my shrewd furtive looks? Did I pass the clubs, the nightclubs, the hotelclubs, the hotelmotelnightclubs with all-over movies movies movies books books books cream cream cream eats eats eats gas gas gas sale sale sale ya want a woman ya want a woman ya want a man? I am Frank Err Stein. I am monstrous, but not very solicitous on the old ministrations. Costas. Costas? Costas'.

43

He tears his way out of the cab, leaving, he believes, moolah enough in the alms hand of the driver following a mumbled unction presumably summing up the fare, and crashes desperately towards the fire stairs door with all the delicacy of a baby elephant wanting a leak. Ravel car park. Level 3, all over Red.

This might be the time of the heart attack, the thrombing of the coronary. As he has slowed from taking the first twelve or so stairs two at a time to taking those at around two-and-a-half level according to the wishes of those tight tapers for calf muscles and a heart that is fibrillating to its own tom-tom beat. His ears fill so full that perhaps he is going to explode by internal combustion and leave ragged pieces of his own flesh and guts dangling from the ceiling or from the banisters like escaped unmentionables from women's hospitals' incinerators; his my own cloud of gas might start a nuclear war. Somebody's dropped the bomb. If I die here I won't be able to help my brother. I won't be able to finish my own manuscript. If I can't finish my own manuscript, I won't be able to assassinate my father, 'My father was...', then I won't be able to help my brother.

Not able to look even level-keeled anymore, just as he had given up looking upwards at Level 3, Frank Stein casts his peepers downwards. He is in a hard well of sharp-edged, soundsome concrete, so all-over grey that it could almost mean the total abandonment of all colour but ashen. He is skugged within a sounding shell; each gasp he takes that punctuates each step he has to hill-climb is made stentorian. The very air seems to jangle with each sound; this could be the first-and-last, the stairwell to the Judgement Day and all is recording, all is fearfully impersonal yet all eavesdrop.

Above and below Frank Stein now the stair rail winds like a blindman's grope, its peeling paint as coarse between his hand as a plague of scabs. His eyes are beginning to water and his legs to rebel. But he knows he is making it. He slows as he nears Level 3. He is not exactly the cavalry come charging to the rescue over the hill in the nick of time, but I have made it Costas, I made it, and as

44

sure as hell I am nicked of time. Hold on, Frank's here, finally. There were a few minor irritations in the path I had to swathe to get here. Did you, could you, ever doubt that I would make it? What the fuck are they doing to you? Who's they?

Frank Stein makes Level 3 of the fire stairs. He is on the landing. His eyes move as cautiously as his throbbing neck muscles will allow according to the science of swivels from his disreputably dirty shoes, along the grey corrugated surface of the bare concrete (it has the look and feel of the coming Holocaust's promise of afteryear), and stops where the first splatter of blood has hit the floor. He pulls away and almost stumbles back down the way so painfully just gained. Shock shiggers in register up and down the stairwell. There is no one there. Costas is not there. But there is a terrifying residue of dried rustbrown blood first plopped against the wall at eye level and shattering down until it just fails to reach the floor, as though whoever's it was, just failed to make it. Stein's stomach now does heave. It is the impact of the image. That it is almost as if Costas's head has been slammed against that concrete there, or a bullet has exploded that mash against there, and the impact has flung it, showered it, rained it into fine droplets upon the floor as though to veil a bloody act. It is all that is there. The blood, so fiercely living against the anonymous deadlife concrete grey, is more horrible in what it conjures than if the deed had been witnessed. Unimpassioned and guiltless brutality in a lonely and final place, done without notice or rhyme or any hope of justice for it. This is the squashing of some bug, is all; penal, left as a warning. Costas.

It is pure fear that makes Frank Stein turn around and flee back down the stairs. It is the anonymity of it. When he reaches the door below and heaves it open (it sucks as if opening to mud) fresh air surges in to envelope him likeasmuchasif the world of night was answering yes by its warm and soothing welcome back to the land of the living. Don't lose your load, old son. He stands outside breathing sobering draughts of fairly clear air. In the frame of that door. I am the thirteenth saint quietly waiting recognition in my own wayside crypt. O'Henry of the oriel. Jesus, I am going to die\ There maintains the silence in that narrow back street. And only one thing wrong.

When Frank Stein has realised that there is one thing wrong and builds up the gumption to look beyond into the world to discover, hopefully not, what that one thing wrong is, he then notices the Toyota that is standing directly before him, parked where the taxi had pulled up in, of course, a very obvious No Parking zone right opposite the fire stairs door a few feet only away from his trembling body. It is Costas's car. Self-preservation has momentarily made him forget Costas and self-preservation makes him momentarily merely stare wildly at the vehicle without registering anything that might be of journalistic habit. His only immediate concern is to try to counter what could well be the second heart attack he has had in, probably, seemingly as many minutes because of the dark shadow of the figure in the car leaning casually against the window. He casts about, but there is no movement in the street, no lights from any homely window, only the ominous stillness of the car left certainly purposefully there and the perpetual waiting of that figure within. Stein's panic is about to mount him with indecent haste so that he might get up an indecent haste of getting the fuck out of there while he still has balls left to swing along a swathing path. I gotta get where I can sleep off this night before it Big Sleeps me.

Funny Costas's car is here where I left the cab. For Christ's sake, funny is not funny. I stand here any longer and they're going to come along and paint a colour target over my heart and give out prizes for the yob who can make me die more than a million ways while they record some symphonia of my screams. If I don't do something, my last dying breath is going to be a technicolour yawn. Reporter Dies An Embarrassment to the Human Race. That's Costas's car there. Booby trapped? Don't be fucking crazy. Move. That's Costas, there. Asleep. He's found you, fond of you.

Frank Stein actually feels his legs moving. He begins to know that his body is moving. He is moving as though he is running across a POW compound under a hail of bullets towards Costas and the car.

He pulls open the passenger side door like it was a half stuck POW hut door. And Costas falls at his feet.

He lies there with his feet still on the carpet of the floorboards of the car and his head resting on Stein's shoes. His dark wide-eyed Italianate gawkers are staring fixedly up into Stein's face. There is no recognition. No surprise. No reaction. He lies there as still as a decorticated chameleon in pathetic attempt at camouflage. Frank Stein is about to scream when only Costas's mouth moves to say:

'Let's diggie it along to the dockery. Let's diggie it along to the dockery.'

Costas Stein has been drugged out of his closed-in cabin to far away. He smells sweet and sour but is unhurt. In his top pocket, there protrudes a piece of paper. It reads:

'We saved this shitcan car from a beating like yours so you can get this shitarse home. Withdraw the book. And stay home!'

Frank Stein reads it all right.

After a night that this is shaping up to be, such that he can feel in his aching bones that 'after' isn't the word he should be using, Stein lets the streets ahead pretty much take care of themselves as he is driving Costas home. It's not my car; let it find its own way home. I'm still trying to find my own, so why should a snot-all car have it all in rose petals?

Stein mainly trying to concentrate on what has gone before rather than what might lie collisionable ahead. But he finds that it is difficult to keep his eyes off the profile of his brother Costas slumped shaggedly by his side. 'Chapter 1: My father, god love his murdered-to-be soul, will be my victim approximately ten minutes after I've finished this book you, dear conspiratorial reader, have paid wonderful lucre for to fill my...' A noble head. A noble Roman

47

head just fit for the wog that is my brother Costas. Pity about the goggles, but I know behind them is that noble conk, that imperial snoz. That wavy hair that he would never lose that has always more than slightly annoyed Frank Stein for its lifelong hold-on. Even his fucking hair has grip. My brother Costas.

'Chapter 1: My now assassinated, in terms of when you are actually reading this book, father never thought *per se* that his adopted second son was a monstrous joke like me...'

Stein is not at all registering how drunkenly he is actually driving the car. As though the breaking down of the alcohol in his bloodstream suddenly reaches a point of heightened chemical apperception, his mind's eye engages the flash of likeness between Costas's profile and the profile of the dead Mario Flocco in the gangster file of the photo library. They could identikit perfectly, this father-and-son.

He did not know why, five years or so ago, he had the unbidding urge to look up the Flocco file down in the basement of the newspaper. Nothing he was working on. Nothing he had seen or heard to raise a curiosity. It was even a few weeks before Stein senior came out in public to demand that tardy justice for his Criado Liyi and when Costas first came to know he was not a real Stein but the biological son of a murdered crime boss whose only connection with his son's life was that he had been Stein senior's Sergeant once. Now one of life's many little bumps-off. Stein just found himself down there in the photo library heaving around with metallic drawers he thought he'd never Be seen dead doing and making a metallic racket such like the drawers were fancifully screeching out here he is come and see him do something he vowed he'd never be seen dead doing. Enough for the bumptious photo librarian, who for the last ten years had sweated on catching him down therein her nest, ever since he never once followed up his promised of leaving wife, kids, fortune, job, all just to get her to come across (she did come and it was well across him) after<;he had hornily dated her for a cappuccino in the then cafeteria one night shift, to hear and investigate. And real sarky she was with it all, too, sparking the exchange (Stein now remembers, too; monstrous joke.)

'That's not the Sports section.'

'I know it's not the Sports section.'

That's Crime and Dealings.'

'I know it's not the Sports section.'

'I don't think you would even know where the Sports section is.'

Such was the notoriety of Mario Flocco that there was a wad of files on him. It was said he had never been mafia, had risen quickly to the top of the drug rackets after the war by the sheer guerilla terrorism of his stand-over tactics. The mobs made room for him. Better to have the madman where you can see him. His gang became known as the Bolt Cutters because they tortured their victims, then cut off a finger or a toe at the first joint using bolt cutters. Great editorial stuff. Wads of files. From drugs to illegal gambling to prostitution. A maverick. Nobody ever did get inklings about where his original stake money came from. By the mid-Fifties Mario Flocco has made it. Clippings of white silk suits and hand-painted ties in member's enclosures. Rumours that his mansion was like a fortress. Paragraphs on how they didn't treat journos and photographers very well there.

Frank Stein sat down with the last photograph and stared at the profile. The police had scraped away enough of the rubbish for the police photographer to focus in on the muck-raked head. The body's mutilated hands and feet were not showing. I had read the clipping on the back again. I don't know why I read the clipping on the back again. I knew the story. It had just stayed with me in all its detail since I was a teenager. At the time I never knew why. On 16 March 1956, precisely, they said, at midnight four hooded men broke into Thommo's Club. It was then the better known illegal gambling joint in the whole of Sydneyside but bribes had kept it going since the Thirties. It was also unofficially called Flocco's by now.

They had sawn-off shotguns and they lined everyone up against the wall -- the patrons, the staff, Flocco himself. They had some big names there, it was said. They had Flocco himself and nobody could ever say how they knew he was going to be there that night. They robbed the place clean. They even turned out the pockets of the sir patrons and the cunny spots of the madame patrons, all steepling their eyes towards the bossman Flocco. But he, too, caught short in options. Caught huge in humiliation. The gang kept laughing in his face. The wads, the jewellery shaken in have your face. To have your patrons robbed inside your own place. Some reported that his fierce face was livid with impotent rage. Some said he was shaking against that wall.

Others said that he began to shiver when, having fleeced the whole joint, they shovelled him before them instead of making for the fast get-away they ought to have made according to lore.

Some added that Mario Flocco just about then, just before he was pushed down the stairs before them and disappeared from his patrons' view, must have started to shake because he must have about then had a premonition that this outlandish burglary was more than it had been to seem to be.

My father stepped in as Commissioner of Police, then, to handle the subsequent demands for ransom made to Mario Flocco's wife, Silvia Flocco. My father was much in the news then. Stein senior moved through the media each day like the experienced troubadour he had become.

My father's homestyle cool each night of the fortnight the story, the drama, made the news on the box. Twice the money was dropped and twice not picked up. On the demands of the third time, Commissioner Stein himself took the pay-off in two carry bags on a train along the western suburbs line. On the third pass through one particular station, the money was taken. My father was never able to identify the pick-up man. Whoever it was had stuffed an envelope down the back of his official shirt. It told exactly where in the rubbish tip the mutilated body of Mario Flocco was. It added that the man had been 'assassinated' the day before even the first demand. Bad luck, snoops.

My father promised all the good citizens that he would use the power of the State to prevent thugs turning our streets into a gangsters' battleground. Of course, he proved as good as his word, wouldn't he? There was no gang war.

Mario Flocco lay like a guerilla shot by a Japanese sniper. But his throat was cut and it wasn't jungle under-1 growth he was sprawled on from the path; it was stinking garbage. He was no Sergeant Flocco anymore. There had been no Criado Liyi, no my-papa Captain Harry Stein VC to protect his flanks that time.

Stein continues to three-parts ignore the road ahead for the fascination of Costas's profile. Still life for the photograph of my brother's real father I once had in my hand down in that moll's library. The time I had her, she was loose as a goose anyway.

'Chapter 1: That's enough. Don't hurt my brother Costas anymore. I know he gets up noses, the peewee, but don't hurt the peewee anymore...'

Stein wields the car into the Stein estate, where the once-white-and-how iron pickets of the fence sweep into the mouth of the driveway, funnelling you down the siphon. It has always seemed to me to be a gummy mouth, and the same old crunching as you go rattling down its gravelly gullet. My father is swallowing me up again. I can never but feel it. How can he, does he, do it? Even his driveway consumes people externally like a jellyfish. Even at three o'clock in the morning. Doesn't his will ever sleep? I can feel him. I want to fall down on my knees and confess. Anything. What does it matter what it is. As long as he would take the time to hear me. It's stupid.

51

Frank Stein fights the car over the slipshod of the gravel, passes down along the side of the main house, where is housed father's reptilean self and his keeper Cowcher, their enclosure fancifully dark and in lurk now although Cowcher will be waking up and registering that the intrusion is a known one at exactly three-o-four according to his bedside clock. Stein passes the back of the main house where he himself has come to bunk in a morbid return to open more wounds to lick. He sweeps around the curve towards the old stables and the billiard house. Where are blazing most of the lights in Costas's abode. They are rude beams of awakedness in this dead of night. Shit. This is going to be no quick fireman's lift and dumping Costas, then trundling off to his own pit. I am not yet finished. I might be Frank Err Stein, but this fucking night has been a monstrous joke itself. Roll on the punchline so I can reap the petty zizz with pretty quickness. My head feels like it has been used for fish guts storage and my mouth as a mop on the floor of the filleting room.

Luce Stein, that Costas spouse, stands in the open doorway. Her long and thin body is silhouetted by the light behind her, the rim of her hair St Elmer-fired. Her otherwise sexless cotton nightie seems almost diaphanous. Fortunately, Stein knows better so that he merely lingers a glance at the crutch region for a brief, and almost insultingly so, passing moment and feels slightly disappointed that the outline of her inner thighs can verify that she at least hasn't got male genitals. As sexless as she has always been for him. It is not so much that she is his brother's wife, but that she is so pithless that she seems an ineffable extension of his brother's vast moral streak -- as something no one in his right mind would want to go after. Instead of pudenda, she might have a cardboard hole and pulpboard nipples. Yet there is the same crazy evangelical light from her green eyes as in Costas's. There is the same nervous intensity that appears to draw her face forward into an elongation that is at right angles to the flat plane of her whole frame. They are good people and they are my family. What is blest has me as the rest.

He feels her agitation from the door as he heaves himself around to help Costas out of the car. Their child Kevvie inside is still smashing up the household, this time with scream-sobbing, even at this time of night. It is as tough his autism never sleeps to tear the house down. The kid mightn't be autistic at all, but got the screaming heebie-jeebies at his parents' goodie-goodies. I'd feed him to a meat mixer. Luce has cried out from the door -- something half-welcoming, half-inquiring, but all edged with nerves. Now she is beside him with a fearful cry of 'Costas' right in Frank Stein's already too-sensitive ears.

'You mind, Luce? He's,' pausing with the exertion of preventing Costas from flopping bodily on the ground, 'all right.'

'Thank God.'

'Don't thank Him, thank me.'

Together they wend Costas into the house, through the living room, through the shattering of the kid Kevvie's screams that is making Stein's head begin to roll as much as his brother's is doing now; a man's only got two bloody hands although I'd trade in two ears for one more right now, and into the bedroom. Stein lets him fall onto the bed and backs out as Luce attacks his shoes and trousers. She might be trying to rape him. He swims his way, careless of the pain in inhuman sounds, into his nephew's room. This is way beyond a godfather's avuncular duty; this is suicide. The boy Kevvie is standing up in his bed. His room looks, as usual, as though the IRA had a special detonative liking for it. It is hard to cognate that that near ten-year-old face, distorted, distressed and as malicious as that of a gargoyle, could be older than the first stormy year. If life is a shout to the shudder, then this brat's going to live forever. The boy Kevvie has obviously scratched his own face.

Stein returns with a couple of tissues. If the kid doesn't stop bawling, I'm going to turn into a glass and shatter all over the walls of this lunatic asylum. As he begins to wipe the boy's cheeks, the wails rise to fever (Stein's) pitch and to banshee. It is hardly possible, yet those cold eyes just stare licitly up at Stein; they could be demanding the response of a complete nervous breakdown right there on the rug. He lets drop the tissues, save for one that he tears in two and stuffs into his ears as earplugs (they don't make tissues as sorbent as they used to) as he walks out of the house to lean on the front door frame.

The wind stirs again. A few drops of rain fall on him. Stein remains there waiting for Luce to come out and talk as it ever must be. He has run out of cigarettes but could not for the saving of the life of himself go back in there to pirate any. Nor it begins to pour. Still Stein stands against the elements. He is saying to himself that this is not the first time by half that I have been pissed on tonight. Like that kid in there, I am a screaming wreck. Thank you, God. Overlook the fact that I've been mugged, drugged, abused, mickey-finned, threatened, had my car mauled, accosted, insulted by indigenes and other useful people being useless, and done my hernia no good carrying that brother of mine to safety. Just overlook this, God. You just continue to piss down on me. Who am I to complain? Why have I got the right to a perfectly understandable human response?

'I can't tell you,' near him, from the shelter of the doorway, not, oh no, having the decency of making those first words an invitation to come in our of the freezing raining miserable cold like she would if I just happened to be a dying mongrel dog, and noticing that the flesh on her thin righteous arms is beginning to pucker into goose bumps, 'how relieved I was to see the car come down the drive. I've never been so scared in my life, Frank.'

The use of his first name gets him. He has never been able to suppress fawning gratitude for any of his family using his first name like they actually want to. Invitations to the inner circle. Stein turns to her, dripping like a puppy not a mongrel dog, kindliness in his thanking eyes, willing to please again.

'Why, Luce? Just a few drinks with the boys.'

'They rang, Frank.'

54

'Who rang, Luce?'

'Them, Frank. They rang three times, Frank. They said that I was never going to see my husband again, Frank.'

'Luce...'

'I'm not joking, Frank. The last time was only a half an hour ago. It got little Kevvie going. It rang and rang, Frank. They said I was never going to see Costas again, Frank.'

'Luce...'

'It was a woman's voice, Frank. It's the book, isn't it, Frank?'

'Look, Luce ..

'You know I don't say anything, Frank. I keep my mouth shut, you know that, Frank. We've had these kinds of things before, but not three times in one night and Costas not coming home, Frank. It's the book, isn't it, Frank? A book's not just a newspaper article, Frank.'

'Luce...'

'It's your fault, Frank. Publishing it, encouraging him. He's all Kevvie and I have got, Frank.'

'Luce.'

'Yes, Frank?'

'Shut up, Luce.'

'Frank, don't you think I've had enough for one night, Frank?'

'Goodnight, Luce.'

After him as he trudges back to Costas's car: 'You should go back to Lorna, Frank. All this trouble's no good, Frank.'

No, not a word about taking your car. You can't bitch about it later if you stop me from borrowing it now, Luce. Just to spite you, I am going back to the bosom of my own family for a bit of sympathy and loving kindness.

Stein, wondering why the hell a unit, climbs the stairs that he once had the right to know so well, to his family's, not now his, unit. I'm forty plus and all I've got to show for it is a unit. Where's the house at my time of life? Knowing those kids of mine, they would have eaten the roof joists and blamed the white ants. That fucking wife of mine would have nightly sent me under the house to talk with the earwigs. Now I'm a near bachelor, how come I don't have the apartment and them three have the earwigs. I'd import them from France for them; slip them in their ears while asleep.

Visions of fire stairs in car parks. His heart thumps temporarily with the remembrance. It and him moving forward to the last few steps. Where he listens by the door for, some telltale sound of familiar habitation or, as he more than half suspects, some telltale sound of unfamiliar habitation. But only the humming of electricity, or perhaps of his inner ear. It is after all four a.m.

Stein now chuckling to himself as he extracts from a secret corner of his wallet the two keys necessary for gaining entrance. She thought that I had handed over all the friggers. 'If you leave, Frank Stein, I want to be guaranteed I and the children won't be molested. Gimme all dem keys.'

The fact that he fumbles loudly-- all the more for trying to insert the keys quietly in the dark -- does not make any within stir. He stands by the door inside the corridor and listens cautiously at first.

'Lorna?'

But all remains stillness, such that Stein has the nerve, mainly out of a rush of rage that she obviously isn't home or is trying to hide something from him, to switch the light on. The apartment remains like a deserted railway station at four o'clock in the morning. I am the Third Man and this is a deserted German street. Moves. Does Stein. He tiptoes down the passageway down which he has often roared and blustered even if nobody in the Lorna and twin-kids stakes had, ever been roused to turn their attentions to him. This time he is sneaking. He edges his arm around the doorway of what used to be the master bedroom, now solely the mistress bedroom, and gropes as furtively as he can and as futilely as he could kill himself for the light switch. If she resists and I have to rape her, I wonder whether I'll end up in court on the way to being on page two? The switch now under hand, Stein hesitates for a prompt breathing exercise, 'r then coordinates a passable music hall routine by leaping forward into the bedroom while at the same time effecting lights.

'Coming ready or...'

Not. No Lorna. For a moment disbelief dispels familiarity of surroundings and makes rise the question of whether he has indeed just broken into the wrong apartment. The bed hasn't even been slept in, and here it is four o'clock in the morning. Shit, she's walked out. I walked out; she can't walk out. Stein whips full around, makes good a slight shoulder charge into the door frame and sallies to the kids' room. My children, my only beloveds! She's raced off with the only things that mean anything to me in this junk world.

But doesn't have to fumble for the light in there. There are quietly intermingled snores from the two lumps brazenly in the moonlight intertwined in the single bed and his anger vanishes into a father's compassion. Poor loves. Erika obviously woke up terrified, probably just after midnight, to find that they'd been abandoned by that slut of a mother. Barefoot waif. Her thin little legs peeking fraily from out under some latterly St Vincent de Paul's handout cotton nightdress, four sizes too large. I'll kill Lorna. Then my little

57

baby hears the muffled whimpers from Jude's bed and rushes to him, her little brother. That's where breeding tells. And reliability on the paternal side. My two lost babes have fallen to sleep in each other's arms. It's all right now, my pets.

'It's all right now, darlings.' Stein leans over the huddled pair and by feeling and sight adjustment discerns them. He sees that they lie nose to nose, Erika's arm under Jude's neck and around his shoulder, Jude's hand innocently cupping Erika's farthest rosebud where her breast might hopefully one day be (if, as Stein used to try to tell her, she didn't keep trying to bind them down intellectually), his knee flung over her two legs much as if he had just toppled sideways from trying to hold her terror down, he naked even around where might hopefully be something resembling a penis (if, as Stein used to try to tell him, he didn't keep trying to strap it up intellectually), she stretched out like a doll three sizes too small for the silk negligee of Lorna's that has somehow got tangled correctly about her body.

He leans close over their faces. They both have similar smiles of satisfaction. Must be those sweet dreams of childhood you hear so much about. In all my years of doting fatherhood, I don't think I've ever actually seen them sleeping before. Funny that. Hours of working; always my nose to the grindstone. Giving all. Stein leans over and kisses her with all givingness behind the ear. She tastes salty as if recently sweating. She turns her head towards him, stirring towards a little consciousness, yawning luxuriously, an homunculus suddenly of a silked twenty-one-year-old at the ripe old age of ten and:

'Mmm, honey,' she murmurs.

'It's only Daddy.' Stein shocked out of his mind when it catches up.

'Yeah, tickle me more, Jude honey,' she murmurs again.

Now Stein is starting to feel as uneasy as his mind. He gently prises Erika's hand off Jude's private part where it has landed as though destined after she has rolled over and returned to purring low. He gently, too, removes Jude's under hand now that he notices it lies beneath the shanks of his sister. The son's hand oozes back to where it was. The daughter's hand oozes back to where it was. Now they are both purring in unison. No wonder the Babes in the Wood got away from interruptions. Oh my bollocks being red, they must've forced an entry and drugged my own two innocent chil'un with aphrodisiacs. What man drakes! This time you get yours, Lorna. Your slutdom goes public as from right now.

Stein walks back into the once-master bedroom. He switches out the light again before groping his way to her bed and crawling under it.

The trouble is, a half an hour later, when he is jolted awake and indubitably bangs his head on the under-mattress springs by the lights going on in the hall and the bray of Lorna's donkey sound he knows to be what she things is s little-girl's oooo-yooo giggle... the trouble is he find himself in dire need of urinating. Looking at his watch doesn't help, either. Four-thirty. Bitch. The man's chuckle as lecherous as ever Stein knows he has heard in his time hiding under her bed and that's *lecherous*. Bastard. Four-thirty. But Stein unable to concentrate on the silence he knows they're tongueing upon each other or to remember his original intent for being under the bed because his bladder feels like it is pushing itself right through the very eye of his dick. It is actually excruciatingly painful. He squeezes his sphincter as tightly together as he possibly could, but this only hurts the more. He has a mad desire to jump up and sprint on the spot; it seems the only remedy to the exquisite torment. Instead, Stein rubs himself fiercely up and down the carpet and forces his feet against the wall, unmindful of the fact that they are doing irreparable damage to a very used tube of KY jelly which must have fallen down from the bed in recent post-Stein times. He clenches his eyes, his jaw, his fist, his very being in willing.

59

They are both not so drunk, Lorna Stein and who Stein will come to know as Horrie Brands. Billy de Wolf; he has a black moustache intended for black ravishings and a soufflé of a head o' hair spun back after egg beating, looks like. These are for modern kills from what looks like a silent movie ghost housing a mortal body upright enough and elegant almost too much, lupine snouted and gaunt as modern virility up front (up, in front!) would consider it. Such is the raffishness in this rake that he can be no other than a lawyer. A bearing, and beelining from the front door straightway for the bed. Direct to the heart of the matter with cool charm. Worse, he is at least ten years younger than Stein. It wouldn't matter if he was twenty years older. He would still be able to beeline Stein's wife towards the sack, presumably even if Stein was home at the time, which he unbeknownst is, and even if she was initially unwilling, which, given the moment, is hardly conceivable, since she has only allowed him to sneak one shoe off at the crush at the door before wheeling him innerwise. Coming hobbling or not. After all, she has already got both her ant crushers off and her silver lame belt and would be showing to Stein, were he on his feet for a sightline instead of under the bed let alone so trapped within piss-desperation as to be certainly oblivious to everything going on totally blind, that she has not wasted the time since his departure some weeks ago when it comes to being able to unclip earrings on the move with one hand while leading jocks across the family demesne with the other. Even Brands, who has cultivated this lady for an unprecedented time of two or so days by now, has to admire the bunlikes of her arse in those black'n'plastic slacks and her urchin ease of walking her mannequin's mould of lush body so cunt-consciously, and the bob of her nineteen-fifties Snow-White's hair and Disney face even without the cosmetics. The thought of having her almost distracts from the thought of having her. Most distracting with only one shoe on. But what a perk of work, and full entertainment allowance thrown in. And it is not just concupiscence that brings a look of rapine pleasure to the face of Horrie Brands as he views the rearform of the wife of Frank Stein. They didn't tell him it was going to be so good when they instructed him to go after her.

Stein only as aware as bladder pressure will allow of them moving straight into the bedroom, minus the preliminaries of show. A flick of his eye from under there certainly lets enough sight of their lower halves into his pain-racked mind that he does register the somewhat oddity of two female shoes, one male shoe and a sock, before returning to the total absorption of the excruciating writhe. Their conversation broken off since the door by mutual bawdic chuckling until, for the Stein eyeline, they are standing by the side of the bed in toe-to-toe and:

'Since when did you turn gay?'

'When he walked out, I got so claphand gay I decided to turn gay.'

Ooooh... Stein.

'I'm gay too, Lorna.'

'What's this hard prick, then?'

Ooooh... Stein.

'I can see from up here you've got a nice clean scalp on the top of your head, Lorna. Wash every day?'

Ooooh... Stein.

'Love the little yachts on your jocks. Every day. Try to lick the problem.'

Oooooh.... Stein.

'My hunger's lickin' good, Lorna.'

'Your finger's lickin' good, you big gook you.' 'Gobbledegook, Lorna.'

'Gobble, gobble, mmmm.'

61

... oooOOOOOHHH! Frank Stein comes up for air from the other side of the bed as though rocketed from a submarine. He has never known such consuming agony before. There is no stopping now the seep of his urine busting the muscular dykes and flooding the known world with an eighth sea. As he tries to scramble to his feet, his hands are already frantically clawing at his fly. By the time he has got to the window, he has got past the fly but is suffering torment trying to get his piece out of the up-out-over-then-down front of his sopping underps while trying to unlock the window latch for to at least spray God's creation of that eighth sea outside for Christ's sake. And there is no way he can take notice of the similar frantic ministrations of clothing adjustment going on behind him at the same time.

For a moment there are three moans in unison and three equally unsuccessful attempts at getting mind-hand-cloth coordinated. States of shock in collective burgeoning. Watched as calmly as all get-out from the doorway by Erika and Jude, never ones to dip out on anything adult farcical, standing hand-in-hand, he naked, she trailing black lacey velvet like a Queen Victoria animated doll. In quick succession, the window snaps up, Stein snaps up and whips his cod out and up towards it like beginning the swing of a lasso, Horrie Brands snaps up unmindful of snatching up a corner of his shirt tail in his fly zip, and Lorna Stein snaps up from her knees and snaps on to what is going on.

'You... *prick*!'

'Oh, please.' All Stein can say in his immense relief. Passing along a golden trail disappearing into the night but making what will come to be in a few seconds an embarrassing loud crackling upon the apartment block's driveway three storeys down. His gratitude to this particular path of biology, now unrestricted, and to a merciful God overwhelming him with pacificism towards the world. Before he strangles the life out of Lorna.

Horrie Brands has backed himself against the wardrobe. Instinct cries out to him to flee, but the door is blocked by two blonde and blank odd shapes who look like they might have once been describable as children and the window is blocked by the frame of the cuckold. Who knows what weapon he might have tucked away besides the weapon he has in his hand. Horrie does not flee. There is his job. There is also the fascination that he has never had an irate husband hiding under the bed before and pissing out of the window to let off steam. He looks at Lorna. She has just registered what is going on and has stiffened with legs apart into a fighting stance already. You've got to admire the way their minds work; she mouths calmly out of the side of her mouth, cross-shoulder:

'Go back to bed, children. It's all right.'

'You...' Erika.

'Aaaa...' Stein.

'. .. kidding?' Jude.

'... aah.' Stein.

The world is back in its uninflamed place again. He bobs in shake, then returns to the world of affairs once more, but anger has somehow gone out of the window.

'Get out, Frank.'

'Naw.'

'How dare you. Horrie, throw him out if you want to.'

'Well...'

'You can throw him bodily out if you want to, Horrie. You're entitled to.'

'Well...'

'You kids go back to bed. Horrie, just don't worry about throwing him out' and now rounding on Stein, 'You get out of here, you bastard, or I'll call the police' picking up the phone anyway and dialling in a daily-occurrence manner, and stopping, stopped by genuine curiosity, 'What do you want anyway, you sod?' giving her name and address over the phone at the same time and with admirable clarity, plus her complaint that she and her two poor terrified children were being terrified by her unwanted husband having broken in in front of a friend who just happened to be passing by at this time of witching hour. And going breathlessly at it all:

'Frank, you'd better leave and leave now go back to bed children as far as I'm concerned you can do your best on him, Horrie.' '

I am in my own home and I don't so much mind the cops coming around as me on the bum's rush end of it. Four-thirty in the fucking morning in my own pad and her coming back with some jack-hard interloper about to grip upon my fucking wife's hairie and me wet-stained in an embarrassing place with cops coming around like some Keystone madness let loose from the other side of the whole wide world upon just me, Frank Err Stein, don't worry he's only a fucking monstrous joke too, and this slack-holed slagbelly of a wife of mine has the ineffable, let us esteemably say the fucking, cheek to be demonstrating to all and sundry that, the shit might have hit the fan, but she's still got everything under control. What a moll. How do you beat that?

'Get out, Frank. You're embarrassing the children.'

'Up the children's. What's that bastard there doing taking notes about what I'm spruiking?'

Brands: 'About what you're what?', a ball-point poised above a pocket notebook courteously. Could be brokering a bid at the Stock Exchange on a slow morning.

64

'Spruiking I said and spruiking I meant. If you're going to take notes, bastard, take them properly.' Stein, having at him.

'What,' Brands, guiltily, 'notes?'

'Bastard, you.' Stein, almost dropping his hands from his damp crutch and making a conjugal charge, sure to acquit me, at the most a mild degree of manbastardslaughter, but survival instinct and a lifetime of cowardice combine, happily, to keep Stein huddled in the corner. With piss-stained strides it's very hard to stand and press home an attack when they're all going to press home an attack of pissing themselves with laughing when they see how you've pissed yourself under the cot.

And Horrie Brands stays against the wall, leaning, relaxing now over his notepad, wondering idly if 'spruiking' has a 'ck' like hrfuck or just a 'uk' like fuk. Infiltration, that whatfor of him really being there, landed so beautifully in his lap. And Jude and Erika stay immobile in the doorway, bland and unblinkingly interested to see if their nonage smirks (of ever-changing Jude) and smirches (of ever-changing Erika), twinned up, can influence adult behaviour. They know they can. And only Lorna bustles about with all the switching on of lights and the tidying up of place needed to be done on the boil. She wouldn't want the cops to feel invited into a place of grubby minds.

When they arrive, the cops find the stasis still in stasis, save for Lorna still in kinesis. All under control.

'That one huddled in that corner there like a rat that peed itself, which the rat has, would you believe, staring at this nice man leaning against the wall there, is my husband who's got no right pissing himself in front of the children. So there.'

Other than what Stein knows is coming next,, he would have otherwise thought the young-likeasif cop to be a nice Anglo-

Saxonish, tanned-brownish, rounded personality of twenty-five if a bit baggy under the eyes and the female cop, new to it, hardlined all along the life and pimple-covering lines out of sheer personal choice, but changes his mind when the female cops stays bemused by it all, while the male cop (he oughta talk) near pisses himself with:

'Pissing himself?'

'Pissing himself.' Lorna, in delighted and ratfaced and ratting affirmation.

'Tee hee.' The male cop.

'You can,' Lorna, 'laugh', buzzing around him in total female, 'I near couldn't stop myself,' control of it all again, 'either', the what-a-moll.

Finally, though, it is the adverse effect on the children that sways against Stein. It is their testimony. It is their distress of the old papas-and-mamas. Coming out like (after Mother's entreaty to whine for chrissakes to *them* since that's what they pay them for and the female cop on one knee solicitously inviting them to have their word in a great big adult and brutish world half averting and half not-averting her eyes from Jude's growing poker):

'Distressed?, are we,' Erika, scratching her crabber thoughtfully through the black velvet.

'... distressed? Are you', Jude, his finger self willingly running itself up and down her central nates path, '... kidding? That pater is a real splatter.'

'That Daddy is a real diddle. It distresses our pre-teenage selves that he, whom or which we prefer to call It, can exist'

'... in a world of genetic engineering and eutectics. Even when he's not living with us. Community scorn...'

66

'... oh, community scorn such that it would melt your hard police hearts, sir and lady, that we have to live with him being our father!' Erika.

'... Sir and Lady, distressed?...' Jude.

'... Mortified. Have you smelt its miasma...?' Erika.

'... Confused and bitter. Would you want to walk across a schoolyard with It?...'

'... Sickened and disheartened, sir and lady. Have you asked him some simple abecedarian question on the state of the Arts, for example...?' Jude.

'... Distressed is putting it mildly. We would say...' Erika, with lips pursed.

'... more amused, methinks. But I will admit it's very distressing being so amused by one's own gene line.' Jude, finding a way of greater pursing of his lips.

'We don't want to, you see, sir and lady, your Lord and Ladyship, grow up into cynics...'

'... with such a disability in a world hard enough as it is...'

'... just because we have such a dog of a Pater. Pitter...' Erika.

'… Pater.' Jude.

'GO BAG YOUR HEADS IN YOUR MOTHER'S FLESH!' Stein.

Poor Frank Err Stein. A *monstrum jocus* for his own kiddiwinks. There are, between themselves, almost peeing themselves as Stein is led away.

67

'Luce.'

'Frank? Frank, it's six-o-five. In the morning, Frank.'

'I can hear kid Kevvie's still got the bawls, Luce.'

'He's upset, that's all, Frank.'

'Poor little screamer, wonder he hasn't had his throat cut really. How's Costas, Luce?'

'Frank, it's….'

'You've told me, Luce. Six-o-five. Listen, don't worry about your car, all right?'

'Oh, my God. What have you done with our car, Frank?'

'I told you not to worry about your car, Luce. Think about my car.'

'What about your car, Frank?'

'It's smashed to fucking smithereens, that's all, Luce.'

'That's no consolation for what you might have done to our car, Frank.'

'Okay, Luce, then don't ask me how my car's been smashed to fucking smithereens. All I'm saying is don't worry about me losing yours too, Luce.'

'Oh no, Frank.'

'It's nothing, really, Luce. I had it parked outside Lorna's and the kids' and by a quirk of circumstances that will remain nameless, Luce, these two kindly cops escorted me down to where I'd parked it and ha ha, Luce, no car. I know how you might feel, but think of how I felt, Luce, being driven home in a patrol car. I mean,

68

somebody might have seen. Luce. I mean, fuck, it's the second car I've lost in one night, Luce. Not bad, eh, Luce?'

'Oh, my heavens a-rotten-bove. How am I going to tell Costas our car's been stolen too, Frank?'

'Why not just tell him, Luce?'

'I can't, Frank.'

'Why not, Luce?'

'He's sleeping too peacefully, Frank.'

'Well, tell him later, Luce.'

'Excoose I, Frank. Losing the car is not something you tell *later*.'

'Goodnight, Luce. Try cotton wool down the gob with Kevvie, why dontcha? Works wonders.'

'Frank, all I want to say about you and our car and the state my Costas is in is…'

'What, Luce?'

'Just this…'

Luce Stein, wife of beloved Costas, crusader against crime and headliner on the national scene, screams down the phone at Frank Err Stein, enough to probably even quieten autistic kid Kevvie. Upstaged. It is a bloodcurdling scream of rage that doesn't articulate much, apart from what it so graphically articulates.

As Stein puts the phone down as slowly as he can, given acute oral pain that is standing his body on screeched-upon tiptoe, Frank Stein can only sadly think of how stunned that young kid Kevvie must be to find out that autism must be just a common old gardenlike family trait.

What the fuck am I doing? Reading this rubbish that I've written about last night when any lesser mortal would have had his hummingly tired head down long ago. You would have thought that last night was as big a joke from the word go as I've been from the fucking word go. Well, ho ho, I've only had a sickeningly worst night of any poor Jaycee Citizen could possibly ever have, that's all. I've got the Mob crawling down my neck, cars oozing from out of my hands, stale alcohol and some concoction of a mickey finn edging destructively towards my vital one'n'only central nervous cord wherever that is, my whole life suddenly slipping away with my wife going like my job in the way of all fannies. What am I, a writing insomniac? I mean, I'm shit scared, Father. I've got jelly for knee blobs. It doesn't take an Einstein to work out the Mob's not too sweet on Costas's book. Last night they were letting me know they know and they don't like and they can reach and I'm lucky to still have my cods in one piece if the truth's known, Father. They could have used them as genuine leather petit-sou purses and my sausage and Costas's sausage for gravy at an Old People's Home charity barbecue. Dear sweet Jesus, protect me. If I didn't know better now, I might have thought it wasn't the Mob, but divine retribution on account of me deciding how to make my million bucks out of assassinating you, Father. I know that's not so, because if there was any divine intervention, I'd get the million bucks for having thought about it, let alone having to have the pain of writing about it before I do it.

I might be a Frank Err Stein
And not a Sweitzer
But wouldn't it be a monstrous joke
If I pulled in a Pulitzer?

Frank Stein, in the brayingly grey mid morning of that next day sits on the floor leaning against the door frame of his father's front

70

room. He has the few motley pages of his manuscript on the floor to his right. He is writing longhand as fast as he can, knowing that soon his bum is going to get intolerably numb soon or that Cowcher is going to return from his usual putt-putting around the corner shops to have at him and piss him off quick smart. Or both simultaneously. Frank Err Stein looks up and gazes again upon his father there.

The old man is snoring like an old dog. Above the scarf, his bottom jaw scoops bonily at the warm and empty air. Stein swears he can hear the crackle of the jaw hinge like some faraway electrical storm making portents of aeolian life on the horizon's comeback trail. That great head nodding. That great substance now inexpressive except for the dry articulations of bones sedging through dry serge of flesh, once, too, great and flourishing. That great being that was and is my father. That mind, that achiever, all that encompassing. The power has left him. I will be assassinating him only as if I was husking wheat , dregs. Stein: senior hunching in the nidus of sleep or semi-consciousness as though the day outside was midwinter, not near-summer. Reptilean now and shrivelling on the form that was once oakishly erect, huddling around seemingly a few hot spots left in the centre of his being. My father's planet's cooling. Stein can see the mini-mountain range of the Stein senior's clenched hands under the blanket binding those once strong legs to that wheelchair with Navajo design. The injuns got him at the stake by a tight weave. The clothed nobbles of the knees. Stein senior farts. Did someone squeeze the empty plastic detergency? Again. That gaggly bottle.

And again, automatically for being on the multi-million dollar royalty fancy, Frank Stein's hand makes light of the composing work on the life of his father. It begins to skim the flat page again in saying: 'Chapter 1: My father will be assassinated the day after I finish this manuscript.' Hope that's before I fucking peg it, erase that. Here we go again. The Nip orderlies used to enjoy going about the hospital with a bottle of chloroform and a 10 c.c. syringe administering the chloroform intravenously to patients chosen at random and watching the subsequent convulsions and death. My father lay on the hard boards that comprised his bed recovering from the wound from the Liyi ambush and would struggle up on his elbows whenever Jap orderlies looked like they were going to stop by him. He feigned being too healthy. Defying them with getting-fit eyes, his size, my father's sheer presence.

The hospital was to get worse in later years. This was in early 1943, and the rations and the POW's health and their morale were all still pretty good, adequate for survival. Their close-up hatred still slowly, inexorably turning to slavish dependency for their Japanese "hosts". The patients lay end on end along hard wood platforms that run the length of the long atap hut. As my father looked down those lines for these, the first few times of sighting, the other patients were still lumpy human forms, still of substance. In less than eighteen months time there would be twice as many forms, but all of skin and bones, shrunken as though a fire had consumed them from within. The gnawing of the guts. This was then the Australian hospital. Not very much later, they would lump the English, the Americans, the Ghurkhas, the Kiwis and the Australians all in together. My father's in-and-out place. His VC coming through even then.

My father also told me this story: that one time one of those Nip orderlies killed one of the patients by putting a pick through his skull, apparently to see how effective a weapon it was.

They didn't know whether they were awarding the VC post-humorously or not. It was more than two years after the fall of Singapore that any sort of list of prisoners reached Australia. I wouldn't know what the impact on our family was when we heard he was 'safe'. What family?

Wet clothes, incessant rain, mental strain and sheer exhaustion in the mountain country of southern Portuguese Timor was lowering my father's men's determination to carry on with the strike-and-strike-out tactics that they had been using against the Japs for four months already. They had to keep moving between their supply dumps, sliding and slipping in constant mud and slush now, aware that they were beginning to set up a pattern of movement as they were doing so. There was the edge of nervousness that they were becoming predictable and therefore ambushable. They, the hunters, were beginning to feel hunted. Who would be the first to betray them? When the Criado Liyi went back to his village was he about to turn? How did they know he went back to his village those times, and not to the nearest Japanese camp?

My father could feel this atmosphere. Most of his men were sick in some way. Each other day, when they moved, it was more slowly, less mobile. Each time there was more who had to be helped because of malaria or dysentery or who just psychologically wanted to be left behind, to have it all done with finally. There were only twenty of them left, but that had been effective over the last few months. They were killing and not being killed. The Japanese had posted them as outlaws. Obliterate on sight. Vermin. And now he was losing their morale and he knew they would soon be lost if he didn't do something about it.

He did. He decided that they should engage the enemy face-on. You wonder how I can assassinate this man, my father, in this premeditated way? Let me tell you of my recollection of my father's reasons for taking this course. These were something like: 'Fears, suspicions, disease was cutting us apart. Liyi was beginning to get on their nerves, coming and going like that. I had to knock that on the head. Then there was how to get us back into being one single unit with a common objective again. The only way to do that was to lose a few men. They were letting the conditions get them down. A couple of deaths would change all that.'

That was, is my father. You call me a monstrous joke.

So he decided to follow Liyi one night with Sergeant Flocco so that he could reassure the men and to throw his force against the village of Babau, where there was a hospital and consequently medical supplies. Kill a few to cure a few. It was, of course, a brilliant success on both fronts, especially for my father.

I cannot believe he could have, but he maintained that Flocco and he followed Liyi through the dripping bush at night without the Chinese knowing. It could have been; it might have been. I find it difficult to believe. But they did discover that Liyi actually did return to his village, where he talked in low tones inside his hut for some hours before going out into the fields behind that hut to do some tending. For a time, my father said, he disappeared into some nearby cave, but didn't elaborate on what he meant by that, or why he ever mentioned the fact to me. They were able to go back to the guerillas and tell them there was no worry when it came to Liyi. What they saw was what he was.

The next day they moved ten kilometres north-east, down the mountainside to take up positions outside of Babau, across maize fields. They were about to attack, at 6.30 in the afternoon, when another platoon of Japanese were seen riding their bicycles into the village. My father ordered his men to wait. Obviously, these were new troops in the area and could probably be caught by surprise as they billeted down for the night. He called Flocco to him and ordered him to wait until he heard firing before attacking the Japanese positions across the maize fields. He then slipped away without further explanation.

By moving out to the west, and back in again, my father was able to scout around to the road "entrance" of the village without being seen. He only had to wait there a few minutes before a native came riding up with bags of rice tied to-his bicycle. My father stepped out, pulled the man casually off the bike and carefully put the sacks of rice on the ground. The Timorese was so amazed that he merely stood respectfully by where my father had put him as though, with the sacks at his feet, he was waiting for a bus to come along. My father jumped on the bicycle and pedalled it right towards the village. He was on the newly-arrived troops before they knew what hit them. All but a few of them were off the track and bunking themselves down in the huts there. He remembered yelling at the top of his lungs as soon as he opened fire with his Owen. It was over in less than two minutes. By that time, my father had emerged out of the other side of the village. Behind him was carnage. The

Japs found eleven of their paratroopers dead back there and another dozen or so that they would soon leave behind, presumably to die as well. Miraculously, my father not only had not been hit, but could not remember ever even being fired upon.

But he had not finished. When Flocco heard the firing, he sent the rest into the maize fields and had cleared two Jap machine gun posts with hardly a shot being fired before being sighted from positions in the village outskirts. They pressed on the attack, losing Maddern, Armstrong and Kinneally before they reached the building that seemed to be the enemy's headquarters. Flocco, Hunt and Stevens moved in under covering fire and killed ten paratroopers, including the Jap commander. Meanwhile, my father returned into the village by moving out around the left flank and advanced towards his men. He established himself in a building and enfiladed an enemy group, drove it off, killing another five.

Two hours later, my father and his men slipped out of the village and moved back into the mountains. They had taken all the medical supplies they wanted from the hospital; they had replenishments of food and ammunition and they slipped away, led by a respectful Liyi, in high and renewed spirits. They had lost three men. My father had gained a Victoria Cross. It was to be another two months before my father was shot during the ambush that led to Liyi's execution. They were eight brilliant guerilla weeks, marred only when father had to take revenge on one of his own men... That was when he gunned down Signaller Sergeant N. P. Ellis who was chatting amiably with three Japanese paratroopers at the time.

Frank Stein is now in the lee of his own room. He knows he should be out on his feet, but still he can't lie back on the couch and get some shut-eye. Far too excited. His typewriter waiting willingly before him and alongside of the yet-small, but-growing pile of manuscript pages about his own coming assassination of his father. Apparently, there's nothing that can beat this publishing racket for making a quick quid, what what what? Who would've thought that the book o' brudder Costas'n'me has been plastered over just about everything it could get plastered over this lovely day. First the TV coverage last night on three stations, okay. But to switch on the ole crystal set and hear it mentioned in the good old national bloody news linking it with the finding of the Moffitt Royal Commission on Drugs and to hear it on just about every current affairs programme this morning, state or commercial radio. You name it. And to hear from a woozy Costas, who's so run off his beautifully arched feet by this station or that on the phone to him for interviews that he hasn't even mentioned a word about last night, as though being slipped a shiner and losing your wheels and your brother having his wheels done right over and your wife in a state of sheer panic because of all the phone threats she's getting... yea, as though these were the most natural things on a little nightly whiz about town these days. Lovely money, money, money. Makes a guy itch to settle back down over the old writer keys and tickle out his own merry best-seller tune, to the tune of a million bucks. 'Chapter 1: My father will be assassinated the day after I finish this book about assassinating my father...' Don't let it bug you, Father; you strolled in on Mum and me the day I was born and took one look and walked away to call me Frank Err Stein, the monstrous joke, funny bloody haha, so, Dads, an I for an I, I'll use thirty bucks from my first six-figure royalty cheque to buy a ticket in the million dollar lottery and I'll put it in your name, Pops. 'Dear Father', I'll call it. And the joke is, it'll probably fucking win, so I'll have the monstrous joke of having to balance a second million bucks in small denomination notes on top of the first million from royalties I'd just stacked so neatly despite the fact they too were in small denominational notes. Not a red cent will go to my wife or the twins unless they beg me to piss on them from a great height. Work, Steiny, work.

Stein does. But the first attempt is thwarted after only a few words by Cowcher's unceremonious entrance into his room and a voice that doesn't stand on too much ceremony either by the way the succinct is used to paraphrase what could be a pretty complex situation:

'You.' Cowcher's finger-aim would draw between-the-eyes bead were it not for its shaking, just as though inarticulation of cold rage was the only thing preventing him from fetching the mob onto Stein, 'Phone.'

'Dear me, Cowcher. What happened to courtesy to one's betters, care about not stepping out of your lowly station, and all that?'

Cowcher, quite unperturbed. 'Phone.' And disappears. The phone conversation is not much better:

'Stein.'

'Steiny-weiny, afternoon.'

'*You*, from last night.'

'We hear you disgraced yourself under a bed.'

'What do you want?' Stein unable to keep out the squawk.

'That's no way to speak to a lady, lovey. They only want your hide.'

'It's the book, isn't it? I'm calling the cops.'

'Don't call the cops, Steiny-weiny. Call Costas. They say for him not to go for the ABC interview tonight. Nasty.'

But not even this exchange has upset Stein's enthusiasm to get on with writing his own manuscript about his father. The sooner finished, the sooner assassinated, the sooner the royalties roll in. He is back at his typewriter and already beginning:

Signaller Sergeant Ellis had been with my father's company, but had been loaned to a party of Portuguese, led by Lieutenants Pirez and Santos, who were the first to go back into Timor after the final withdrawal of the main Australian unit either through surrender or pick-up. My father had taken pity on this pretty pathetic bunch of excolonials; they were obviously ill-equipped to stand out against the Japanese Imperial Army for very long, not the least because they even trotted about the countryside playing at guerilla warfare, but with their wives and friends. He instructed Ellis to go with them, ostensibly to be able to maintain contact between the two parties in case of trouble, but more particularly to keep the Portuguese under some sort of surveillance, since they knew so much about the remaining Australian dispositions in the country. He also instructed Ellis not to get involved with heavy fighting, but to pull out when he guessed that the going was getting too tough.

It only took three days for my father to receive Ellis's last message: "Japanese attacking. Am burying radio.'

They had been captured somewhere to the east of Dili. My father replied with two challenge messages but, when these went unanswered, had to turn the control over to the Services Reconnaissance Department headquarters in Melbourne. It was learnt later that, down there, a Signals Corporal stupidly sent a third message deliberately using the challenge word "Slender" three times. Meanwhile, the Japanese had captured Ellis, tortured him, recovered the radio and, with the code in their hands, made Ellis receive all the messages, including this last one from Melbourne.

When they found the message with 'slender' repeated three times as the obvious authenticator, they tortured Ellis again until he revealed what it meant -- it was the code name for dropping mare troop?, and supplies within the next few weeks to help my father harass the enemy. But nobody knew that then.

Four weeks later, Ellis suddenly broke radio silence with Darwin to inform them that he had escaped, had recovered the radio and: was living reasonably well in the mountains with his Timorese friends. At least he could report that Operation Slender remained undetected by the Japanese. There were two prongs to the Operation -- the first was a small, advance party to go in by sea on the south coast on 29 June 1943, followed by a paratroop contingent of 100 men on the 1st of July. Ellis was messaged from Darwin of the strategy and the dates; he was ordered to meet the advance party on the beach, lighting three fires as a signal.

The inevitable happened. The advance party of three Australians: and three Portuguese nationals were led into an ambush and annihilated.

At 17.30. hours on 1 July, a Liberator flew over the south coast of the island and headed for the southern slopes of: the mountains. The paratroopers jumped at the prearranged position -- a large cleared area surrounded by dense jungle. The Japanese waited for them to land and to gather together before pounding the group with mortar and machine gun. fire. There was not a single survivor nor, it was reported, eventually, even the slightest wound to any Japanese soldier.

In the meantime my father, who had been monitoring all the radio messages, was getting suspicious that something had gone wrong with the code. When he heard of this massacre: and of strong rumours that the Japanese were vastly enjoying themselves because HMS *Darwin* continued to supply stores on the instructions of the Japanese sent through Ellis, he radio'd Darwin and convinced them to send a further message to Ellis that a second landing was going to take place on 9 July. The message said: A recce for Methos II will be made next two days followed by supply drop at last light on D plus 2 STOP Same place and signal STOP. Ack.

Twenty-four hours before the supposed drop, my father, Criado Liyi, Flocco and two others moved to a point only 200 metres upstream of the site and hid in metre-high grass. At 16.00 hours the next day, Ellis appeared carrying a Lucas lamp in its box and escorted by three Japanese soldiers. He appeared in good physical condition and was wearing a clean shirt and trousers and web belt. He sat down, set up his lamp and waited. The Japanese went into hiding. With two hours to go, my father sent Liyi out to reconnoitre. He returned in an hour to say that the Japanese had taken up heavy position around the fringe of the cleared area. Machine guns and mortars. Ellis still remained cross-legged on the ground.

At dusk, when he knew Ellis's and the Japanese attention would be on the sky, my father crept forward. A hundred or so yards from Ellis, he stopped, set up his rifle across a stump and waited again. Eventually Ellis repacked his lamp, and sounded a whistle three times. My father could just see the Japanese escorts begin to move out of the jungle when he shot Ellis through the head. The .303 flung him virtually at the Nip soldiers' feet.

My father told me this. It was never officially recorded. Not that my father was ashamed of murdering Ellis. It was just that they all agreed it better kept secret for the memory of the 100 men who had been cut down without a chance. That was my father. That man. He's done a fair bit of assassinating himself. Time of war, imperativeness of duty and all that, sure. You have to admire the shot, though. A 100 yards, plus. It's not so easy being out of point-blank.

He got his two weeks after that. Just to keep this chronicle of the amazing exploits of my amazing father within amazingly tight style bounds, I can report that he estimates he got his from three hundred and fifty yards away, but that was with a machine gun. It seems important that the difference is made.

The extraordinary thing about the bullet he coughed up only last year, forty years after the dastardly deed wert done, was that the bullet had actually began to rust inside him. Oxygen in the blood, I suppose. Cough it up, biomechanics.

Frank Stein had seen the car in the driveway and had recognised it, although rather surprised it should be waiting there for him. He had looked at his watch then and broke the relative inactivity of trying to think what next to write about by realising time had gotten away from him. He was an hour late for work already. But why the

Editor-in-Chief should send his own car around to pick up Frank Stein just to take him to work was something that Frank Stein could not, and did not want to bother to, conjecture. Probably wants to get near to the sweet smell of publishing success, rub shoulders with a genius with an eye to the big day in royalties.

So, Frank Stein has got ready for the office, has left his manuscript, has deigned to give the world a little measure of his company by strutting up to the chauffeur-driven veteran Caprice of his Editor-in-Chief waiting for him. It not the Chief. He opens the door without even raising even one famed eyebrow of inquiry towards the chauffeur and works his way across the frictive and now creekbed-cracked leather of the back seat. Very creeky.

'Not you,' goes the chauffeur.

'Me, who else?'

'Shiddalmighty, all this waiting for *you*. And I ain't cleaned my teeth yet.'

At his desk, the reception carried through when he is unallowed to even sit for a moment's pause along the glittering road of success before he is physically heaved to his feet by the sixty-year-old copyboy who'll never change... this supervised from feet away by the Chief's secretary, herself so sawn-off as the copyboy but with largesse of contempt to spare. As he is being lifted into the air by a theoretical sixty-year-old weakling, she has only grunted and pointed and snapped her rotten little square and sawn-off fingers in the direction of the Chief's office. And the olden little twerp has merely nodded at her and with a chuckle far beyond his years swept Stein's desk quite clean with one arm while preliminarily heaving Stein up by the collar with the other.

'March.' She, with her tail up.

'March.' Copyboy, by way of echoing her instruction, propelling Frank S. towards the door beyond the two lines of lowly cheering fellow journos and copy-editors lining the passageway. Dressed in spiritual imperial purple, Frank Stein, smile on wry, shakes himself free of the fucking juvenile delinquent's over-zealous attention and strolls past these his colleagues for what he knows now to be a request for an audience with him by the Editor-in-Chief Ed 'Dognuts' Bradley. Undoubtedly wants to curry favour or start up a new general book division with me at the helm. Watch your back Dognuts; Frank Stein's on the way up. And how.

The outer office to the Editor-in-Chief's office is Hollywood in neo-fact, with its walnut panelling and Polynesian decor from the last freebie trip that Dognuts Bradley had something like a decade ago. In her corner, doleful Secretary looks, in turn, like a piece of the Polynesian decor from face or mask down to her wooden clogs or clumps of balsa.

Frank Stein waits in the outer office of his Editor-in-Chief, very mindful that the man has sent his personal car and personal chauffeur and personal secretary and personal invitation for to get him here. It is six forty-five in the evening and it would seem unfortunate that he has forgotten to shower or change or shave or sleep for nigh on two days, last night being last night and today being the day of book and author-demand. Who needs sleep, though mere mortals might.

Frank Stein is now beginning to snore slightly in the opposite corner of the outer office. Loud dark looks and disapproving clearings of the throat from the Secretary there could never matter at a time like this. He drifts off into the cocoon of silence where there are only small human noises in a long muted distance and a ticking of a clock tied to an eternal rhythm. He has his hand full of pieces of shattered windscreen from his own car, each shape becoming vastly blue and vastly solid, and drifts into tropical ulcers as big as a saucer, malaria, beri beri, atoxia, dysentery, typhus, cholera, protein oedema, sores and boils, eating snakes between fish and rabbit, inflamed and festering feet, no boots, meals of rice in Japanese and jungle-leaf flavoured water, the vines around your feet when you're trying to escape, the hot fermentation in your nostrils of rotting

82

leaves and jungle underfloor when the Jap patrol eases past a few metres off to your left or right, when he is jolted awake by:

'Whitey, you couldn't stay awake even if the Bears were physically mounting the Bombers. But here, you old whitey you, do yourself a favour...' Flash Gurton reaches into the breast pocket of a very natty pinstripe number and extracts a black Moroccan leather wallet that blends with his Languines grey silk necktie of another number, all very much looming over Frank Stein with a considerable smirch on his Polynesian-type mug. From his wallet of surprising Opulent bulge he extricates from a sticky wad a one-dollar note which he transfers by the very fingertips to the torn top pocket of Stein's sad tweed sports coat.

'... Buy two units to win I'm A Special, number 5, Race 8. A bit of luck and you might be able to buy a capsule of cyanide from around the traps.'

And then is departed gigglishly before Stein can come full attention. Slow take. What is all this? Why me here; why Flash G. too? And hardly even managing to get himself registering that he now stands inside the inner sanctum of Dognuts Bradley's office, somehow got there in the slipstream of Secretary's abrupt whistle from the opposite side of the outer office and her finger pointing get-in-there-mugwump. Am I writing this so it's *funny*? The boss is already talking to him, but Stein rallies from the doorway with a natural shout, learnt from years of practice across that vast mahogany'd space, that can only make himself heard as one so jolly:

'Dognuts!'

'Who?'

'Ed, baby.' Show 'em a bit of compassion.

'Mr Bradley or Your Majesty will do, Stein. What are you, some kind of joke?'

'Monstrous, actually.' Stein, magnanimous to Fate, and sinking himself in it further, can't help it: 'Dognuts, Your Honour, was that black dill just come out of this fucking office by any chance Flash the Peewee Gurton?'

'How long have you known the tribal lad?'

'Fifteen years. After last night, thirty years at least.'

'You known him that long, Steiny-weiny?'

'What you call me?'

'Steiny-weiny...' Again, that exchange. That mock conjuring up, as if his name wasn't a real monstrous joke as it is. Dognuts Bradley, laughing as though he has just cracked the riddle of the Sphinx from behind his desk, so crassly carved in the shape of a boomerang that he hates it so much he wouldn't part with it. Even as much as ten seconds passes before the strain of keeping a smile on his face for that long tells on Bradley and it slips from the curtain of expression as it would if his face was really just a curtain of expression rather than a metaphor of being a curtain of expression. Now, with his upturned eyes peering over reading glasses after the manner that he looks at everyone who comes into his office, as much as to say you've got two seconds to say your piece, get the answer no, and get out. His heavy and squared frame settling, too, in behind aggressive elbows on the desk. Judge and juror. And Dognuts Bradley going on:

'Steiny-weiny? Forget Steiny-weiny, Steiny-weiny. Some people have been telling me...'

Frank Stein immediately loses Dognuts's voice. The silverine luxuriance of the man's mop of hair. Does that make an Editor-in-Chief, like a measuring tape makes an Ambassador? They say that it proves that Ed Dognuts Bradley came up the easy way without ever having had to roll his scab-hiding sleeves up, the fact that he still has all of his hair. Any decent ascender to the top from the pits of early journalism would have torn his fucking hair out by now, cum laude A million other newspaper skinheads can't be wrong. My father lost his head of hair at first when they shaved his head on account of ringworms in the first two months of Changi. His scalp, when he first looked at it in the piece of broken mirror he had scrounged for his own private use ('I used to be fearful that I'd contract a dose of crabs from the latrines and needed something I could hold and inspect myself under the balls with'. That's what he told me once, delighting, I felt, in being crude with me and shocking me), looked like it had been sucked by the great moon crater-maker in the sky, he told me. And the second time he lost his hair was about a year after that when, in the swamps of Thailand on the Death Railway, his hair fell out during a week of acute fever or thankfully mild-enough myxoedema. The Nipponese guards would bring them out of their shelters they called huts every morning even so and make them pass muster. You had to be dying before you were allowed to be declared unfit for that day's twelve hours' hard labour. My father worked nearly one hundred sogging, mud-ridden hours that week, each day dragging himself the two miles to the railhead and crawling back in the mud in the dark of night. He weighed eight stone, a dummy for a medical student's classroom, but his face was all swollen and his hair and eyebrows fallen out; despite that damp that pervaded everything, his skin was parch-dry and yellow and he could not hear except what seemed the roar of a mighty waterfall in his ears and they had to keep beating him where he lay with wooden pick handles to get him wake before the guards came and shot him, he was so drowsy all the time. His own friends beating him, his own mates. He was so dull-witted from diseases that he could not think everything could have ever been any different. This is the man I am going to assassinate. My father was... What's Dognuts going on about.. ? It was this:

'...a funny idea that we're supposed to pay you for trotting out wrong results. As I said to The Man, what I guess and it's got to be a guess because who am I to be a know-it-all, but what I figure is that your beater ain't exactly in the pocket of this newspaper if you don't even get the one-nil or three-one shit right. Even your union agrees. If we put out a vote on you, Stein, the rest of the joint would probably walk out if we kept you in. I mean, we've been working together for a decade and a half now, right? I even remember when you could have been described as being reasonably normal good-looking and halfway to intelligent when we both applied for this kinda keyboard penpushing out of uni, right? But, jesus, I'm telling you, Steiny-weiney, it's embarrassing to, yes, me and mine to have the shagragging copyboy, yes, ring me up and say if there's ever a vacancy of Stein in the Stein department, he'd do me a favour by filling it.'

'The little cunt,' Stein can only get in, 'must have been talking to my kids! Going the diddle for all I know.'

'I'm not talking about that. I'm talking about some people telling me that maybe I shouldn't be carrying you or your brother. Your brother I know I can carry. Your brother's got the looks, the youth, the talents and, thank Christ, the following. What have you got, Stein? Tell me. It's important I should know if I ever have to put a footnote concerning you crazy two in my autobiography.'

'Listen, Dognuts...'

'With that, you've just fired yourself, Steiny-weiny.'

'Okay, so listen, Dognuts, bastard, I got a best-seller, which you ain't having the serial rights on, no way so boo hoo, and I've got the outstanding and distinct prospect of a million dollars give or take in royalties in a little thing I've got writing up right now. Who needs you?'

'Who needs a senior journo that can't write what's between an A and a B?'

'Ha. What're you paying Flash Gurton to turn traitor and come over here?' Stein on the unfair nature of things.

'Twice your salary for a start.'

'Very fucking funny.' Stein even more on the unfair nature of things and: 'I knew you when you didn't even rate the name dognuts, Dognuts.'

'Let me give you a bit of advice. Some people say lay off with that book of your brother's and you. Let it lie doggo, Steiny-weiny. No interviews, or so I'm told. No film, no fucking TV rights. Bury it. No handing it onto the Fed's Royal Commission going at the moment. Above all, what I'm told by some people is get Costas to forget about demanding the government sets up a Crimes Commission. That's dumb, or so I'm told. I'm only passing it on because I've known you fondly as a dumdum for more years than I want to remember. I repeat, some people have had it passed on to me that Costas is becoming embarrassing. I don't want to have to bow to pressure to fire Costas. I'd rather fire you. You're fired.'

'Fucking thanks.'

'Don't mention it. Bye now.'

'You're throwing up my whole life's work, Dognuts.'

'Well, that's not much to write home about, is it?, which is what I've been going on about. Thank you and out.'

'If I had a final word to say to you, Dognuts, I'd stuff it right up your dognuts.'

'Thank you.'

'Don't mention it.'

Back at his desk, Frank Stein sits silently in the webbing of noise that will produce tomorrow's edition. There are no condolences, sympathies, you're better off out of this loony bin you zany bugger you. None of that. Embarrassment and then, presumably because he hasn't come back to his desk and broken down into a thousand shells of a man, frank regard turning to frank disregard has ensured that the wave of goings on now sweeps healthily over him after but a few minutes of eddying around, and the like.

Stein remains there pinching the tear ducts at the top of his nose as though he was frozen in the removing of a pince-nez at high-tea time, so elegantly cocked are his third and little fingers. But Stein is thinking. He is thinking that, monstrous joke or no monstrous joke, oh Jesus, I can feel, what's the metaphor? I can feel dark clouds on the horizon. Something breathing down my neck, and I don't like the smell of its breath. Suddenly I'm tired, and suddenly not much is a joke anymore. Nature always sides with the hidden flaw. I have to pack up this desk and leave here now. I feel like somebody has shot a great cylindrical hole through me, right where my heart used to be.

Frank Stein goes starchily through the motions of clearing out his desk, while thinking of ways he should be rewriting his life somehow. Now the phone, once a familiar, now a travesty, rings. For some reason, he looks up at the copyboy before daring to answer it and gets a curt nod back that he may one last time. This is not at all pleasing to Frank Stein.

'Yeah?'

'You still in the building then?'

'No, this is Mr Stein's ventriloquised dummy, you dummy.' Knowing he is speaking to the telephonist downstairs and always knew the bitch would fold if ever given caustic curry back. She does by switching the call straight through and Stein feels already the better.

'Frank?'

'Yes, Luce.' He can't hear her voice for kid Kevvie breaking glass in the background but knows it's his sister-in-law's voice because it

88

must only be kid Kevvie breaking glass like that in the background, meaning wholesale.

'Frank.'

'Luce?'

'Frank?'

'Luce?'

'Dear God, Frank, why did you go home last night? I just heard what you did to Lorna and the kids, Frank. Weren't you ever potty trained, Frank?'

'A long time ago, Luce.'

'Frank, Costas couldn't catch you. He left a long note for you, Frank.'

'Oh, good, Luce.'

'A long note, Frank.'

Oh, Christ, now this. Sighs. 'Luce, what's wrong, Luce, Luce, Luce, Luce, eh?'

Luce Stein breaks down instantly, as though her brother-in-law's sympathetic sigh came thundering in to pound her in the middle of the back, knocking the shoulder straps of her dress off those bony ridges, flinging her dry hair down across her face, knocking the literal stuffing out of her. To Stein it sounds very much like she is transformed into wailing ecstasy amid a fanatic attack by Muslim children on a Christian glasshouse. But then he would. And he has only to wait for the blurt:

'Frank, I'm trying to pull myself together.'

'Pull yourself together, good idea, Luce.'

'Frank, I don't know what I'd do if I didn't have you, Frank. It's those phone calls again, Frank. I've been getting more of them and I honestly think I'm supposed to be impressed by the number of ways they're going to get at me. I'm not, am I?'

'What, Luce?'

'Supposed to get impressed, Frank.'

'Not really, unless you want to, Luce. Do you?'

Frank Stein stops trying to find more paper clips to pirate in his desk drawers by way of principle. He pulls the receiver in from where he had been trying to nestle it between jaw and shoulder, a la Humphrey Bogart as Philip Marlowe.

'Frank, there's been three calls. All they said was for Costas not to go on TV tonight because if there's talk about a crime's commission they knew, Frank, where Kevvie and I were. It was the same, but different voices, Frank, know what I mean? Frank, you know what Costas is like.'

'Yes, Luce. He hasn't taken any notice of it.'

'It's worse than that, Frank. He hasn't taken any notice of it. I hate you and that book you made him write.'

'How's the royalties, Luce?'

'One wave of my Mastercard and gone before they've come. You expect me to call those royalties? What's not to be beneath my contempt?'

90

The man sits at his usual place in the corner of the bar at the Journalists' Club. They haven't yet taken my membership away, just my embers. This is Frank Stein's sixth gin and tonic, a drink he has told the barman, he only guzzles when he is fired as on really special celebratory occasions to get oblivious to. Good for the internal itches, gin and tonic. A bit poofy, who cares. While the place, while between journo shifts as it were, fills up with those either doctor-certificated as too sick to work but boozable or those of the majority of them on holidays but with nowhere else they would conceivably go. This is reporterland, flytrap-tacky land. At least a man can sit here getting miserable and only be half as miserable as half of them here.

Neither was the time ripe when he was much able to look up as yet and look the world in the eyeball-to-eyeball. The commotion that suddenly went on behind the bar just out of his downcast reach soon changed that difficulty. Before he could say, 'I refuse to look up to see what that holy fucking row is,' he had looked up and seen an unholy row going on behind the bar under the television set a few feet away from him. He was already hearing mingled grunts of male protest and a sort of female:

'No bugger's gonna come on top of me!'

This time she is dressed in a lipsticked mouth that, in its wide distortions of line and such shocking red in form, is the whole of what you would ever notice at first. And she has just broken through the regular barman's defense with a swift knee to his cods that has him already doubled up and backing off for reinforcements or the nearest workers' compensation claim form, or both tied in with witnesses. So much, Stein observes as she triumphantly reaches up to switch on the television and to get the ABC, is her face a flabby mask of lines and her hair a prematurely-grey matted mop that she might well have just emerged from some horror-film's makeup wardrobe had he not recognised her before anyway. He has reacted little because there are very few surprises left in the fortieth hour of sleeplessness. She already punching the tip of her forefinger on the top of his scalp where he is going thin as a rag golliwog and bouncing the other hand between patting herself palmfully on the slope of those considerable knockers and flipping upwards at the TV with a dismissive back of the hand, saying:

'Name's Milly Hunt, not silly cunt. I know what you wanna watch, lovey, eh?' and giggles when Stein looks up languidly into her blue eyes that are startling in their similarity to cloudy cat's-eyes marbles with flecks of red. 'Ain't I ever going to be your writing princess, Steiny-weiny, but you can call me your saviour.'

Stein, waving the apparition away drunkenly: 'I know, you're not here; you're always here. You're my doppelganger. How do. Go away.'

Amazingly, she does while Stein thinks himself to blink but equally as amazingly she appears at his side as, more amazingly, the image of Costas again appears on the screen. Ah, Costas. That elegant nose calling up barristers and noble beaks; those dark and searching eyes despite the glasses. My Costas has them out of their drawing rooms and into the palm of his hand. He should have been a politician. He could be making a political speech right now. How can you stop that big Italiano lug? Who'd want to? What a man! He's a journo, a pro. He'll be turning all those dumb questions around to what he wants to talk about. The crimes commission. For sure, he's saying we need a Crimes Commission with capital letters, because until we do big time crime bosses are going to feed off us and I don't care whether little bro of mine is still living in a dream world of Humphrey Bogart as Philip Marlowe, like I keep going on about myself. If that's what you have to be to stay naïve and a force for good, then I'm for that. I'm for my brother. I love the big bugger. Look at him. Sweet evangelist. Go go go, my Costas, go.

Stein dimly feels the elbow jab into his biceps and feels it none too kindly. From the upper corner of his eye, Milly's mouth looks werewolf bloody and looming gonnagetcha, as though it had come from outer space for a chewy landing on his ear. Instinct has him in sudden flinch, but instead he hears:

92

'How much you paid him to write that book? I could do better, Steiny.'

'I told you you're too old to be a writer. Go bad fruit.'

'I'm going to ask you one more time.'

'You haven't asked me the first time yet.'

'I wouldn't demean myself.'

The voice in his ear is suddenly chopped off and Stein hears the rapid departure of Milly Hunt that, as a bit of stealth, might have been the Last Rush of the Elephants. In her place, under the somehow winking cameo of Costas on screen above him, are two uniformed policemen. Strangely deferential for articles of constabulary in the hallowed hall of despicable journalism. The usual thump on the shoulder or the audio blast into the ear replaced by a gentle laying on of hands upon the Stein upper arm and an as-gentle manipulation of the glass from out of the Stein grasp.

Stein looks up. They look down. They are then speaking to him.

'Frank Stein? Stein?'

'Here.'

'Would you come along with us, sir, to make an identification.'

It is not a question. Of course. In the circumstances. It is only, in fact, two blocks away where, in front of the television station not far removed from Gotham City in outside architectural style and inside intellectual age, they have finished up by the time Frank Stein is helped as gently as a rich maiden aunt out of the back of the patrol car. If one was surprised at how few citizens of the street had gathered there around the arc lamps and the ambulance and police vehicles red-and-blue pulsings and also how finely muted the whole scene was, Stein might also be surprised at how many employees of

93

a station still on the air could be leaning out of lighted windows, two or three to a window. Gargoyles leering at me. They have not told Frank Stein what this is all about on the way there. He has not asked them what goes.

As they help him out of the car he notes that their touch is too morbidly considerate. There is something to do here that is of me. Think. He can only think: My father spent three and a half years in the hell-hole of a prisoner of war arena called Changi Goal and the Thailand-Burmese Railway. That my father survived and that any man of those 85 000 originally taken prisoner by the Nips survived, is a miracle.

In that small street, the scene was frozen as very much like a filming conceived inside the adjoining television station. It is as though with the arrival of Stein all there recognises that the principal has arrived to give the final affirming performance. Wait for it. Frank Stein walks past the two ambulances parked wedge-shaped nose-to-nose and all of five police cars. The small crowd of onlookers has parted a way for him as if moving to an unseen cue. The soldiers and the cops huddling around the car have stood up almost to attention and moved back a pace as if caught in the act of doing something embarrassing. The car is a Toyota. The car is Costas's car.

Frank Stein stops before it and nods to it as if identifying someone in an identification parade. As if. As if. As if the word has just reached them, the ambulance men and the press photographers and the police photographer he would suppose and the hand-held TV camera crew with an exclusive he supposes since it is right outside the front doors and the uniformed cops and the un-uniformed cops and a man in a tweed sports jacket he supposes to be the police doctor or someone really straight out of a TV police drama... as if, yes, the word has just reached thrift of Stein's attendance, these huddling people stand up too and move away respectfully too from the body on the ground there. They even have a TV-style white sheet covering it.

94

No. Stein hears the word begin to come up from his very soul. No.

The man in the tweed sports coat has moved mysteriously back to beside the body. On one knee. About to give artificial resuscitation? This is a surf carnival. No. This is the R & R event; the beltman and the patient. No. Stein feels the word coming up, nearer, for air. No.

The sheet is pulled back from the head. They have been kind enough to wipe the hole in my Costas's forehead free of blood. Stein nods to his brother. No. And is turned away. No. There is a mysterious voice at him for his attention, calmly, no, and gently, no, insistent, no no, saying about it being a high velocity .22 killing, what they take to be the killing tool of a professional, maybe a pro hitman, instant, but the bomb didn't go off only the detonator, perhaps the car and clues. No.

It, the word, reaches the surface with the violence of vomit. No. No. Frank Stein howls it out. He pukes the word to all of all the black void above him.

'No!'

Frank Stein bellows like a beast in mortal pain.

Costas.

PART II

1.

Even before the police are called in to investigate the disappearance and probable suicide of Frank E. R. R. Stein, Les Cayley of the Investigations Department of the INP Group of Insurance Companies, a sturdy middle-aged man much given to the importance of his specialty of investigating car claims in the (to him) not-so-much-wider world of insurance generally (he uses generally with a diminishing back-hand wave), has already documented what is going to be discovered by the police anyway.

Normally Cayley has it as a point of pride that he hardly ever has to get up off his bum platform, as he calls his lottery-won, self-imported leather captain's chair which acts as a platform for his bum during working hours in his particular niche called office in the INP building, big enough by any standard, inner citywise and worldwise. This is Sydney. It might heave, but for Les Cayley it rarely heaves. A win of $50000 in the smallest lottery available to citizen-kind three years ago has formed a buffer between himself and heavings, even potential heavings, for, as he has maintained, he would have even got a divorce had he been married. Instead he grew a moustache and anointed it with wax as a definite affectation of being one of the lucky chosen few able to sit at work in a leather captain's chair and extol the devious effect on otherwise honest human beings that car ownership has.

However, there are few enough cases of car 'bashing', in which it could be said that the vehicle has been so totally demolished without being in an accident. This, the vehicle in question belonging to a Mr F. Stein, who said he was a monstrous joke on the claim form but obviously must have meant the damage to the car, had evidently not so much suffered vandalism, but murder. And the chance to investigate a vendetta just happened to marry happily with Les

97

Cayley's avidity to prove that car insurance really was the skirts-up of all the insurance hemline.

For the first time since winning the lottery, he got out of his captain's chair and did the investigatory rounds with tape recorder and notebook instead of remaining behind his desk and saying no, absolutely no, to all claims. He had always wanted to compile what could genuinely be called a dossier on a case and immediately smelt the possibility here of finally being able to do so. A car actually 'murdered' not damaged! And he managed to near complete his dossier before he was found in a side alley in King's Cross with his head split open but his life assurance fully paid up. At that stage of terminated life Les Cayley had been through the various evidences of one Frank Stein's family and had begun to investigate that actual murder of the Stein vehicle with heavy wooden posts that one dark night near the Krondyke Bar in Kings Cross.

If he had been able to talk to the one Frank Stein he might not have taken his investigations so far. The single trouble, if not the singular fascination of the case, was that at about the same time as the claim form came in, the one Mr Frank Stein went out missing. That the deed had certainly been well and truly done by vandaleers (as he loved to call them) and that the police report was firmly and correctly before him and that each and all things were pretty above board was just not enough for Les Cayley. It became a matter of pride to fill in the holism of the thingumabob, to show those life insurance investigators, finally, that theirs was a pale pursuit in comparison to the exciting world of ear claims.

So Les Cayley took a leaf out of the 'lifers' (as he called them) book and, having taken all the testimonies of the family circle quite unnecessarily and perhaps illegally, then extended his fierce probe into the area of the who did it and why.

The police never ever linked the matter of Cayley's investigations with the fatal bashing of him. The INP Insurance Group never made the connection because Les Cayley's successor, a long admirer of the captain's chair, eased himself into that bum platform and unconsciously vowed that he would not even arise from it for metaphysics, let alone hard core reality.

The Cayley successor stamped 'okay', let the car be fixed and he returned to the Stein residence, where it remained in-the open alongside of the Costas outbuilding for many sad days. The murder of Les Cayley remained unsolved and his investigations unresolved. Only the autopsy discovered that he had been shot by a high velocity .22 rounds out of an undoubted long-barrelled pistol before his skull had been stoved in by an indubitable blunt weapon. And all the vomit on the ground around was the finder's, not his.

The Cayley Tapes (as Les Cayley called them himself, for the quaintness of it), which remained yellowing in the INP filing cabinet and definitely not ever in the police files, showed ex-Les to be high on the personal dredging but low on admissible facts. They established sections, like the seating plan of a theatre -- but did not lay down the how and the why of the Frank Stein's disappearance. Also, it was a pretty sparse dossier indeed; the whole evidence lasted only forty-five minutes on tape, together with a separate typescript that one would want read aloud anyway; his successor's covering summary of the pile was as much as there was meatily in there anyway; in essence, it went like this:

Frank Stein's movements after the murder of his brother Costas first came to the attention of his sister-in-law Luce when, she recounted, there was a knock on the door of their outbuilding house the next morning. Around seven, give or take. Luce didn't answer the door. Her aunt from the North Shore did the answering for the little bereaved darling by waddling her stocky frame over to eventually fill the open doorway like a large mole in a small eye, eyeing Stein whom she didn't know in actuality, let alone because she was too remorse-indulged on display for the fifteen other distant relatives there to have been bothered about him anyway.

Frank Stein looked over her shoulder and found it sufficient unto himself to witness the relative flock gathered about the distraught yarns of Luce floating on her cloud of grief so very real that kid Kevvie, the orphaned child of my Costas, my once Costas, my only Costas, sits at her feet wide-eyed and wide-opened in mouth and quite beyond the callings of autism for this time. And Frank Stein perceives in that instant of gawk that neither the one or the two of any of his brother's relatives-in-law are there for anything but the closing of ranks, the family renewal, the genetic imbroglio. We forgive you for marrying a man who got murdered. Stein has already said to the aunt at the doorway:

'Goodnight.'

'I beg your pardon. This is a bereavemental, do you mind?'

'Well, goodnight.'

'Some people.'

It is recorded on Les Cayley's Cayley Tapes that Frank Stein then has already turned and is plodding his way back to the dark moonless side of the house proper of Stein senior, the last sighting of him of the aunt in question who had never seen him before anyway and who wouldn't have invited him in anyway even if she had been properly introduced, because she had almost instantly realised that when she said 'bereavemental' she didn't so much mean bereavement, but that this was a sheila's turn-out you man you, plus there's a child present and he might start screaming his frigging little pig's head off again if some deadbeat like you suddenly fronts up. If she wasn't a refined lady in her fiftieth anniversary of the Florence Nightingale Cup. Stein's shoulders were hunched and he shuffled like an old man. There was a silence, the aunt reported, about him, and a redness of eye that made him look like he was going for the nearest virgin's bedroom window with long claws that would do for a jemmy. And it was recorded that she added that had she not been right out of any further wails at the time, she might have given sway to a sudden impulse that she had at

100

the time and wailed after him. Why? Why, cause there was nothing left in his eyes that was seeing, and not even an old man should look so old.

The second incident was recorded with the voice of Les Cayley himself. Given that he was evidently talking to Cowcher, it is apparent that that crusty manservant of Stein senior had forbad the devil of the recording instrument to come into the house, up front where the old man still sat seemingly hardly completed in his wheelchair there. Cayley began with a whispered aside that he recognised who the old man was from pictures in the newspapers and on TV. The Commissioner of Police. Real cop work in those days, real men doing the job before drugs and organised crime -- especially when it came to fabricating evidences on ear insurance claims, oh, yes -- began to hit deep within the ranks of the police. He was clearly impressed and the whispertone of his voice on the tapes indicates deference to the venerability of the old man.

Cowcher recounted on the Cayley tapes that Frank Stein had earlier come to announce the death of Costas Stein or Flocco, whichever, to the old man. At that stage Stein was reeling as though he was drunk as a lord and trying desperately to hide it. He was so drunk his eyes were watering or he had been crying like any returned soldier should not. Frank Stein was not an ex-soldier. That's why, Cayley speculated, the man Cowcher looked upon Stein with contempt, or something inscrutably like it, and refused to let him get past the threshold to the father's room by physically planting himself in the doorway and refusing to budge even though Frank Stein did come to resort to beating on his worthy chest with his fists. They had heard. There is no need for you to come here to relay the news of this terrible event to your father. There is no need for you to come here trying to upset your father. We have had a phone call from true old friends in the Force long before you had decided to come here and upset your father with this terrible news. This is the type of news that my master does not need. Let him sit there and have a few peaceful days at the end of his life.

'FATHER!' Stein, it was recalled.

He can't hear you. I think he's asleep, but he's got the habit of sleeping with his eyes open these days. I have already broken the news to him of Costas as gently as I could and he took it like the true old soldier and Commissioner of Police that he was and always will be. He is in deep grief. Go now. Your father is licking the wounds of sorrow like any loving father would at the loss of a truly beloved son.

'I am the son! Tell me what he's thinking. Tell me what he says!' Stein, said to have said.

With dignity and honour as a true leader of men can only do. The Commissioner might be sitting down but, gentlemen, he is standing up with head held high and shoulders pulled back and his back as straight as all VCs should. Did someone else ask what did he say? It is hard to say, gentlemen. Moments of shock. Time for it to sink in, etcetera. Not even the great men among us are immune to that and those, oh no. But as far as I can remember, gentlemen, the Commissioner said nothing.

'I am the monstrous joke, not you!' Stein, recounted.

Cut out going on like this, Junior. Gentlemen, this is Stein Jnr, the Commissioner's son. Although the eldest, he's the mostest in the monstrous jokes area of this family. Unfortunately he is now the sole heir as monstrously laughable as that may seem. His name is Frank E. R. R. Stein pronounced Frankerrstein, that's a monster joke. It's the only big thing about him, gentlemen.

'Costas, father. *Let me talk to him!*' Stein, echoed as in stress.

Ah, Costas. We will never forget Costas. The favourite and the achiever of the issue, gentlemen. Stop banging on my chest; little boy. You are not going to get in that way. Costas, gentlemen, is one of the great tragedies of our time. That such a pre-eminent, young and rising star in journalism, with his sense of decency and social goodness, with his young wife and nervous child of such vocal chords, a family man standing for all that is worth preserving in a democracy such as outs so under siege from so many unsavory elements, with such a famous father as the Commissioner and a family name that is redolent of justice coupled with compassion, gentleman… that young Costas with so much future before him should be hounded down like a dog and murdered like a cur so openly in a public street outside a television station… Think on that, gentlemen. That is all for now.

'You gone crazy, Cowcher? Let me see my father!'

As Stein senior suddenly jolted as though prodded with an electric rattle jab and cried out in what came out as a triumphant ululation. It was one word and it was as final as could be imagined. The old man settled back in the chair; he could have returned wearily to earth in an eternal time to come back to his ever-gaze out of the window across the lawns and Cowcher's flower beds to the brick walls of the property's boundary. The movement was enough to send Cowcher reeling like a top from the doorway to the Stein senior wheelchair where he knelt administering to the blanket across those shaky knees there.

Frank Stein, it is reported, had not moved into the room despite the sudden opening. It was as if his father's single word has knocked whatever stuffing there was left in him out of him. He merely asked:

'Did he say, "Criado"?'

'What,' Cowcher venomously from the chair; there was no wrong here, 'about it?'

Frank Stein was reported by Les Cayley to have turned away from his father's door and left them. He was not reeling. He was shuffling. Cowcher's voice is heard at the end of the recording, in answer to Les Cayley's:

'Was he really shuffling?'

103

'Since the little sod was first monstrously sprogged, sir and gentlemen.'

The Cayley Tapes then made reference to the importance of reading here eight leaves of closely-typed transcript that Frank Stein had apparently typed just after the visit to his father and just before his disappearance. There was no explanation as to why these pages were separated from Stein's inchoate novel writings by either Cayley or Stein himself. Perhaps Cayley saw something suspiciously vehicular in only them:

'Chapter 1: My father was assassinated by me the day after I finished revising this first draft of my book about going to assassinate my father when I have finished revising the book. The reason, you ask. The reason is money. I'm going to spend ten years in a loony bin for the criminally insane and then come out laughing maniacally while I dig up the million bucks, as they say in publishing circles, in royalties I got in the first six months alone of the book coming out. My father was someone you all would have known at some stage in your lives. He was hero, politician, soldier, tall poppy cop, VC, you name it. He was a household name. As I write this, he is a household name. But you know what they've gone and done? They gone and done in my brother. They've done Costas. They've taken his life. They've rubbed my Costas out. How can that be? How could anyone do that? Is that what it's come to? My Costas. Because he had written this book called Australian Crime Bosses and was justifiably well-known enough to make a big noise about it, they snuffed him out like a candle. My beloved Costas, the only human being I have every truly loved, and that's what they did to him. He was the most unique human being I have ever known and yet they wouldn't have even missed a puff of their after-dinner cigar over killing that unique life. Where is the right in that? You tell me where the God is in that.

He lay like a bloody piece of meat on a butcher's floor. My brother. A bit of bloody side.

I'm sitting here writing this with my heart as aching to bursting as they tell you in booby books it can want to. Finally, there is no success or failure, nup; there's only the sham of it all. There's no more Costas. So why has he bothered in the; first place? He has bothered because there has only been his one-man war, as we all only have our one-man war when it all boils down. There is no success. There is no failure! In that one-man war. There is my father sitting there as dumb and proto-martyred as any first ever vegetable growed up in virgin time. That's his one-man war and who now gives a stuff. Nobody, except me, his assassinator.

At the end of his one-man war they gunned down my Costas and bashed all the virtue and all the champion qualities out of his head. He might have squealed and 1 did not hear him.

My turn next.

Between the success and the failure the only reality is that you're going to finish up a bloody mess. And, oh, I'm scared. 1 know 1 have death upon me. It is, you know, plainly fearsome. Each word I am writing now is a pain of concentration away from its presence. Willbeing, nowbeing, wasbeing. That those stinking bullies think they have the right to dictate when we have to endure this annihilation. That my Costas has had a human decision made on when he is going to die...

But most of all I feel ungrateful. The ingrate. My despair looms my losses at me... the loss of my Costas; the loss of my family; the loss of my father's affection I never had; the loss of any maternal affection from a mother I never had to ever lose; the loss of my job. The loss of my Car they fucking pounded into the dust. I feel all of these things acutely at a time like this, when my turn is coming up. 1 am an ingrate at the last bus stop. I might be even complaining it's running late.

'Chapter 1: My father is going to be rubbed out like my brother Costas was by hoodlums some weeks ago. He is going to be assassinated as soon after I have finished this manuscript and got it on the way to a rich and generous publisher who will recognise its lucre-lucrative qualities. I am returning to the writing of this my real-work manuscript before they come for me, too, since I can't think of any other way of waiting when I think of it.

Once when my father was patrolling the Timor jungle with his Criado Liyi, they heard some arguing on the trail up ahead. Liyi motioned instant caution because one of the voices was speaking with an unmistakable Japanese accent. They skirted the track and come up on the left of a group of three men -- two Timorese from Liyi's village and a Japanese soldier prodding them with his rifle. He was going to rob them of the pig they had trailing behind them. Liyi held my father back when he edged his rifle forward, then slipped across the ditch and came up behind the Jap, where he plunged his knife into the man's neck, twisted the blade and severed the head. There was hardly a sound except the plopping of blood and the hissing of air. He threw the head to the pig and dragged the body off into the bushes. My father said he went on his way, knowing that Liyi would catch him up. He did not want to stay watching the villagers calmly watch the pig eat the head.

I am writing about Criado Liyi because my father seems to have become obsessed again lately with the injustice of Liyi's military execution. I have just come from him to try to console him about Costas and, for the second time in so many weeks, he has cried out the word "Criado", the only two words I have heard him clearly utter for years. I don't know why this is so, but it is why I'm going to kill him.

Another legend my father told me once about Criado Liyi was that he had really killed more than the 57 or 58 Japanese he'd been officially accredited for. There were also the Timorese officials who had been collaborating with the Japs for months. He spread a rumour around that these selfsame collaborators were not to be harmed at any time because, in actual truth, they were really working for Liyi and supplying him and my father's guerillas with information and supplies. He said that every time they heard of an ambush, the villagers should secretly thank the collaborators. Such

106

was his reputation amongst the villagers of the whole region that the rumours were passed on from one person to another with total conviction, until the inevitable Japanese lackeys heard them and relayed them on. The Japanese responded by executing twenty of their most loyal agents.

My father's Criado was his local guide, and comrade in arms. They fought alongside each other for over eighteen months with Sergeant Flocco. I have said all this. It doesn't matter. Liyi was Chinese. He was not a local Timorese. He was a big man for a Chinese. He mostly went bare-footed; mostly he only wore shorts. He had a barrel chest covered in black hairs, unusual for a Chinese. He liked to have his shock of black hair caked with mud. He was a fierce fighter and a formidable sight, yet when he returned to his village, he could don a lap-lap and look as weedy as any poor suffering coolie could look. I don't know why I am writing about Criado Liyi or why my father keeps calling his name. This spectre that I have never seen, but often heard about. This wart on my father's conscience. This is how my father told me they met, another bullet he coughed up years after:

After the battle for Dili, the remnant forces of Australians, Portuguese, Brits and some American artillery joes struggled south-west towards the centre of the island hopeful to link up with those forces operating in the Dutch sphere further to the west. They were being pursued so hotly that orders came that all troops capable of carrying on the withdrawal should do so (my father was one of these) while those too infirmed to go further should surrender to the enemy forces. (As my father told me many years ago, he was not going to surrender to anybody, Japanese or Eskimo, who was riding on a bicycle -- as most of the Jap paratroopers were doing; indeed much of South-East Asia could be said to have been overrun by troops on treadlies. Bikes were ideal for fast movement over jungle terrain; advance assault troops, for example, merely carried their transport on their backs when they wanted to cross such obstacles as rivers, paddy fields and so forth. My father was not going to surrender to a treadly as long as he was able to put a spanner through spokes, he said, but I still don't know what he meant.)

107

Through Liyi's own ordeal, my father discovered what happened to those they left behind.

These men, most of them Australians, did not actually surrender, but blasted away with bren guns until the Japanese finally surrounded them. Only then did they lay down their arms. The Japanese were not impressed. This motley group of barbarians had held up their pursuit of the main task force and this, since most of the captives were barely-walking wounded, was definitely loss of much face. Firstly they herded the Allies into a circle. There must have been at least a hundred men there. The Japanese made them strip and then did the rounds bashing, kicking and prodding their prisoners with bayonets. It was reported that many of the Nip soldiers seemed to delight in kicking deliberately at an open would -- the chest, the stomach, the ulcerous leg -- and if the victim showed any sign of pain, then the boot or the rifle butt would go in again and again. After a couple of hours of this, they were then jabbed and kicked into a small copra drying shed which was already overcrowded with thirty or so native villagers. They were just piled on top of one another.

At sunset, they were all roped or wired together in groups of three or four. Those who were left for dead were bayoneted many times just to ensure they were dead. The Criado Liyi was among those led away. He was tied to two Australian and half-dead soldiers.

My father remembered he was eating something as uninteresting as corn beef when they carried the Criado Liyi into his camp. Of course, he knew there was a group of villagers bringing in two wounded Australians and one wounded local but he could never have imagined the effect on his life that the native would have. The three of them smelt terribly of petrol, so much so that my father moved away to finish his meal while the medic looked after them as best he could. The two Australians died. The Criado Liyi recovered in almost an indecently quick time. He told them that, after being shackled together and taken from the shed, the Japanese had moved away from the groups to high ground and machine-gunned them. Being tied together, being mostly wounded, there was no hope of running for any of them. As it happened Liyi had managed to sever the cord that tied him to the two Australians just before; it was as though that much' extra movement, however small, allowed them to avoid being killed outright. Instinctively, each of them fell and feigned death.

The Nips then came down and poured petrol over everyone. There would have been over a hundred men in that place alone. They burnt slowly after the initial conflagration. The smell of suckling pig; the Criado always maintained to my father that it wasn't a bad experience. Just bad. Just bad and like suckling pigs. Criado Liyi was like this: He did not say one word to anyone when he was first brought in. He did not even acknowledge food and drink brought to him. Four days later he was gone when they woke up in the morning. Fearing betrayal, my father moved camp up along the mountain ridge where he could watch the ravine from three sides and be out of sight from the air. Yet, despite these precautions, they woke up three days later to find Criado Liyi sitting silently there on the edge of the clearing. The sentries had not noticed him slip in and they could not believe he could have got past them. Criado Liyi merely nodded conspiratorially to my father.

The third incident recorded by the Cayley Tapes related to a commiseratory visit to Frank Stein by his estranged wife Lorna and children, who Cayley described as 'fenders of full chrome'. He did himself warn that certain parts of this narrative might be somewhat exaggerated and, should the listener not find them exaggerated, perhaps the listener might have a history of putting in too many car insurance claims to know reality anymore. He continued on to mention that his young informants kept blowing polysyllables at the time at him beyond what he would call normal for their ten years of age -- also, their constant mutual pudendal manual exploration seemed to be more advanced than when he was ten. Cayley did not mention Frank Stein's twin children Erika and Jude by name but such various background intrusions as heavy metal rock accompanied live by the pluckings of an educated violin and the systematic contrapuntals of goose-steppings which Stein would have recognised as Jude in a tap-dance routine on the dining room table again did not need mention.

As it went, it seems that Mrs Lorna Stein and the twin children named Jude and Erika Stein appeared two days after the supposed wrecking of the claimant's car at the temporary bachelor residence of the claimant. They did not visit the claimant's elderly father who owned the residence and who, with the domestic help by name of Cowcher, is the subject of another part of the Tape, nor the wife of the claimant's brother, named Costas, who had been killed by foul play a day and a half earlier. A link between the murder of the vehicle and the demise of the brother Costas has not been ruled out, however irrelevant to the claim that might be.

The wife Lorna Stein first appeared at the doorway of the Frank Stein bachelor rooms around the back of the mansion of Stein, his children apparently reluctant to get out of the car, being more interested at the time in unravelling the wiring diagram of the vehicle electrics as given on page 67 of the owner's maintenance manual. Apparently the wife had come to commiserate with Stein for some reason that remains a mystery to the author of this tape. We cannot rule out the cause of commiseration as being the death of the man's brother or -- as, more likely -- the sad mutilation of the family charabanc called car. The wife found the claimant Stein deep in the works of writing, a sample of which has just been tasted by whoever has got this far. The wife and the claimant said not a word. The claimant merely looked at her from across the room, his stubby hands poised clubbishly above the typewriter as though he was caught red-handed in the act of vandalising it. He was seen to nod ever so slightly. The claimant's wife was also seen to nod back at him ever so slightly. She then turned and returned to the second family car called runabout and forcibly ejected the progeny of their union from out of the back seat where they appeared to be lying on top of each other and groaning sweet childish nothings into each other's ears. The claimant's wife then returned to the claimant's bachelor rooms with the children, whenupon she nodded ever so slightly again in sympathy in answer to his renewal of a nod ever so slight. The children sucked their teeth and shook their heads

110

disparagingly. The dispersal of conversation seemed to go somewhat as follows (if any proof is needed of the genuineness of the claim or the vehicle-in-question's cause of the pain then your investigator recommends close listening to the agony of the refrains, no refraining back!):

'I'm sorry, Frank.'

She, the claimant's wife, waits for an answer. None comes. Nor has the claimant moved, his hands still like waiting cranes above the glassworks of the typewriter. She moves in the wake of the twin children, who have long before moved into the bachelor rooms and are now examining with tutorial snorts some of the pages that the claimant has finished typing before dropping them to the floor to be beneath their contemptuous feet. She moves to her once family and gently prises the pages from beneath the said feet of her children, picks up those pages that have landed on the floor, remakes the stack of pages into a neat manuscript pile, then gently, gently wipes the tears from the eyes of the Claimant Stein. She holds his face in her hands and tenderly invites him back home so that forgiving can forgive and so forth. Carefully she motions to the children that they should leave now; the boy answers with a silent yawn, and the girl answers with rolling her eyes skywards. At the door, the wife Lorna stops with a second thought and:

'I mean by the invitation to come back home, Frank: after all this is over, pop around sometime for a cup of coffee.'

'Yeah.'

'Don't get any ideas, that's all, Frank.'

At this juncture, the claimant's children return to their father and produce a wad of legal tender, some of which they stuff in their father's top shirt pocket.

'Merely, Pater, a little portion of the old crackle...'

111

'... for you to, some hope and...'

'... sorry about this current split infinitive, for you to hopefully get your teeth fixed first before popping around. Hairline...'

'... corrected. Clothes replaced by something of the last twenty-five years. Back straightened. Mind...'

'... sharpened, if only a miraculous teeny weeny bit. A prosthetic job done on thou bladder, embonpoint, etcetera, etcetera...'

'... before we find out too late that whatever thou hast is really infectious and we poor offsprung unfortunates wind up with dropsy of the parentage.'

'Oedematose, Erika...'

'... as all fuck, Jude, my spunky.'

The Cayley Tapes also mentioned that it was a common rumour that a black man of the Australian indigenous variety paid a visit to the claimant after that night's football match under lights, but this could not be confirmed because (a) there were no witnesses and (b) the Claimant Frank Stein has not been seen since.

The last piece of concrete evidence we have from the claimant is a hastily scribbled note written on a scrap of paper that was screwed up but not thrown away. It contains mysterious sentiments laid out in equally-mysterious ways of what seems free verse written as though it was one single sentence. It is reproduced here:

'Feel like I'm leaving feel like I'm collecting bones feel like Costas feel like my brother feel like my turn feel like creating my own monster always been coming to feel me.'

At the time of finalising what seems to be everything available on this case, one should add riders of the singular publicity that the death of the claimant's brother, namely Costas Stein -- or, hearsay,

Flocco -- has created. That publicity is not for me to record, except to comment that it is now dying somewhat down. It was fanned, of course, by the disappearance of the claimant only three weeks after the known demise of the younger brother, at which time it popped back onto the front pages, not to mention the media news bulletins, with headlines like: FRANK STEIN MISSING: Older Brother Goes Way of Crimebusting Younger Brother? or Organised Crime Link? or FEARS FOR CRIME FIGHTER'S SAFETY: Second Brother Missing After Crime Investigations, even down to JOURNO NSHOT OR SHOT THROUGH?

It is of note too that all the newspaper and media reports have the US mafia being involved through their Australian connections. The protection of the illicit drug trade and the Stein's championing of a Crime Commission are said to be the prime causes.

Signing off now, but what really gets my goat is, okay, they can do what they like to each other, but why do they have to drag innocent cars into it? This is a sick, sick world.

The men could only be half seen by the diffusion of lights coming from the interior of the Stein mansion as they made their way down the driveway. This made them only discernible, not identifiable. They moved with the confidence of knowing that, and having gotten used to knowing it. They did not try to hide themselves; they were not even moving diligently.

They were big men who moved roughly in swagger and they were moving quite openly in swagger now, despite having orders to just ascertain where Frank Stein was and leave without being observed.

They stopped at the dark portion of the back of the house. They knew where Frank Stein was bunking down since the separation from his wife and children. The way they moved up openly onto the porch to peer into the window indicated that they also knew not to expect Frank Stein to be in.

113

The taller of the two was a huge man. His shoulders were set so square that he looked in silhouette to be wearing a jacket with spatulate padding in the shoulders. When he turned to nod to his companion to go ahead with the door, his heavy jaw immediately indicated that his weight, his strength was all bone, not fat. His eyes white blue, reptilean. As he turned to casually ensure that their break-in wasn't being seen, he actually did lick his lips, but this looked to be stifling a yawn as much as anything, a gesture that was as incongruously gentle as his American Bronx accent was rasping.

'Don't box around with it.'

His companion didn't have to box around with it. As a matter of reflex he tried the door, found it open and amused himself by standing in the open doorway without saying anything while the American stood his brief guard before turning back. The companion, the smaller man but still big-man size narrowed oddly to a weasel's sharpness of face and form, did not wait for The American to assert authority by way of displeasure over the little joke, but moved into the Frank Stein rooms first.

They didn't care about switching on the lights. Being seen obviously wasn't a worry to them. They were merely looking for Frank Stein. A walk through the two rooms was sufficient.

The American nodded and they left, the smaller of them casually sweeping the back of his hand across the phone table as he passed. Not much of a clatter. No worries at all about leaving the lights on and the door open.

The two men walked further down the driveway to the place that was once Costas Stein's. They moved openly across the centre grass of the roundabout where the horses would have once turned the carriages about and they moved openly up to the front door. And they stood proprietorially.

It was past midnight, towards the half hour.

This time the big American knocked until the lights went on inside. Instead of stepping slightly back as Luce Stein made her way to the door, the two men pressed perceptibly closer. Yet they remained unmoving when she opened the door first smally ('Who's there?' and crazily not waiting for an answer, all so neuro-motored) and then largely. With the light behind her and the outline of her body so solid against the screen of her nightgown, Luce Stein could not have been more visually nude. The light at one and the same time gave substance to her thinness, classic form to her flatness. She was all girlie magazine. All swan neck in cock, hip in thrust, legs in funnel, shape in soft touch, breasts in seeping, female for fuck; if the men heard the voice of Luce Stein's immovable aunt calling who is it Luce? from inside or the whiney stirring of young Kevvie in there, they made no sudden movement.

She could have been held mesmeric by the reptilean eyes of the huge man. She did not try to move when he swept her up. She only nodded impassively, as though he was collecting a debt when he picked her up and strode into the place that was once Costas Stein's.

'What are you doing, do you mind?' This was not Luce. This was the aunt standing old and grotesque in the doorway of the second bedroom, her ginger hair moulded into a starched disarray by sleep and her freckled whiteness blotched by the returning here and now. Her nightgown was heavily woollen; She was a lump unfemale inside it. When the two men appeared with Luce Stein in carriage, the old lady cried out her hey! but herself did not move from her own doorway there. She opened her mouth in surprise but the loose gel of flesh there made her only seem to gobble. Then, instantly, there was no possibility of moving before the smaller of these two fearfully sized men slipped quickly to her side to hold her arms pinioned with one hand and mouth gagged with the other. She smelt the musk of him and she tried to scream. The man hardly registered that she was trying to struggle, and, just as automatically as the American hefted Luce Stein into the bedroom he lightly frogmarched her to the doorway of that bedroom.

The American had the wife that was once Costas Stein's up against the inbuilt wardrobe that was once Costas Stein's. He had her held up from underneath the armpits so that their faces were level pegging, his tongue at her mouth and plainly and rudely scouring it. Her legs hung down stiffly towards the floor, the point of her toes so well above a purchase, angled out across his body. He had rucked her nightgown up so much that he held it puckered between her armpits and the cradles of his hands.

Her ribs showed through so. Her hipbones showed through so. Her breasts were stretched into a little boy's chest. Luce Stein's nude body looked like a lean carcass on an abattoir's meat hook.

She was spiked in midair on the American's solid dork. Silently. Both. He had only unzipped halfway down. It was all, seemingly, that she deserved. A dry violation. Come on. This is what you knew it would always be.

Luce Stein's aunt tried to bite the hand that stopped her from crying out. She tried to turn her head away. She tried to turn herself away bodily. But, like her niece, she too was held in midair. Aloft. The man felt the fat of her push up from his arm that circled the buttocks and he felt the fat of her push down from her breasts. He felt, as he watched Luce Stein being rodded against the wardrobe, that the fat of the aunt in his arms, pressed against him, was meeting lusciously at her middle as though he alone was concentrating all her enfolding flesh where he alone wanted it. He felt the surprise stirring upon the image of he alone being able to awaken a quiver in her sweet flub, her juice flesh, her sucking folds. He spun her in the air to better face him and moved over to the bed that was once Costas Stein's where he pushed her head and shoulders back onto the rugged landscape of blankets, kept his hand over her mouth while he unzipped, raised her fat, disfigured and disgusting (his manhood flicked at the thought) thighs high to meet him and entered, with difficulty at first, the old lady. In a few strokes he was gasping with the effort of prolonging the ecstatic release. He had already moved his hand from her mouth, but she was not screaming. Her neck was strained backwards as an old turtle's, her face thrust up as a receiver

116

of a miracle, she was rocking her head from side to side in time with his heavy thuddings against her. Her body was bouncing with judders of its own and she was smiling passed the grim grin of a skeleton.

It was left to the kid Kevvie, in his room across the living room, to cry out against the dark forces he could only, unseen, imagine.

When the two men emerged from the place that was once Costas Stein's, Cowcher was waiting outside. He was standing directly in front of, but away, from the front door, just in the light from inside. In that nether of light and dark, he looked even older.

The two men stopped and watched him carefully. But Cowcher did not move for a long time. The smaller of the two men went to move to him, but was held back by The American. Finally Cowcher walked towards them to stand searching their faces for an instant before moving around them and into the house. Again, The American held his companion back. His nod and look said wait. Inside, the kid Kevvie was at full pitch.

Cowcher came out of the place that was once Costas Stein's. He passed close to, but did not brush against, the smaller of the other two men as he moved around them to walk back up the driveway. At a nod from The American, they followed him until the front door of the mansion, the door to old Stein's rooms. Cowcher turned and stood impassively on the doorstep. Again, he seemed so old as to look apocryphal. Still he had not said a word. The smaller man turned to The American.-

'We wanna go in there?'

'Now, I wouldn't mind.'

The smaller man nudged The American, winked easily at him, nodded a tag-along and jokishly feinted his way up to Cowcher. With the first kick, Cowcher broke the man's kneecap front on. He staggered back onto the porch with a gargle that was meant to be a

117

scream. The American did not even move when Cowcher moved with surprising agility to the smaller man, lifted his face up towards him by a vicious tug of the hair and gave him such a sharp stiff-fingered jolt to the right eye that even from behind The American knew the eye would be lost. It was so fast, so direct, that it took a fraction of a second before the smaller man's whole being seemed to explode in writhe.

'Go your way.' Cowcher, hard, very hard-edged in voice, back at guard on the doorstep to old Stein's rooms. He looked so old, but The American knew. As he dragged the smaller man back up the driveway, The American said:

'Yeah, sure, I've heard about you. 'Kay, you've made your point. We've made ours, buddy.'

Cowcher did not even cast a glance back down to the place that was once Costas Stein's before turning back to the keepsafe of the old man.

2.

'What'd they call you Dognuts for?'

'Gurton, if you're going to work with us, you show a bit of respect.'

'Who said I'm going to work for you, Dognuts?'

'The contract you just signed said so. No Dognuts, you black person. Dognuts is out.'

'Dognuts, just read what's in front of you.'

'What is this hype, anyway. "Chapter 1: My father is going to be assassinated one day after I've knocked over this book about me preplanning to assassinate the old bugger..."'

They are in the Editor-in-Chief's office and Ed Dognuts Bradley is now waving the piece of paper from which he has just read in front of the bland face, full of Aboriginal causality, of Flash Gurton standing before his desk with arms folded and legs apart firmly planted like he was back in the ring in the right corner for a change. And only the primmish tightness of his lips imparts a pursing of the same that says he is not back in the ring but standing unmoving on the mat waiting for an answer. His biceps are still such that they bulge through his trickish tweed jacket; his neck still thick enough to divert the attention away from old sweatbeds of dirt in the delta folds of the rhinotype skin above his distinctly non-U collar.

The flutter of the piece of paper stays in the air as though it was likely Frank Stein himself would come down and answer for it in person. There is not amusement on either man's face, but the sheer bullishness of Flash Gurton's presumption in his future boss's office is obviously winning the day. His voice, too, is no-foolin':

'Where is he?'

'Who?'

119

'Frankie Stein. Journo once belonga here, man. You gave him the bullet and now he's missing.'

'You agreed to take his job, for Christ's sake.'

'That's only because I hate the little white shit. Keep to the point. Who put the screws on you to hoick him out, Dognuts?'

'Get out.'

'Where were you when my people were settling this fucking country, Dognuts?'

'What?'

'Don't give me "what". Had that tuck-it-away rhubarb ever since I was spitting out my mother's milk, whitey. I wanna know where my new adopted totem, that pig-faced marsupial mouse Frank Stein, a sportswriter's arsehole but me oppo, is. You wanna start a racial war? Who were they?'

'What're you talking about, Gurton? Piss off.'

Flash, his Polynesian features descending into a positive Aboriginal wryness and his large frame going so loose that for an alarming moment Dognuts Bradley could veritably see a black bellybutton following black belly hair out of the lower shirt level atop those flappy grey strides and suffered a cold flush that he might have black nudity thrust upon his person in a most unsanguine manner before the authorities could be called. Whatever authorities there might be for such possibilities. But Flash Gurton merely wags his thick forefinger in Dognuts direction along with the tipping of a wink. Turns, heels and departs as though his request for a raise had just been granted with five grand lumped on top.

Outside, he makes a feint for Dognuts's Secretary's mammae she takes as a feint for her tits and covers up and giggles, though it really isn't her style and a fucking liberty. Where Flash, too and

120

likewise, wags the same forefinger similarly at her, sweetly expresses that he wouldn't work for Dognuts even if he was a cur looking for her cunt, retrieves a waddy he has left in the corridor outside that outer office, and marches back into Dognuts's office before she has time to perfect her fumbling upon the intercom by way of run for your life, boss.

At the sight of Flash Gurton re-entering with that waddy in his hands and seemingly practising cover drives as he enters in upon, Dognuts Bradley loses something that he later considered to be his dignity and makes for the corner of the office with both hands out like Moses stopping the waters. But Flash is making for the desk and with: 'Scottie for the US Open this year' swings the waddy as Number 1 wood cleanly against first one then the other desk leg at the same end of the desk. It drops like a bull brought to the kneel before the matador, with tomorrow morning's editorial fluttering across the toes of his shoes like it would wrap him up with the threats of the future. You can rub me out but don't shoeshine me.

For some reason, unknown even to himself, Dognuts Bradley squeals with terror and then is instantly ashamed of himself, such that it is too late for Flash Gurton (momentarily stunned himself by himself for not having had the common d.f. to step out of the way of the pen-and-ink stand before it slid down the slipway of the desk and spilled its inky guts across his lower trousers) to say:

'Tell me who they were, or you're next, whitey-come-fucking-lately.'

Dognuts Bradley recommissions himself enough to sit down on that spot in the corner and light a cigarette to calm his nerves. There is obviously no way he is now going to tell the startling Aboriginal the whatfor, because it is obvious even to the bellicose Flash G. that Dognuts Bradley has gone well beyond him mentally. With a furious roar of rage, Flash leaps over to where Dognuts is executing a sumptuous drawback on what could be his last cigarette, even unwittingly, and proceeds to swing the waddy against the two walls directly above the Editor-in-Chief's head. Not making one blind bit

121

of difference to the now becalmed, muted figure of Dognuts; chips of plaster falling on his head making him look confetti'd, if not angelic, until, finally, even the racial fury of Flash Gurton wanes to a halt.

'Jesus, Dognuts, they say you go right off when you've got a fag between your kissers, but this is ridiculous.'

When Bradley merely emerges momentarily from his new soak of nicotine to shrug I guess so, Flash Gurton's beef-sorta shoulders slumps in failure. He swings away from his one-time future boss and, with the waddy trailing along the ground as though it was cut from a tree without pith, removes himself from the heady presences of the upper offices wallahs. His brows are knit in heavy consternation. Between the first and second floors he lets the waddy fall out of his hand in a manner that suggests it was just a matter of time before it fell by the wayside anyway. His large shoes scuff across the raw concrete of the fire stairs. His padded shoulders hunch awkwardly. For one of the few times in his minority-race existence, Flash Gurton's body forms a frigged-out S as he walks along. He has failed. He has not come away with the who of the 'they' he was trying to find out about. He has blown his new job, been of no use to his newly adopted totem mate Frank Stein.

But what really hurts is that a good dose of black and threatening rage against a pissweak whitey has had no effect that you would chant songs about to rhythm sticks let alone gain a redress of an injustice. What's the prejudiced world coming to?

Flash Gurton walks past the gatekeeper to the wide open and embracing arms of the land of unemployment. Suddenly the world has taken on grey tones. On the footpath of that side alley there, not ten metres away from the gatehouse, he stops short with the realisation of what he has done. A mug, a white mug, a white dumb white mug has disappeared in suspicious circumstances. Who cares? He wants to know from himself why should he. Why it has come to the head of being symptomatic of being black in this country. He has no answers for himself. He smiles. He doesn't care. It just feels so good to be on the atavistic hunt trail; from his roots, feeling what it might feel like. He turns back and moves back to the gatekeeper; he could be carrying on where they last broke off some recent conversation:

'Christ knows, though, where I go from here, bub.'

Nor is it as though the gatekeeper is thrown into confusion by this stunningly irrelevant remark. He hitches his serge trousers further up his thin and bleak frame, tips his blue cap further over his brow and hawks out from green eyes used to watching many for many a long year so that the downright suspicious has become the sheerly righteous, like it or damn lump it, mate -- all this in one fell movement -- before drawling at Flash Gurton with the expression of voice that a sleepy lizard might have if it could find voice out in the sun during a blazing high noon:

'If you're the black guy that's a journo, then they said to wait here for a parcel.'

'Who's "they"?'

'Don't ask me, mate. They just said you stay put no matter what happens.'

They stood staring at each other with growing malevolence for five minutes before if happened. For some reason that neither could figure out, they couldn't take their eyes off each other, even when the scream rang out from high above them. Finally Flash Gurton looks up, but there is no way of telling from which of the fifteen storeys avast above him came the single cry of pain. He knows that somewhere in that building there would be movement. The going to whatever-it-was; the bustling away from whatever-it-was. The ergates, unseen and silent. Trouble in the nest. Close in: But still he waits as mysteriously told.

It takes another five minutes from even then before he finds out the reason for the scream and the reason for the message. The box is

123

hand delivered to him by a teenager who thrusts it into his hands so furtively that you could tell he has been slipped a few Judas cents to mosey it on down to the Mack guy waiting by the back gate. It is a tobacco tin inside an ordinary brown envelope roughly sealed and inside the tobacco tin is a whole and very bloody thumbnail.

Flash Gurton guesses, rather than knows, that it is Dognuts Bradley's thumbnail. He is not too surprised; such confluences of events and circumstances are animistic anyway. Lodged spirits of places along the new hunting trail. He reads again the scribbled address on the envelope; it says 'Horrie Brands, Solicitor' at the end of a wickedly amateurish drawing of a pointing finger.

'I would've,' he ventures as a matter of fact to the gatekeeper, 'screamed, too, wouldn't you?'

And even if it had mattered at that moment of leaving, Flash Gurton still wouldn't have wondered who had followed on his heels to do this. He has a name. He has no idea what a solicitor called Horrie Brands might have to do with the no-more Frank Stein. Anyway, right then that is a thing of the future to discover, and somewhat pale in significance with the current somewhat problem of how to dispose of Editor-in-Chief Bradley's dognutty thumbnail with the proper ceremony due to it. Fortunately, only a block away, he has come across a trash can that it fitted.

But it was really more the maddening thing of having in your hands the handwritten Stein scrawl going: 'Chapter 1: By the time you read this my father would have been assassinated. He was assassinated by myself one day after I had finished correcting this manuscript, which was already on its way to three publishers by the time my father was assassinated by me and which is all about, basically, the how and why of me putting the old man away for good after I've finished this manuscript, if you see what I mean...'6

And not knowing what the damn thing meant, apart from the obvious flipped meaning.

Frank Stein's father, the adopter of Costas Stein, used to be known as Harold Stein Rhodes Scholar, then Captain Harry Stein, then Captain Harry Stein VC, then just plain Harry Stein when he was that sort of everymum and everydad hero who was always being interviewed on radio or in the weekly soapies of the day as the young and healthy and typical and brave-heroic cop that could be patrolling your area every night when you were asleep or away, protecting your home and loved ones (this was the immediate postwar years), then Assistant Commissioner H. Stein educated at Cambridge University just after the start of the Fifties, then Commissioner Harry Stein fullstop. His name has been a household two-word. On the ever-eve of his retirement, he held a press conference. He upstaged even the Prime Minister leaving for a State visit to the US for first-spot news item. When he left the dais at which he stood avuncularly answering their questions, there were tears in his ageing grey eyes and he caught them all so on the hop by suddenly looking old as he walked away that even his old journalistic adversaries stood to cheer his departure.

Then he just became known as the old man Stein, because, sitting there in lowly solitude and in constant trembling, heatless, with his skin stretched like a temporary shelter across bony pontoons, as though the body couldn't fill its fleshy confines anymore . .. because that was all he was. An old man. The old man Stein.

Waiting.

His blanket over his knees and his knees together and his hands resting in his lap looking like a small monkey's hands and staring out of the window across the front lawn of the mansion to the high enclosing brick fence over across there.

And waiting.

Only Cowcher does not call him the old man Stein. Cowcher still calls him Commissioner. He moves around the old man Stein as reverently as he has ever done when Harry Stein was working at his desk on something that was quite beyond Cowcher in importance. It is the same now as then. Cowcher waits on the old man waiting.

But even Cowcher knows that much of what had to be accomplished has now been accomplished and that his purpose for the old man Stein might be at an end. Or that, now that it has been done, the old man might die where once inconceivable. Same thing.

Cowcher waits, watching the old man Stein now mostly.

He does not need to fuss around the old man Stein now. He knows it. He waits, waiting for what the Commissioner is now going to do, now that the thing has been accomplished. Cowcher has no fear. He has guarded well, has done what had been asked of him a long time ago. Cowcher just waits.

He has told the old man Stein about Costas. He feels in his bones that the old man Stein understood. Cowcher has not mentioned the disappearance of Frank Stein, the son, or the night visit of The American and his companion to the place and the wife that was once Costas Stein's. Those things don't matter now.

The most noticeable flaw in a body noticeably flawed in many other ways is her mouth. It seems for all the world that she is perpetually smiling by means of an invisible wire hooked into the left hand corner of her upper lip and pulled upwards, as much as if she is grinning and bearing being the only fish in the big wide ocean always on the dangle. It gives her sometimes the look of a smile and sometimes the look of a leer, but it is always lopsided. On the left side of her mouth, her lips are like two ruddy curtains drawn back to display the grim yellow slabs that are her teeth. They somewhat matched the colour of the blotched powder of a past cosmetic age upon her cheeks. Yet her eyes are green and twinkling Irishly

126

beneath the drawn-up brown hair which sits on her head with its tentacles limply falling about her face and neck like a stranded octopus there.

It is Milly Hunt and she sits on the seat in the concrete concourse evidently waiting for someone. If it wasn't for the stains on, and the unfashionability of, the duffle coat she is wearing, she could almost be regarded as a perfectly ordinary lady of mature years sitting there waiting for someone, rather than a frump who you wouldn't dare even regard unless you were looking for a mouthful of abuse right up your alley. 'Names Milly Hunt, not silly cunt! No bugger's gonna come on top of me!' Old snail trails of snot make the lapels of the duffle coat glisten in the early afternoon sun; the ash from her cigarettes make it seem that the duffle coat is going prematurely grey in the odd scabulous place.

It is Kings Cross. The pigeons around her could be reflecting the shoppers moving up and down the à la mode shops opposite, so frenetic are they pecking, paddling, jigging, squabbling, picking and plucking. She is not the only irritant among them but she could be, and when she sees Flash Gurton roll his frame around the corner she becomes visibly agitated the more, because he is not finding who he is searching for. She even has to call him back.

'Here, you silly bugger.'

She has said it in a voice so loud that even Flash can't fluke an instant non-recognition. And Milly now right at him, powdered nose to puggy spread.

'Milly Hunt. Not silly cunt, buster. You don't even know who Horrie Brands, solicitor, is.'

'Who're you when you're home?'

'Milly Hunt, so open the ear flaps.'

'Listen, whitey, I ain't got time to delve you. Find some other customer.'

She has already hit him a straight left hook to the guts and sunk him to his knees before he has got his ringside instincts going. Difficult to defend yourself when your eyes are suddenly level to the purple blotches showing through the stockings on the shins of your opponent, and her getting rounds of loud two-handed clappings from a seeming million or so goody-goodies suddenly appreciatively appearing in the first couple of eye-witness rows around, fuck em. She is graceful enough, though, to let him hang on to her legs while his' body commits all its self-preserving forces to overcome a unique but universal apnoea fell-swooped she has made him suffer from down there. Hearing above him:

'How's bloody Dognuts Bradley's thumbnail gonna help you bloodhound bloody Horrie Brands, solicitor, you silly cunt you?'

Flash can hardly believe that his own voice should sound so normal so near to the ground, saying as only a low-slung croak could:

'Phone book look up.'

'Don't apologise to me, you black person you. No buggers gonna come on top of me. That's my bastard third or fourth cousin, that Horrie Brands. You're lucky you can come with me. Now get up and no foolin' with the hairy silly of Milly.'

And she has actually driven him before her by the twigging of the left ear lug before Flash thunders her off with exceedingly dark looks rising above clenched fists that would certainly blackout any part of her, hairy or not, silly or not, coming ready or not.

'Slackbum.' Flash Gurton.

'Hoon.' Her.

But said with a winning smile on the better side of her mouth when it comes to teeth population and swinging away with a swish of her hips, not a little unsplendid when all's said and done, which they probably have. A little coquette from the back end. She leads him from the square of the El Alamein fountain as a safe route out through a clubland that is passing this daytime, like any other daytime, in respectable show when people should be safe to walk the streets without indigenous persons getting aggro with unfortunate white ladies of the seemingly underprivileged variety.

Fortunately for his reputation he only has to follow her three blocks down an obliging hill before she turns into an apartment block no more than three storeys high, featuring iron grilles to the windows and hand-wrought iron gates to the main entrance that truly promise all the sumptuousness of Victorian living for those who might have enough sumptuous padding around the cheque book region if ever one of the twelve apartments ever came onto the market by way of glide around the ever-waiting list. On a hill it might be, but in the high belt it was. Where she soft-shoed to a halt, extracted a key from a meaty dive into her bra with fingers that looked like they could have been dipped in vast decadence even before they were perhaps used in experiments with nail polish dips too bloody to contemplate, unlocked those iron gates there with proprietorial ease, and swung them open like a seraglio's tent flap for Flash G. to enter if he was man enough by naked eye to sight sights unseen by the same. The hold she has suddenly gained upon the waistband of his strides has helped somewhat as well.

When in there, in the cool glade of the entrance hall and on the lushy verge of that deep pile there, she backs him up against an oriel containing a statue of Apollo Belvedere and proceeds to grind her pelvis into a gap that approximates to his own were it not for the bulge of his vast guts above that still-snagged waistband demanding a contortionist's nightmare. The stain of her breath putting the sprig of garlic around his neck to a fast wither:

'This is where I live, you silly cunt. Kiss me, lover.'

'Never!'

'Don't ever ask me again, then, black bugger you.'

'You've got me word on that, honest.'

'Come on, Milly'll show you something. And don't think I don't know.'

Suddenly, in all this luxury, she doesn't look a ham sandwich half-devoured by a rabies dog. But Flash G. realises too late that he could stir for the boodle in it for him, beyond the poor poodle in her, for she has slipped off him and slipped before him up lush stairs with a swishy swagger environmentally fitful. He stares and trundles after. His sense of taste screaming at his sense of decorum.

She seems to shed powder gunk as she goes. Trillingly. By the time they have arrived outside the great oak door, 'this one Milly Hunt is no longer a silly recount, but is bearing for him metaphoric images of pure wool twin sets and pearls. It has made Flash G. speechless with the gigolo possibilities residing within that apartment and her indoors transformation. We should all spread a little Aboriginality around among the white crazies and richies. We should lament lost friends like Stein from afar. We should write .long inquiries to the Lost Person's Bureau from 'leather confines in circumstances of a kept man, rather than float around like some dickhead aggro-ing ordinary poor slobs about Stein's whereabouts. So what happens, is all, is that they get their fingernails pulled out to the tune of a very-upsetting-for-all scream being a bringer-down of newspaper employees' confidences and a filler-up of trash cans otherwise known as rubbish bins without the discarded human parts. If kissing her might be like wiping your mouth with a bats' cave entrance, so what?

The door opens before him. Munificent whiffs of Chanel. Flash G. enters Milly's apartment by way of following his nose.

In there, from down the corridor that could lead to a gigolo's dream, from behind a locked door down there at the end, he thinks he has heard a cry for help. Some small piping lament. Once and hardly no more, but Flash G's too busy trying to mentally rehearse for a big seduction scene to worry about minor things like human cries for help. His Hollywood saunter leading him into a lounge room all white in Swedish where she sits drooped mawkishly across some just-right-for-two, swigging five-star straight from the bottle.

What does a thickly desired man do?

She does not invite him to sit down. And he might have waited there embarrassingly unsure given the gigolo he has just decided to be, if that small piping lament did not come again. Somewhere off, dull and muted.

And it is only to pass the time of day for her leaving him standing in the doorway like a shag on an ugly rock that he pipes up a casual what's that, some pet parrot remained unfed waiting for mamma to have come home? Did I hear an attempt at pounding upon the door back there too? As much as mascara plastered sodways across bagshot eyes can reflect a twinkle, her mascara refracts back at him:

'What you don't know can't hurt you, darls.'

Ah, she's talking at last. So gigolo Flash G. takes a number of a couple of swaggering strides into the room without him really quickly being conscious of the fact that his mind has turned from sexual phantasms to suddenly remembering where he had seen her before. Frank Stein, oppo. The Journo's Club. Her behind the bar at the Journo's Club talking to my new totem Frank. Jesus. Come this. Come Dognuts Bradley's thumbnail definitely out of the position it ought to be in. Come some lawyer's name, name Horrie Brands. Come her bailing me up and mentioning this lawyer's name writ large alongside of Dognuts's forcibly-withdrawn scabber.

And now Flash G. is suddenly finding himself moving to guzzling Milly to knock aside that bottle of five-star with a bearish swipe.

131

Plants his left size twelve on the area of her chest where her breasts might have been seemingly sixty or more years ago and pushes her back beneath his contempt. She giggles like she might have done seemingly ninety years ago.

'Gimme some answers, sweetheart. Horrie somethingorother, lawyer, who?'

'My flunk of a third or fourth cousin, keeps trying to say he's my brother.'

'Poor old Dognuts Bradley's thumbnail.'

'Gone missing in the shitcan you threw it in.'

'How come you know that?'

'Name's Milly Hunt, not silly cunt.'

'Talk.'

'Stop tickling me.'

'Talk, so help me.'

'Nobody's gonna come on top of me.'

'The Journo's Club, you and Frank. What've they done to the bozo?'

'There was an old lady who lived in a shoe, the silly old cunt...'

She suddenly flibbers beneath his boot like a puppet with string demolition. Flash's heart in a real sense jumps with the thought that it's probably life to crush to death a white sluggo against a cochineal velvet cushion with one foot of the lightly touching kind, when she suddenly swoons to snore drunkenly even before his body has followed his heart in a pronto retreat from her. Relieved to notice that only her mouth resembles a real corpse. They could slide whole slabs from the morgue in and out of it.

Gigolo? Christ, like that, she looks as inviting as a half-filled bean bag would look inviting. Things getting all very confusing these last few days upon the old sleuth trail. Never thought the whiteys lived as chaotically as they played the racial game.

When there is a far greater change in the cry somewhere off right. A cry for help more hapless than hopeless, yet surely now positively within the apartment itself. Flash G. turns and moves back to the door at the end of the corridor and doesn't try it for he knows that it is locked. There are scratchings within that can only come from someone locked within.

He moves back to the front door and has determined visions of the best rugby tackle he ever once did see. That door is gonna lay low. I'm going to assert black power here'n'now upon the unhinged in this fucking city, when:

'All right, all right.'

It is Milly, not with a .45 but a key in her hand, and as suddenly wide awake as she is still giggling in a sort of contemptuously snoring way. Her timing such that he hasn't even had time to get a good head of steam up, before she has opened up.

And in that sudden open space of a room there before him, the first thing Flash G. sees are the many tin plates of disturbed foodstuffs littered about the floor as though a SAS platoon has eaten there a whole year before scattering. Then he notices the sorry naked form silhouetted against the window frame, its outline so uggers that it might be a survivor from Bergen Belsen. He hears her:

'I gave the silly cunt a rope out of the window if he wanted to climb out. All the chicken shit had to do was drop the last two floors if he wanted out.'

133

He sees, does Flash, moving a whole curiosity closer, a poor thing of a man. Standing there with one hand over his privates (easily covered) and the other held supplicatingly out in a plea for rescue.

And he was gagging so with relief that perhaps he is a survivor from Belsen, that monstrous joke of a place a dross time ago. Like Frank E. R. R. Stein.

PART III

1

'Where you been at? I've been looking all over for you, bozo.'

But Stein has already sunk to the floor. A whimpering show. Relief's dog-end. The rescue has hit him between the eyes with a belated KO that could do justice to a sudden an overwhelming divine uppercut. Not that flash G. is taking any notice of him at all. He has turned to her instead:

'Everybody's thinking he topped himself.'

Milly burps, as though she herself is inspired by divine afflatus, and giggles. Drinks explode in Flash's face. But she is not again what she was seeming to be; suddenly she's on the rational splurge:

'Silly cunt was going to throw himself over that cliff at The Gap, wasn't he? He... ' and she was nudging Stein with the toe of her shoe to elicit a blubbering bagpipe effect of air from him, even asonorous for a whine, and she wasn't stopping: 'was sitting on the edge, silly cunt, with his toes dangling over the edge, knees knocking. Blue as a plucked chook. Have you ever seen a grown man cry? Silly cunt, he was sitting there all nude, his clothes neatly piled back about where I was. Silly cunt didn't even see me. Mean, you look like him, you should be putting more clothes on at a time like karking it, not taking them off.'

'Should've pushed the bozo. It would've saved me a lot of time.' Flash, booting the bagpipes from the other side. Second wind.

'Oh, the silly cunt was going to jump all right if my name ain't Milly Hunt, not silly cunt. So what I did was simple. I picked up them there rags of his and ran away with them, then turned back and laughed at the silly cunt. Nobody's so dopey they can do their useless selves in when they're being laughed at, not even this silly cunt. I got him and he's mine, so you can piss off.'

At which she places her foot on the back of Stein's neck. A monstrous stroke. Yet Flash G. is not displaced. He clumps his own plate of meat on Stein's bruddied back. If this is ownership, it is onerous, and:

'Uhuh, white bint, dis fella plurry belonga me. Get it? I've got me no job on account of this bozo, and I had to discard no less than Dognuts Bradley's thumbnail from my person on account of this bozo, and it's paying too much black lip service to a whitey-run world to let go on a principle. He's mine. Get your shitkicker off, Milly Cunt.'

'The name's Milly Hunt.'

'Silly cunt.'

'No black bum's going to come on top of me!'

'Get off. Why were you following him, eh? What you want him for?'

'Because,' because she has to talk when her right cross to Flash G.'s genitalia misses wildly because of the difficulty of keeping her right foot anchored on the crook of Stein's neck, 'he's gonna make me the limousine lady I'm cut out to be, that's why. I'm gonna write the million dollar bestseller, and he's gonna publish it. My publisher. I love the sweetie and hate the bastard already. Me in my furs going to the premiere of the multi-buck movie based on my book. You can laugh, you silly cunt. ..'

'I wasn't...' Flash G., but can't finish his honest protestation at such an outrageous suggestion in this serious moment due to a laugh a minute coming up each micro-second.

136

'My name's Milly Hunt, and I always knew I was destined to have my own publisher eating out of my hand. There's gonna be Russian silver fox furs at that premiere, too, but don't ask me what length. How do I know what the temperature's gonna be?'

'Ohhh!'

This is Stein junior surging up from the prostrate to the kneeling, flinging clodhoppers off him so as to be very upsetting to both she and the other he, in a position that supplicants to the very Gods. This man is not whimpering anymore. There are tears of great ruined-self seeping from his Stein's eyes, cloaks of liquid pain. Stein in great grief.

He bawls. Stein bawls. He howls aloud for Costas. For the murder of his beloved brother. For the brother he probably caused the murder of by insisting on paying for the publication of that book. That blown-away beloved body. My father was... What I touched did go all that way shittily unto my brother Costas, and I haven't done myself in. And whoever did it is free, got him, nearly got me.

'Shaggit!'

That, yet again comes out of Stein -- different way, same sentiment -- to their fairly-impressed impressions. Before them, the man Stein has gone through grief. He is standing. Now on his face is rage.

'Get off me, you two whackos!'

Stein in chrysalis. A new moth.

Stein, now with a gritty jut to his jaw, Milly, hers half on the slattern slant and half on the innate breeding, and Flash G. with his on the wonder how as much as a bored black can be with such paling company, are interrogatorily in the lounge of Milly's Louis

Quatorze (or some parts more present) lounge. She is stubbornly beefing it up to their beefing it up of her.

'What do you think I am, some silly cunt? If I tell you all I know, what's left for my million dollar best-seller?'

Stein: 'I once had the same thought. If you must know it was about my own dear Dad. Now tell, or guts gets smashed. Have you ever seen yours spilled?'

'Sticks and stones. You're just talking like a publisher, you sod. Trying to rip me off already. No way are you gonna know, nup. I'll give you clues. Tell you where to go, but the million dollars is mine. I'm already writing it in my mind. That's the deal.'

'Oh, shit.'

'Don't swear in front of me, you silly cee. I picked you up from the gutter.',

'You really ought to talk.' Stein. With his fist at the junction of her meaty lips, but Flash G. (back metaphorically in the ring but as referee) at the strong hold so he can't draw that fist back for an effective punch to the lipstick that would send the geraniums to the wall in sympathy with her teeth.

'I talk. Oh boy, don't I talk, like haven't I already told you all I'm gonna?'

'Say again.'

'I'll say again. I'll lead but that's all. They got at your brother because of the book, sure. You want to know more? Friesman is the guy you're after. He paid me, some pittance you should see the miserly cunt, to tab you all over, like that Journos Club you shouldn't oughta wanta puke in let alone grog on in. That was me a coupla times, you silly cunt. Picking you up, slipping you a mickey that night.'

138

'Why.'

'Don't whine, I can't stand whining. If you're going to make a fortune out of me by publishing my book, just don't whine. Look on the silver lining.'

'Why? I'll kill her.'

'Who's he talking to?' Milly is giving the judication to Flash G., who nods as appropriately as he stems Stein from the assault, mainly because he really doesn't understand what this white trash is talking about either, 'I ask you.'

'Don't ask me, keep talking.'

'The book, of course. What fucking else, you silly cunts? He tried to warn you off. Even paid my brother to have it away with that slack arse of a wife of yours, and what does he do?'

'Dunno,' Flash G. has to answer because his hand over

Stein's mouth doesn't allow any other question from the floor of the house.

'He pees himself under the bed, so I hear.'

'Get off.'

'No bull.'

Flash G. earnest himself to Stein's face looking like it's got a blood stoppage. Sort of. 'That right, bozo?'

'My brother told me right up. Friesian did his brother in.'

'Friesman?'

'He's a heavy.'

'I used to live with the silly cunt when I was two stone lighter. I oughta know he's heavy. Now, I ain't gonna write my best-selling novel if silly cunt here doesn't track down who killed his wowser brother because I've decided that's going to be the theme of my best-selling novel, so I'm gonna help. But only clues. He's gotta find, so I can write about it. That's fair.'

'Balls.' Stein has broken free by probably breaking Flash G.'s instep.

'Don't give me balls, you.'

'That's all you're going to get, you tart, if you don't come to the cops with me. That was my brother Costas.'

'Stiff. You find, I'll lead. That's the deal.'

Stein couldn't refuse it a great deal.

He is outside the iron gate of the house and is shivering with that anxiety that comes from not knowing how he will react if he is confronted by the scenario that he has come there for... ie, Frank Stein. He hopes, I hope that if I can collar fucking Friesman face-to-face I get so homicidal I can tear the prick from limb to limb.

He and Flash G., there, don't even really know why they have taken up Milly's clue that they should stand outside Friesman's mansion. They both know that there's going to be no comely neon flashing out above the front door across the sweeping driveway, and the swept lawn through there informing the world that I (Friesman) Bumped Off Fuckwit But Gutsy Costas Stein, Ole Monstrous-joke Stein's Younger Brudder. That wouldn't even turn a head of an ironing-board brigade anywhere anyway. Even if it got flashed on telly. But it is a clue and it was a clue from Milly that they should come/go and see, like the silly cunts they are. Perhaps Stein gets the chance and gouges Friesman's eyes out and feels better already because that's about as much chance as he's gonna get to bring down Morrie Friesman, the silly cunt.

Someone is at home. From each of the three storeys of the Friesman covey are lights. They eye the grounds. They cast highlights at the three-metre wall that surrounds the large surrounding flats gardenesque. They drive luminous flooks at Stein and Flash Gurton. Lairising leers from the hated lair.

As Milly Hunt knows. She watches them, shivering with those emotions, at the gate of the Friesman house, from a safe distance across the street many safe retributive paces away and along. Her face has not the sluttish turns about it now. Milly Hunt is seriously in bate down there, unmoving and not even writing in the notebook she has to record, as she would have it, what goes for her million dollar best-seller on the run.

They have been there for at least a half an hour by now, tied to that indelible waiting outside the Friesman place. There has been long ago the opening of the front door to let loose the broad, fair, gaiting man they did not then know as The American (but who Luce Stein had known by blur, by rape, by kid Kevvie's screaming as he pounded her in midair against the wardrobe), who came, smugly caricaturing a hometown Hollywood shamus, with all the lip that his wide lapels inflected, softly across the lawns to front them up there. In his wake followed another anonymous two. Wayang shadows against the house lights. Puppets with hats. More flat as hoods, a few paces kept deliberately behind. The American:

'I don't wanna know what you two cripples want. Probably I-got-no-Jesus Lefties you'd be. Just beat yourselves oft somewhere off, Mac and Mac.' .'

Stein doesn't give ground. He is still shivering from the encounter long after The American has stared silently at them from behind the iron gate and turned back into the house; but I didn't give ground. Oh God, let the rage happen at the right time. Let me revenge his brother Costas. *My brother was...* In that house is Costas's murderer.

And silence again. There is not even cars along this street. They must all count their string pearls and cuff links after dark within this boulevard's ranches.

If this is a spell, it is Flash G. who finally breaks the spell by pumping Stein's arm from the elbow and, while Milly begins to write furiously in her notebook again:

'Come oil, whitey bozo, you. There's nothing here.'

'I'm staying. He's going to know.' Stein, not so much shivering now. It might happen right.

Certainly they did not see the front door open, if it ever did; yet the Merc in the driveway starts up and moves dolefully around the wide arc of the driveway to the gate. Stein and Flash G. physically feel the incision of its high beam on their persons cutting them out of the background of the night. Flash G. is surged with the need to run, but cannot seem to be able to let go his hold on Stein's elbow. For all the world he could be trying to dampen Stein's quaking. And it is as if by the power of the forces against them that these twin grilled gates glide open before them and it is as if by the immutability of the powers before them that the Merc slides by them without even so much as a need for the smallest of a growl. There are three in there. Stein seems to recognise the silhouette of the man he doesn't yet know as The American sitting in the front, but not driving. Even the gate has shut again and the car quite down the road near where Milly Hunt is before either of them can move to turn around. It didn't happen; I should've kicked the windows in; I had the chance.

Not so Milly. She begins to run for all that her ludicrous spike heels will allow. Now the car growls. From where Stein and Flash G. are, it seems to merely bound up to her; a slight diversion; a slight pinching of the brakes; a slight flurry of movement around the doors. A slight jerk as it takes off again. But not so slight is Milly's

142

scream. And by the time they can move towards down there, she and the car and The American and the other two with him are together turning off the main street a block away. Any whatever speed surprisingly too quick for them.

Stein runs as hard as he can from an untidy start burdened by a black man who still won't let go. His rage coil-sprung at last. They run as furiously as they can after the car, that Merc., Friesman's hearse. Stein is crying out; he cries:

'Bring her back!' He doesn't hear himself. Flash G. doesn't register it. Only a pretty silly cunt would have said it.

They are so far behind already, it is already a cold trail that block away, just about.

It would have taken them fifteen minutes to belt around the block that contains the great home of bastard Friesman. As it is, Stein and Flash G. arrive back at those front gates in a little under a half an hour. They had scoured the scrubby verges around the block, tearing away at the winter, poking branches, knowing, just knowing that that car had been around there. That it had not taken Milly for a joy ride. Stein frantic. Flash G. more recidivistically acceptive. A moonless night helps not at all.

Back there is no better now. No passing cars still. The lights in the house now out. The house a vague, heavy outline. There is the hum of the city behind them and a mute orange tone from its lights in the sky. But these feel like the things of an air-raid in some past war. Stein and Flash G. could be the last two people alive.

'Let's go get the cops.'

'Get nicked.'

'Okay, okay.' Flash G. realises he still has some mental hold on - Stein, like an invisible grip around the elbow. But he can't seem to figuratively pull away. He feels Stein's innate' rage might blow him away. For Stein, himself, too, he seems to be held back by some invisible hand from bursting upwards' and outwards and overwards to crush Friesman and his house and all Friesman things. So he screams his out-rage as outrageously as he can:

'You bastard! You bloody bastard!'

Unfortunately, the effect of this is stunningly contra. As though the house of Friesman had a schoolmasterish intelligence and now catches out, gotcha you little beast, the boy who has shouted a dirty word out aloud, the floodlights to the lawn and that front gate switch on. They must work sonically, tripped by abuse. And there stands The American in the middle of the lawn, legs apart and huge arms akimbo, in the light the tips of his hair a white halo around the head of his form in silhouette. What they see, too, is the Merc has returned. What they both feel is that The American is staring at them with the cold eyes of a fed snake -- a casual, visual licking. This is too much concentration camp from within the perimeter to rage against, too much cold confidence from the ones who control the effects. I can't hold onto my rage. It won't come forth. I want to run, Costas. What have they done to her, not her too? Flash G. is in no two minds:

'The cops now, bozo.'

Still Stein shakes his head. He is trying at least to stand his ground. Flash G. mentally releases his grip on Stein's elbow and turns away. But no more than half a pace before he comes up hard against a body that makes even his own great lumbering self a relatively small lumber.

Such a huge figure so darkly in his way and so silently so close makes Flash G. cry out:

'Speakee the lingo?'

before he even realises he has done so, let alone, himself, know why he has done so. By that time sheer fright has cannoned him off the figure back against the now turning form of Stein. His astonishment is so shaped that it could almost be theatrical. For before them now, but obviously behind them unnoticed just an instant ago, is an unmistakable Chinese unmistakably mountainous. Even when his height is compared to Flash G.'s oromorphic gut breadth. That's saying something. I am Frank N. Stein. Even the Fifties suit on the man, with its shoulder pads like wide wings held up by skyhooks and its pinchings at the armpits and the crutch, looks like a vital prop out of Frankenstein Lumbers Through The Refugee Camp. Big gaps between the trouser cuffs and the largest-size sneakers.

Yet the man's face is round and, even in this barely light, Chinese kindly, such that when he moves up to them faster than either Stein or Flash G. could have thought possible for such a fleshy edifice and has taken them indubitably by the upper arms, both of the same time, and has led them off down the footpath, they feel great strength but not menace upon them.

It has happened so fast that neither has uttered as much as a grunt. Nor, now, does either feel that he should. This is a power of a presence that commands an awe instantly overwhelming. The gold in the man's teeth is now your vulgar gold.

Neither has the Chinaman said a word, not that they would in the least expect him to have to, somehow, but smoothly drives them before him into the lane that runs by the side wall of the Friesman's grounds. No more than ten of their skipping paces and perhaps five of his own, the Chinaman brings them to a halt and quarter-turns them towards the neighbour's wall there. And when they take far too long to adjust their eyes to the greater darkness of there, he shows a first sign of fearsome annoyance, as little as the gesture is, by bending their heads over near to the form of Milly on the ground.

She is propped against the wall like an unemployed puppet; her eyes wide open, lidless marbles shining rheumy now to their seeings.

'Aw, fuck.' Stein's heart sinks, but not, apparently, with any measure of eloquence. It is for pity and for the no-rage.

For her arms are already swollen from the many cigarette burns around each of her inner elbows. She sits like a beggar long tired of seeking alms. She is so roughed-up that even if you did know her usual way of dress and way of gashy make-up and ways of different B.O., you would immediately know the difference. Her mouth schlossy, more unbelievable than what normal could possibly be. Not the greatest suckhole. Milly Hunt in hurt shock. Her eyes shining with single tears.

Released by the Chinaman, they move to her and try to lift her. Stein lifts at her shoulders but only her arms come up (she whimpers with the pain) from the dead weight of her body. Flash G. singles for her legs but they reflex more easily to open wide than to elevate virginally together. It is as though her bum contains all her weight. So the Chinaman flips them backhandedly away from her and lifts her as pleasingly as he would a small child. He must be from the land of a thousand million, thinks Stein, where he seen anything grotesque that human flesh can throw up by way of Nature's amazing variations. And she, she only mentions blandly once, as though in casual passing:

'No silly cunt's gonna come on top of me.' before laying her head upon his huge chest and falling asleep.

He walks with her, Stein and Flash G. following lappishly, back to the street and along to level with a now-seeming tiny Toyota where, by classically-minimal head gestures he gets Flash G. to open the back door, gets Stein and Flash G. to seat themselves side by side in the back seat and lays doll Milly across their laps. It is hardly possible to imagine he could fit in behind the steering wheel, but he does so with an agility that must be a monument to the ability of human beings to fit in with strange environments.

There is no hurry. All is smooth and somehow in expected order. His driving is of no hurry and as though all is, yes, somehow in expected order. I am dreaming all this; what is missing. What is fucking missing is that I'm sitting here-in a confined space with unbridled Milly on my nose and helpless on my lap, with half a fat coming on and that's disgusting, next to tribal-bro Gurton, my minority competitor for all those years, in a car that compared to this Chow whale up front sitting there seems like a sardine tin, and I've just seen what you wouldn't exactly call a normal night's happenings, yet I don't feel that screw loose in the air that I've always felt for years every time I've stepped outside my own bloody front door. Even behind my own bloody front door.

The Chinaman does not say a word at any time driving them back to Milly Hunt's apartment house. They do not ask him how he knows where she lives. It seems natural. He does not get out of the car, nor even look around, when they struggle out with her. Thankfully she does not wake when they drop her on her head on the footpath and have to scramble to pick her up.

They must know about sporty takes-off from the kerb side even in China.

The Gang. They are now a gang and they know it. Stein is feeling the luxury of being missing presumed dead. I wonder what my father is thinking. I wonder if my father can think. My father was... No feeling the need to start the book about his coming assassination of my father anymore. The sheer luxury. My wife Lorna and those two pricks of kids. I'm not talking about conscience, either. The Gang. Flash G., the only other emotional tie he's ever had with another human being was with his trainer when he was a punchbag in the ring, until Flash G. caught him humping the only girl-friend he ever had in his life and that trainer only thirty fucking years older than him at the time. Nice boost to the ego, that. Goes to show that whites really do fuck up the world. The Gang. Milly Hunt, thickly bound at the elbows like the mummifiers started but quickly gave up when they took a good look at what they were working on, at home, on her couch with two grown men not even looking like they were

147

trying to make for the door. Ruffed up in pillows and in a state of queendom not experienced since her days as a delicious tart who made the big-spenders like Morrie Friesman priapic and all bunches of flowers. Her quiet smile so smug that it almost doesn't look like a lopsided leer. Never mind getting hurt last night and losing her notebook; she's still got a few brain cells left functioning on memory and her two men grist to her million dollar bestseller mill. And Steiny-weiny, like herself, alone in the world as an outcast member of a snobbish family, up their wowserism with a big wow. The Gang. Looks a bit of a Yid crossed with a Heiney, but I bet a snap of my fingers could get him kneeling and drooling underneath my dress. I've never seen anything animal vegetable mineral that looks so uggers but the local chemist has got to have some paregoric to sight and smell that'll make her as lovely as she looks to me now.

The Gang. It is the next day. They are sitting with their comforts in silent camaraderie. Fitting in, each, after so long. At home, yes. They have stayed with her overnight, taking it in turns to watch over her. The Gang holds a palaver:

'I never saw that Chow in my life.' Her.

'I don't like hearing,' Flash, as irate quick as a Flash, 'a Chow being called a Chow. What would you call me?'

'Fuzzy-wuzzy.'

'Steiny-weiney.'

'I never saw Chow before in my life.' Her again, strident, stoic, not to be come on top of.

'Year 2008, at a guess, Chinese Republic National Men's Basketball team, you bet, and combined with the weightlifting reps to save the national gross domestic product. Would've walked over the Aussies even without playing them. Weak as piss comparatively, you bet too. He might've defected, been lying low these years since and just breaking out to wreak further public destructions.'

'Year 2007'

'Eight, Bozo.'

'Seven. You never could write up a game of tiddlywinks after you got yourself punch drunk and that was before you started to write for that rag of yours.'

'Dognuts Bradley wanted me in and you out, you white dickhead, because people read the obituary column before yours. What about last year when you turned up a day late for the Grand Final? The thing is: are we going to the cops?'

'No!' Milly, thinking of her name on top of the bestseller lists all over filthy-rich Land of the Brave.

'No way.' Stein, with his jaw so set that it could almost be noticed and hurting again with the thought of Costas bleeding from the car. I want my Costas to forgive me, not Friesman on a minor charge, not Friesman let off because I can't get the evidence. Not Friesman and the cops and all that corruption in high friggable places that Costas used to talk about, wrote about, died for.

'No.' Flash G., a moment of his defenses being down in agreeing with an opinion of any two others and only wanting to stay with them. 'So what next?'

Stein turns hard with her. 'You tell us. You've got it on Friesman. Tell it. It's my Costas.'

'No way. Name's Milly Hunt, not silly cunt. It's my book and you're my publisher.'

'You couldn't write better than he here could. That makes a simple postcard beyond you.'

'Clues only. That was the bargain!'

149

'Okay, okay. What a moll still.' Stein.

'So what's next?' Flash G.

Milly in sulky pout, but still managing: 'Horrie Brands, Friesman's lawyer, who else?'

'Where do we find that bozo?'

'How do I know? He's only my up-himself cousin or brother, who cares?, I told you.' She jerks a thumb at Stein. 'Ask this double-crosser who wants to double-cross me.'

'Why me?'

'Because,' said as petulantly as a ten-year-old, 'even though bloody shag Friesman has warned Horrie to lay off after Costas, he'll be still shagging Steiny-weiny wife in Steiny-weiny's own place, so there and ha bloody ha.'

When the lawyer Horrie Brands lets himself into Lorna Stein's, once was Lorna and Frank Stein's, apartment with his own key which he has had gold plated so that it can hang, for the occasions of visiting here to pump upon Lorna Stein, upon the hair of his chest ever since he learnt that that monstrous joke of a missing husband of hers is or was as hairless as a Chinese handmaiden. He knows that she and the terrible twins are out. He stands in the passage way and smiles at the thought of how wicked it is of him to have made this his own private concubinage whenever the spirit moves. Take it and leave it. Whenever he wants, she's in the' palm of his hands. Any part of her. Her buns probably the most passable for a spare afternoon. Tied with those two little horrors, she's lucky to get anything at all.

Enjoys the luxury of the moment, then he ambles down the passageway, looks into the bedroom (once the shrine in which Frank Err Stein's manhood rested, occasionally stood), fronts up to the bed just so he can crudely rub his crutch Italianately to serve up to

150

himself visions of pinning her against her will at first again, moves back out to the living room where he will proceed to put away a goodly amount of the scotch she has bought for him and where, now, with glass in hand, he puts his feet up and the telly on for the kingpin's-home-baby effect in it. Nice and wicked but nice. Raises one's standard just to think of it. Here's to good ole Friesman. Horrie and Morrie, mates together.

What Horrie Brands hasn't heard when he left the bedroom was the muffled scuffle from under the bed behind him where Milly and Flash have flung themselves upon Stein as much as is possible in the confined space defined by the frame of a bed and its mattress springs. Some part of the body of Milly has nuzzled off the clatter of what he is trying to splutter out and some part of the body of Flash G. (an ore in motion) has clammed up the clammer of Stein trying to red-beret his way out from under there and from between them to killkillkill this interloping fucker in his home.

Finally Stein settles down enough to turn his head to look into the eyes of Milly from a distance of about one very close centimetre. She shakes her head in silent warning of let's not blow it but Stein has already decided that nothing, not even the gut-wrenching behaviour of that bastard Brands in my own bed pit where nightly I was undoubtedly magnificent as a bull or would have been if Lorna had a proper cunt rather than a mine pit or if Jude and Erika didn't keep giggling at me while they rubbed each other in the doorway, no nothing can be so dreadful as looking into lovely Milly's technicolours from this close so I'll stay here and kitchen knife Brands later. Dear father, if you were still Commissioner of Police, you would have sent in the cops by now to save the family honour. All left up to me. My father was... *My Costas was.*

And it is only little humpy jerks of the whole bed that give away any little thing of the immense struggle that goes on under there for a time. Soon quiet again.

There is not much time to wait. Children's chatter and the weary mezzosopranic whining of Lorna soon on the landing and the door opening, allowing to burst through the twin-exhaust of the Stein twins:

'Mother, do hurry up or get...' this is Jude,... those varicose veins bypassed before they begin to show and...' this is dear little Erika, 'start to embarrass us going out to the Shadow Plays of Indonesia with you again' this is Jude again.

'Shut your gobs for just one moment, will you, you little sods?' Lorna, dragging herself down the passageway after them. That's terrific, fucking Lorna you, you throw a man out of his own castle just because he wanted to take to those superbrats from out of that super-splatty belly of yours with a meat axe and here I am, having to listen to such abuse that no loving father should have to hear under the conjugal bed that made them. The sight of your ankles now...

'Oh, do look what the cat brought in.' This is Erika down the passageway from Stein and at the door of the living room.

'Hi, kids.' Horrie, brandishing the remote control.

'Don't you "kids" us and...' Erika.

'... get your atrocious clodhoppers with those appalling fuckwit Italian leather uppers off our New Scientist mags, thank. ..' Jude joining his sister there and slipping his hand automatically inside her blouse.

'... you so very much. Mother!' calls Erika in a fit of cooperation, 'your loverboy's here.'

'Horrie...?' Lorna's ankles move from the six eyes sizing them up from under the bed and out of the bedroom, so that they can hear:

'Hi, dollface.'

'Mother, if you don't throw the bum out, Jude will use martial arts, won't you, Jude?' Erika.

'You just can't walk in here after all these weeks, Horrie.' Lorna.

'I just wanted to talk, Lorna.' Horrie, trying to get a word in edgeways.

'Talk? He wants to distend that euphemistic snake of his and get on the slide between your glands, that's what he wants to do. How you...' Erika automatically sliding a second hand across Jude's butt and he stimulated to add: '... can allow the copulative act upon your person, which by some act of gross random chance produced Erika and I, without any intention of procreating the cause of the nuclear family is quite beyond us, Mother, especially when we have just been to see a passable representation of the Dong-Son culture of Indonesia on stage...'

'Well, we'll discuss later whether,' Jude in very shocking mild rebuke of his sister; must be catching up in the puberty race, 'it was or is passable or not. However, having it away, as the more common expression by those quite hot rid kids at school would have it, with this creature here...'

'... who's ludicrously dressed ten years younger than he should be and that's not passable, Jude.'

'Quite, Erika, my throb. With this creature here, with presumably only the most basic pass in Law, Erika and I really really wonder....

'... we really do...'

'... whether you should not have walked out with uggers Daddy quite a while ago, instead of staying to make our cheeks go red.'

'You two monsters, shut your clackers.' Lorna, now a bit torn between throwing Horrie Brands out or defending him smirking! Resplendently at her now her virtue's been put on the line.

153

'It's a pretty pass,' this is Erika, 'when this family has come to this,' this is Jude, 'and frankly we've got to warn you, Mother,' this is Erika, 'that if you're going to poke in the middle of the afternoon, we're going to watch, aren't we, Erika?'

'Poking oath.'

'Are they yours?' Milly, truly shocked for the first time in many a year, whispering into Stein's pinkie. And he only able to answer by rolling great cow-eyes up to the heavens which, in this case, are the undersprings of his once heavenly marital pit. Hearing now Horrie Brands, half getting up and half finishing his drink, all chirpy good-fellow, if not new-Daddy material:

'We've all been out to a kid's matinee movie, have we?'

'We have been to see, if you must know, a wayang kulit performance to which we had to trot poor silly goose Mother along... or do you want to enlighten this adult human being, Erika?'

'No, Jude, do proceed but don't stop scratching.'

'... along because of some inept and personally offensive regulation of the Management, probably thought up by some immature, adult legal mind like yours, m'sieur.'

'Would he happen to know what a wayang kulit was, do you think, Jude?'

'Tell them to shut their clackers, Horrie; don't be shy.'

'Mother, I'm trying to explain to horny Horrie,' this is Jude, 'thank you very much,' this is Erika, her eyes like her usual daggers, as keen as they are a matching grey. 'Do carry on, Jude, but tickle between my titties.'

'Thank you, Erika. The shadow play is the dame of life, the Buddhist-based peace of the inner world in microcosmic spheres. It

154

is a moral instruction upon a mythical plumb. We were particularly pleased to see that the visiting dalang priest was a senior one from the wayang school centred around the Prambanan temple complex which was built during the period of AD 732 and 928, or was it 927?'

'I think the former, Jude dear.'

'And, frankly, that meant that his performance would not be disappointing for us.'

'Jude, I don't think this yet-another buffoon isn't listening.'

'Listen, for God's sake, Horrie, or we'll be here forever.'

'Sure, I'm,' swallowing hard the scotch he was swilling around his mouth and actually taking his luxuriating eyes off Lorna's lower parts, 'listening. Who's in Wayland Cools It?'

'Dumbo, I don't think we even want to watch you fuck.'

And then they cakewalk a humpf off not at all shadowy.

'And clean up your room like I told you!' Lorna, saving for herself a little motherly dignity with the necessary last word before she swings back to round on Brands. 'Horrie, what are you here for?'

'Well....' He would nudge her were he near enough.

'After not hearing from you all last week.'

'Let's go somewhere private, Lorna.'

'Definitely not.'

'Into the bedroom.'

'Oh, *all right*. Why didn't you say?'

155

Now The Gang takes its collective breath and spiritually holds it. They see the pairs of brogues and high heels move into their lines of vision, meet toes-to-toes, his assertive, hers fidgety, if they have them right.

'No. You can't come in like this and...' Fidget in her voice too.

'Come on, Lorna,' his voice husky with a miff mission now, 'you know I couldn't.'

'I don't.'

'I told you after that brother-in-law thing of yours happened, my boss told me not to associate. Think of my position. Feel my state.'

'I will not feel your state.' But her toes edged up to his. The hands of Milly and Flash G. settle weightily upon Stein. The stomach of Stein knots mightily. They hear:

'Oo, what a state you're in, too. What about the door?'

'If they have to watch, let them watch.'

'*Horrie...*'

'*What?*'

'I wanna call you Frank. Can I call you Frank?'

Now the ankles before The Gang's eyes take, to the left, worsted wool trousers and, to the right, denim dress, then cotton briefs to the left, then spun cotton black scanties to the right and the hand of Flash G. moves off the body of Stein to run lightly around the left-to-right breast of Milly and even her hand begins dancing a caress upon the small of the Stein back as those two sets of ankles trip and trip to the bed on high above them down there and the bulk of Flash G. is virtually pinned upon beneath the mattress spring sag. For much of that moment he doesn't look like he cares. Grunts and

156

slurpings and suckings and iron squeaks as though Heaven Above is having some Rio de Janiero carnivale.

I am Frank N. Stein. A monstrous joke. My father. Costas. I am not some fucking joke. And with a bellow that could have almost warmed the cockles of his rage-wanting heart, Stein heaved himself up and out. It isn't he who upset that bed like a fruit cart spillage, though, for in doing so he delivers a swift knee to Flash G.'s knockers who yowls and literally hits the roof -- bed, bodies and all.

Lorna and Horrie, still joined but not now coupled, hit the wall beneath an avalanche of doona, mattress, bed, cod-grasping Flash Gurton and Nemesis Stein stacked upon them by a down-pouring of just about every known form of human guttural. There are, instantly and semi-nude, too, Jude and Erika Keystone Copping to a stop in the doorway, copping out the lot in a moment of joint amusement they would never admit to, especially when the gashy and gaudy form of this frump they could never know as Milly Hunt swoops down upon even them even before the debris of arms and legs and bedding in the corner has the dust settled up it in turn to haul them, clucking she croaking they, into her hoving bosom (two cushions cut low in red mottled flesh pink-kinda) protectively as if suffocation of the innocent-aged was about the only way to keep the smile or smirk in innocent eyes before it dyes.

The Gang rampant, what a mob!

And Lorna's angry screeches rising above all. The shock of finding on top of her a welterishly nicely-acceptable Polynesian-shirted Horrie body traded for a white rangy one in dervish.

By the time rampant Stein has torn aside all between him and Horrie Brands below, Horrie Brands is no longer, though, the rangy one in dervish, for shock in kinesis has bolted forth not a passionately thick cream of gism but an ejaculation of urine do flooding and so not-ended that Lorna's first words are scientifically flip:

'Horrie, you've peed yourself too!'

157

before she has sunk her teeth into Flash G.'s soft underbelly to send him back the way he has come just as swiftly and just as painfully and before Stein, with a manly blood rush that his kids must have surely admired if they were not fighting asphyxia in Milly Hunt's folds, has Brands by the Polynesian-shirt front and heaved to his feet and jammed into the corner there and before the urine stench of storpored Horrie drives him off a few willing paces.

'Phew!' Stein.

'Mum!' Erika or Jude, obviously back again. Could never be heard under those absorbent folds.

'Oh… *Christ*!' Flash G., back where he started on the floor, minus the bed but with his manhood flowering a bruise on top of it all. Bit of a bugger.

'Lorna, cover,' Stein in full control, the dramatic irony of a little involuntary piddle between a once-upon-a-time and this-now not lost on him, 'up that great slack hole of yours. Hairier than a whore's should be in this age of industrial harvesters.'

'Don't mind me.' Though in yet agony, Flash G.'s eyes are not missing a crack to look through.

Such that even Lorna Stein has to leave off and go by the cover up, and in the momentary impasse rings the voice of retribution:

'Horrie Brands! What's the world coming to? Did or did not Morrie Friesman tell you not to come here again, you buggerlugs, you? My… cousin-brother. Or vikky-verka. Well, a sort of relative. He just thinks he knows his way around this bedroom…'

'I'm going to kill him.' Stein.

'Don't do that until I get dressed!' Lorna.

Stein. 'You're coming to the cops with us, bastard Brands. My Costas, you... *bastard.*'

At the mention of Costas's name, Lorna grabs at Stein, mindless that she has only succeeded in getting one leg through her panties and not knowing that the sight she is giving Flash G. is fast improving his health. It's probably as well she in over-toppling into Frank Stein's arms.

'Get orf!', but it is too late to swing herself away from landing between him and Horrie Brands. Anyway, with a low cunning that can only come from the opportunism of being in the legal profession, Horrie has already hurdled Flash G., mountaineered the perimeter of the amalgam of Milly and the children still struggling boy-and girl-fully, and has his trousers back around his waist by the time he is pealing out through the front door.

And it seems to Stein that there are suddenly too many bodies in that one small room bound up inextricably in his life for him to even bother to try to give chase. Except maybe to kick a few heads in there first before giving the prospect up, figuratively speaking. But doesn't bother with even that. Nor does he bother to chase a now-gone Horrie Brands down the stairs. If I was a blood-hound I could wait an hour and still track him down along the urine trails.

The first other thing that Stein comes up against when he manoeuvres himself past the polymorph of Milly'n'kids back into the bedroom (seat of once grievous, but at least striving, excesses) is the wrath of ex-wife Lorna accusatory:

'I've got an insurance claim in on you!'

'I'm not dead yet, Lorna.'

'You could've saved me the trouble of putting the claim in.'

Stein: 'I think I might do you in in front of witnesses, you dingbat.'

'Oh yeah?' Lorna.

'Yeah!' Stein.

The Steins back together again. Chest to breast. And their angry red faces could be kissing, as in love does bite.

'Put her knickers back on first, bozo.' Flash G., as a sportswriter, used to a good thing going past. And Milly, too, almost jumping as she comes out of a motherhood gnosis of herself as Miss Heinz Baby Foods not realising that she is loosening her protective grip around this Jude's and this Erika's mouths as she rebukes across her shoulder:

'Not in front of the children, either.'

Yet loosed the Steins are and before Frank Stein and Lorna Stein can round on her, the defty twin-duo has rounded on them all. This is Jude: 'Mother, get this obese cunt off of us and get...' this is Erika: '... that unimproved specimen of a ghost of a father from off our expanding horizons...' And this is Jude again: '... and, while you're about it, kindly ask that simian-type of melanous authochthon of a minority racial group either to show his pass or stop looking rape at my scantily-clad sister.'

'Oh', being Milly getting in her outrage at the cheeky little buggers in first, 'it's like that, is it? Well, sonnyjim, little cunt, you've got to be a man like my friend over there and have a man's sized dork to worry about that, not your wee willy winkle that looks about one year old.'

Whenupon Jude bursts into great baby crocodile tears and fleets from the room and, whenupon instanter, Erika haves at Milly with pounding fists whacking petulancies all in a flash. Though held nonchalantly at arm's length:

'Don't you talk to Jude like that, you fat uxorial!'

'As for you, missy silly cunt, you've gotta have something to *put* it in other than a slit that'll never get offers from slip knots.'

It could have been a king hit that does make a gal flee, too; flashes of thin waiflike Erika legs beneath a very fat and ripe quivering upper lip.,

In livid silence, now paradigm mum Lorna Stein completes the full elevation of her panties as though she is a street fighter rolling up her sleeves, my wife up and down with her knickers like a street fighter's sleeve, and makes no mistake as to her final, irrecoverable meaning:

'Frank Stein, you and your "friends" get out of here forever.'

'I'm going, Lorna, and I'll tell you why I'm going. Because, Lorna, you've always been too dumb for me.'

The Gang in cohesion again. With a concerted action, they impressively withdraw with all banners aloft and almost nearly get right to the front door before the door bell chimes. Christ, I tried to make a home and ended up with an empty church. Flash G., an actual street fighter, rolling his actual sleeves up, and pushes past them both into the vanguard:

'Leave this lawyer piddler to me'.

He unlatches; he sees; he growls; he chokes back his on-growl; he retreats like a billiard ball to the rear of the line. This is not Horrie Brands. On the doorstep is now the blocking frame of the Chinaman, silent as death and equally inevitable.

'Chow!'

Not one of them could later remember how the Chinaman signals because not one of them later remembers him even moving but, with a foreboding as wide as his sheer presence, Stein is leading them charily out onto the landing out there where Horrie Brands lies

161

on the top few stairs like a fallen sparrow heart burst before the presence of the living Buddha come all the way from China. The only trouble is he is bleeding quite neatly from a bullet hole in his forehead and the only trouble with that is he is dead.

Frank Stein cannot move as the others cannot move. I am going to die at the hands of a Chinese I don't know. My father coughed up his bullet forty years after. Costas. Oh my god, the blood in that car park. Milly gasps when the Chinaman moves his huge hand, but he merely taps Stein on the shoulder with a gentle olive digit, points to Horrie Brands that was and shakes his head not-me. Then he squeezes himself past Stein to move to pick up the body with a weightlifter's jerk and returns.

For a tearing moment Stein thinks the Chinaman is going to present the corpse to him as though he was carrying something precious on a ritual cushion. Don't lay it at my feet, I didn't do it. I'm just Frank N. Stein and I'm a monstrous joke. Instead he finds that the Chinaman is mutely pressing him to take the envelope that is sticking out of Horrie Brands's shirt pocket. He can't. Milly, does.

'Thank you, Chow.'

Why is she talking to him like that with sweet reason? She knows something that I don't. But the Chinaman is already going from them, taking the body of Horrie Brands away, and in her hand is, yes, a white envelope and on the white envelope is the drawing of a Mafiosa black hand.

The Gang confers. Leastways, when they get fed up and plough into her room to interrupt her writing right effing now for a necessary roundtable, Milly Hunt storms up to take the floor:

'What sort of silly cunt do you think I am? Nobody's gonna come on top of me and my writing. You go to the cops and I've suddenly got terminal laryngitis, Steiny-weiney and you, you other thing.

162

Brother? What brother? Which one of you big shots wouldn't sell your own father, let alone your fucking grandmothers, if you had any, for a million greenies?' (Doesn't Stein secretly blanch.) 'My novel's I-was-there stuff that's gonna make me Whistler's mother. Who fucking cares if I don't know who Whistler is; if I'm the silly cunt's mother, I'm his mother, and by the time I get my book shot of you poor sodders chasing your tails following my clues, smartarse Whistler's gonna wanna know me, you betcha. Your brother Costas? I'll put ten bucks of a millionaire's bouquet on his grave, and that'll be ten bucks more than he would've done for me. So clues, clues is all you're gonna get out of this Milly Hunt, no silly cunt. No cops. You'll do the "shops" how Milly tells you and work out yourselves how to collar fucking Friesman Mr Bigs. By "shops", yours truly means his houses of ill-fame one by one if need be. Starting with the Policeman's Ball. Yep, is what I said. On this Satdee. Fancy dress. Keep your eyes open and you might learn something. And, if you don't get the goods on him then, you silly cunts, you ain't no Milly Hunt and we're going to have to do the rounds of his "shop" until the penny drops. I'm a reasonable broad: I only demand that you take it in turns to sleep with me each alternative night, starting right now while I'm in the middle of a sentence, appropriate to my coming status.'

(Don't Stein and Flash G. openly blanch.)

The Gang has conferred, but what a terrible conferment.

The Policeman's Ball, on this one Saturday night of the year in Sydney Town Hall, turns out to be a real cop out. Het up. The night when cops are coming in off the streets dressed up, not dressing down. This year Keystone Cops and train drivers seem to be uniformly in fashion. Later there are some doubts as to whether there will be a next year, but for tonight all that glitters is not a policeman's badge under a strobe. They have come from all corners of the globe that is Rose and Double Bays and climbed their ways into the great hall, banquet-laid and dance-floored and big-banded

163

over. It is only an hour and a half after the official starting time and already the early birds have begun to arrive, some dressed as early birds and some, with the three or four wedding rings to identify them, as their worms. The Lord Mayor of them all is due to arrive soon with his wife as Pacman and Ms Pacman, such is the nostalgia for the Eighties high on the agenda. From the lowest constable who drew the short straw who had to come as Captain Invincible to the highest Commissioner who couldn't go in the ballot for Captain Invincible and still had to come (his wife was Punk and he was puny), from the quiet-type money-launderer who delighted in the opportunity of rubbing his A1 Capone shoulder pads with the greater of the criminal class for one public night out of three hundred and sixty-four ones he had to hide his face (he came as sweet Confessional Bliss) to the low-down-society maid with the greatest build (she came on an arm and left on a promise), from the lawyers who came so they could tell their corporations they have looked the defenders of law and order fair'n'square in the eye (they tended to turn up in marks so it was difficult to tell what was different about them from the everyday) to the simplest of con merchants... they were all there and conning, if they were still yet coming. It is all so exclusive that the ticket hawkers are doing a fine illegal business on the footpath outside. This was such an affair that the floodlights on the Town Hall's tower could have come as the finest of Sydney's prison searchlights. A gift from the lads who couldn't make it.

There is a rumour abroad that Morrie Friesman in a blue velvet suit is coming and he is coming as He Who Sits On The Lord Mayor Left Hand Fittingly. As usual, this year the rumour is only different in the colour of the velvet.

At nine-thirty exactly there is a crowlike screech at the very door to the festivities when a ticket inspector (dressed as a traffic warden which he was, but moonlighting) tried to grab hold of the duckfootlike hand of Milly as she, Frank Stein and Flash (Harry, as he was decked out) Gurton sailed on past him with an entry that is reminiscent of gliding swans which they aren't dressed as. It stops the band and it stops the waiters (dressed as waitresses so as not to

164

be confusing providing you weren't female) and it turns fancy dresses all over the place. And it does so for an instant. What does so very much longer is the dress of the trio. For they each are matched with hula-hula skirts made of spare covers of Costas's book *Australian Crime Bosses* and they all absolute all, except for the placards, large as they are large writ and as crude as they , are crude writ, hanging from around their necks. Flash G. trying to rumble in and along there as the lead with a bumbling Polynesian imitation of a Polynesian hello-how-are-you dance from his own ancestral island which he remembers seeing on television once. And around their necks these placards read:

for Stein: MR BIG'S VICTIM'S BROTHER'S ME!

for Milly: MR BIG'S HAD ME, TOO!

for Flash G.: FANCY THAT FRIESMAN!

Given the night of the social stars, there is not one present who either does not know or does not hear from aft whispering from his or her left or right that Mr Big is theft, dupey name given on the half joke to Morrie Friesman Who, as all there again know, is due for his annual self-amused grand entry waving his cheque for his annual five thousand dollar donation to the Police Boys' Clubs in about two seconds flat. His blue velvet suit's going to turn green when he sees these jokers.

In the middle of the dance area, Milly Hunt curtsies to the assembled revellers there and then moves to join Stein and Flash to lean backwards with them against the VIP table facing the main entrance. She# positions herself considerately between them so that Morrie Friesman does not have to strain his eyes when he comes in but can easily read from left to right. They wait. The whole hall is in waiting. There are only one or two pockets of sibilant conversation break out and these are brief. Nobody wishes to miss anything he or she is likely to miss anyway; their heads swinging from the Gang to the main entrance in quite admirable unison, a ghostly tennis match.

The American precedes Friesman into the hall by force of habit, a suavely matching tie to his regular suit the only concession to fancy dress. Naturally off-guard at this moment, he enters a good full ten paces before lamping onto The Gang's reception committee up at the top table. By this time, the wonderful azure blue of Morrie Friesman's suit is very much in evidence inside the hall. Indeed, he has already let drop the thing (a dish of all gams very quincy in matching satin blue) on his arm and is ground to a halt that only comes when some outside observer tries desperately to read in it something between the lines. One further glance around the hall at all those faces turned towards him then he turns on his heels and departs as quickly as the matching blue rises from his gills.

And, while his boss Morrie Friesman has left without a word, The American looks momentarily at The Gang as though he would have something to say on the matter later, before leaving with his professional pride in tatters. It's a well his costume intended the tattered look. Which is not a bad outfit for a fancy dress ball, when all is not said but done.

When the white Merc deliberately rams into the back of the taxi just after it pulls up outside Milly's apartment block and, while the taxi driver is trying to spill out, The Gang as fast as even a taxi-driver's outrage would spill out were trying not to spill out, the Chinaman steps out from the shadows of the apartment's portal and moves quickly to the scene. It is as though his shadow falls across the two cars in the instance, a great lodged spirit aroused. The doors of the Merc have opened but now, when his presence is *there*, shut quickly again. The great car backs up, then thrums in swerve around the taxi to move off down the road growling predatorily.

Inside the cab, the driver is beneath the thrashing body of Milly Hunt suddenly and Stein is beneath the sky fallen in in the bodyform of Flash G. At the time the Merc is leaving, the cabbie is yelling out of both the horror and the ecstasy of being suffocated by Milly's flesh which gravity is moulding to his every contour, and Stein is praying silently that the floor of the cab won't collapse beneath him and Flash G. And Milly is crying out to the heavens or to any rescue team:

'Nobody's gonna come on top of me!'

a statement that the cabbie will question about himself, did-he-crack-it or didn't-he-crack-it?, all his life… every cloud having a silvery looking lining. He is hanging onto the steering wheel for dear life, as though it is the only thing to stop him from drowning.

Without fashery, with slow compassion, the Chinaman opens each of the front doors and extracts them (more than half-pissed, more than near-nude, more than the cabbie has ever come across). The way he stands them up on the safety of the footpath, it races through Stein's shickered mind that we are dolls and Chow's gonna dust us up. Dear old Chow.

Chow doesn't. He just walks away. They watch him sloely.

A smart amateur photographer snaps them standing there in what looks like hula-hula skirts made out of old book-covers, looking after him and will get the photograph in the next American edition of 'Would You Believe?'.

The Gang confers again. Leastways Stein wakes up swathed with a cold sweat from a dream in which some dark identity is in the room to kill him. When he sits up in bed and sees, he cries out in fright. Reality is worse than the nightmare. No endeavours to thrash away from the horror of it all, but Milly's legs continue to fasten his own to the sheets and her arm refuses to uncoil itself from his. One of her eyes open in a face that sleep has turned into a mask crudely dipped in a collation of all impossibly possible cosmetic components and then allowed to set. Though it is evidently alive, the eye is certainly not at all better. It rolls at him, as it seems to Stein, like a pulsation of the aurora borealis. Her tongue rolls around her lips, as it seems to Stein no less than the eye, like a worm searching for a bit of a breather from the juices of the skull. The wafts that come from her mulled femininity makes him wonder whether it is himself as incontinent. She is droopingly nude.

167

All this does not help Stein's gurgling panic to come fully awake and escape the ultimate succubussy nightmare. He manages to the gods:

'It wasn't my turn!'

'Wasn't it hell.'

This could be, too, a nightmarish apparition of even an incubus, but in fact it is Flash G., his large black head which appears over the bottom of the bed a sorry advertisement for alcoholic products and. with what's left of the book-cover hula-hula skirt draped over one shoulder imperiously.

'Cover yourself up. Get off,' Stein, the nightmare getting worse; he just can't wake up, 'off me. God, what have I done?'

'Don't blame me, dick-led.' And, with a low groan, Flash sinks back to the floor at the foot of the bed, gone now from sight.

'God, we've got to go to the police!'

'You do and I'll tell em it was rape.' Milly, quite seriously.

'I don't mean you. I mean about Friesman. Get off me!'

'Silly cunt.'

The Gang; continues to confer, but she won't budge, from on top of Stein, nor budge from the writing of her million dollar best-seller on the hoof while they chase the pearls of clues she casts at their feet. The next stop to one of Friesman's 'shops' is all she'll say. And it is not looking like no-one on God's nude earth that is making her coy, either.

It is somewhere around this time (he doesn't know exactly) that Stein first feels the stabbing pain around his kidneys and knows instinctively that he has become impotent once and for all. Wouldn't you, if you were me, Father?

This night she is certainly not recognisable. She is wearing a sheer red satin, number cut low back and front and such high silver high heels that it seems the very rigid elevation of the hods themselves must be pushing up her nates and her breasts so that even they sit acceptably curvilinear within the straining fabric. She moves up the brick-inlay path to the front door of the terrace house with such confident' defiance of equilibriums and centres-of-gravity that she looks the horny part. The night, of course, is a near moonless one; has to be.

She punches, does Milly Hunt, the brass doorbell beneath the credit card signs beneath the Club Finese sign illuminated appropriately by naked bulbs and waits no longer than ten seconds before she punches it a couple more times. This gal won't be kept waiting. When the door opens a sassy young thing who could be brandishing her pop-art lollypop as a protest placard against people who come to your door uninvited gets unceremoniously shoved out of the way for the inward carriage of Madame Hunt, the best manageress this joint ever had, you silly cunt. As she sails past to the inner auction floor where she falls into the arms of Madame Fifi, who has been brought from behind the bar on the trot by the near hue and cry from Lollypop.

'Milly, you silly fanny-lost-its-tone!'

'Fifi, you great hairy box!'

Expressions of bonhomie, or bonnefemmie, and general plushings of similar endearments not mutually expressed since the age ago when Milly retired from the game and protégé Fifi took over from her. Including Morrie Friesman who always practised good carnal staff relations. They break, and they look in the soft rose lighting

169

like two aunts at the social dance who have decided they might as well get up to no good anyway.

'Quiet tonight.' Milly.

'That's only because we've had put in pink bats under the carpets in all the rooms.' Madame Fifi.

'Lots of quiet little mouses running into pussies' mouths.'

'Full house. What're you here for, you old moll?'

'Thought I might come back on the game. See what's going.'

'There's a lot of preverts around these days, Mill, but I dunno if there's that many preverts.'

'Up yours! Give's a real champers, and I'll just sit in the corner so I don't have to look at all the cracks coming into your face. That way I can keep quiet and enjoy the old place again one last time without getting noticed by having to die laughing.'

'I hope the bubbles go down to your furry funnel and cause seepage.'

It is indeed a lull. Almost immediately, three clients come down the stairs and two new ones come in. Milly is left sitting on the corner stool of the bar. She observes that it has not changed. Club Finesse is still for the higher class naughty little rooter. There is still the feeling there of discretion. A client somehow feels that if he is going to get blackmailed at work or at home by having his driver's license or something copied when he's on the job, at least it's going to be done with that measure of class called discretion or, alternatively, it's going to be the bigtime boys who are going to do the blackmailing. None of the risk of smalltime crooks. The ones who have come down from upstairs even staying quite comfortably for the drink post-coitus (presumably) on the house; the new ones coming in with an unbrashy, perhaps even sober, mien, wallet-

170

confident and languid for the pouch. Milly Hunt feels almost nostalgic. You knew where your next belt was coming from... around fat, rich bellies coming through that door. She shakes her head to clear it, must be the extraordinary combination of real champagne and this atmosphere. Nor is Lollypop a sudden friend. One of the newies has just got up from the velvet chaise longue when she is halfway through question number three in the manual about what exactly does he do in the job he's given as an answer to question two and is now leaning against the bar in front of Milly as a fatherly figure who would never do any wrong to her:

'What's your name, little one?'

She sees his glasses in their case inside his breast pocket. 'Names Milly Hunt, not silly cunt. And no bugger's gonna come on top of me.'

'I was thinking of the other way around, too. Can I buy you a drink?'

'Blow.'

'Okay. How much?'

'Fred, put your glasses on.' Madame Fifi to the rescue and gliding him back to Lollypop, who has complained but now has been suaged down.

When Fifi comes back, they make a bargain. For the rest of the bottle of the real champagne, Milly will sit behind the bar in the corner with her legs together and her lips pursed primly and make like she is only there to attend the coffee machine. Also, she can only stay until Morrie's money collectors come in around midnight.

As it turns out, it is half past eleven when the police raid. They come through the door, with either precise or dreadful timing, in an exact lull in the proceedings, when even Madame Fifi is plying her trader upstairs to help siphon off the excess demand and poor

171

Lollypop (it isn't her night) is on the door again. Lollypop is so stunned by the bust that she cannot even create a little Cain, let alone use her Lollypop in defense of Club Finesse's reputation for reliable confidentiality. This is no bordello to board.

But they do. The five of them -- three in uniform and two in civilians -- arrive in the reception area to nothing more than a quaint burping giggle from a female shape in the corner by the coffee machine who could only be there for the making of coffee, even given the range of likely perversions by the male members of the human race. They ignore her. Yet are nonplussed by the emptiness of Sydney's most celebrated brothel, when even the ceremonial pool with its outdoor palmy area looks like a deserted confectionary ad set, and, apart from that burping giggle, the quietness.

'It's the,' chiding them through the burps and the giggles, 'pink bats under the floor spreads.'

Still they ignore her. One of the detectives waves his men upstairs as he wards off Lollypop who has just decided to spring into action with her lollypop against his head (for a moment she was stunning) and the forces of law and order spring into round-up time complete with cowboy yippie aye ayes and a heavyhandedness which makes resound their boots on the pink bats all over upstairs. In no time flat these are joined with doors banging and women (even those in momentary dominating roles up there) squealing and shrieking and male cries that leave no social, occupational or marital horror left to the imagination. Milly does not imagine for too long, but takes the golden opportunity of diving for another bottle of real and unreal whogivesastuff champers and starts shouting the house down too when she can't get the cork out.

Within five minutes, where once five minutes ago it was coconut-bar placidity itself, the ceremonial pool and its palmy surrounds is such a place of mayhem that it could be the Golan Heights on a brush-fire battle day. The police have herded all down to there, with the ladies to the right of the pool and the gents to the left of the pool and Madame Fifi trying to land a left or a right foot, either one

172

would do, drive to the agates of one of the detectives only because, in just two minutes, she has literally screamed herself hoarse and two of the uniform cops have her arms pinned.

'Drop her in the pool.'

They do. It doesn't help her voice but for some reason it does help her behaviour. She stands in the centre of it, mute and defiant yet still, as though she has decided that the lake is the best place in the midst of what could fierily consume her. It is much the same for the ladies and gents. The tidal wave that has come upon them, much as if Fifi's watery spirit had departed from her, has dampened so their own that they too stand now mute and still. But nowhere defiant. You can't be so when you've been nabbed in flagrante delicto by the law who won't give you back your strides (the guys) or who won't treat you with the respect you expect when you've got your knickers down (the gals). Who shouldn't be here anyway. What the shit's Morrie Friesman doing anyway? Decent people, they expect adequate protection in brothels with good reputations, m Though not how it is now. The cops there have confiscated most of their wallets and the shorter of the two detectives, who both look like they've been on the vice squad for too long even in this roseate light which would make a ruddy healthy glow out of corpse-skin parchment, is already flicking through one out of the pile. With a practised eye, so that by midnight he has done the same thing to each and every one of those pillars of dayseen society there, he scans its contents, then looks up with a jaundiced glare not colour-prone to the lighting set-up:

'Judge Evans step forward.'

He certainly would not have, but Fifi finds in her watery harbour her defiance again and identifies him with: 'Don't go, Fred.' so that he has nowhere else to go but into obeying, seeing that all the other upright citizens part from him like magnetic poles. When he steps forward he slips on the pool's edge and lands in the drink alongside Fifi, who replaces defiance with disgust:

173

'Oh, for Christ sake, Fred, I said put on your glasses.'

Now it is a very wet and miserable Judge Evans who stands before the two detectives. Combined with the water, the flush of embarrassment that he is feeling all over makes the new welts on his thin pigeon-toed legs look a heavily sore price for an expensive little pleasure. It hurts all the more to have many pairs of eyes running over them and titters running all over this kangaroo court.

'Judge Evans,' the shorter, whiter detective says to start the humiliation that is to come for them all, 'cat-o'-ninetails got your tongue?'

'Shouldn't be here. Don't arrest.'

'Shaddup. We've got your name and we've got your number and we're going to keep this little piccy here of your wife and kids, Judge,' the sneer now rising to a verbal fury that threatens police violence to anybody who might dare move a finger, the Judge near fainting as this detective goes on: 'You talking to me, you old wick-dipper. Who else is there to go to if we can't go to Judges to help clean up this town? I had a good mate. He was a good reporter. He said the right things and he went out on a limb against the mob and the Friesmans of this pricking world. He had a wife and a kid and a family. And Friesman shot him. Friesman murdered him. His name was Costas Stein. Morrie Friesman did that, and we're going to get him. Hear that? All you losers hear it?'

Naked nude like that, the Judge doesn't seem capable of denying it; nods foolishly. He is not alone, either. The detective steps away from him; he could be counting to ten; then turns back to his fellow dick:

'Shoot him.'

'Aw, come on, Frank.'

'I said, shoot him.'

'Aw, waste a bullet.'

'Shoot his dick off.'

'Okay.' With a shrug.

Somehow a gurgle manages to escape from the mouth of the Judge (it is a dampened tintinnabulation across an empty landscape of a sudden) as the second detective, not even taking the chewing gum out of his black mouth, steps forward as he pulls out his gun, aims at the opulent, therefore not at all judicious, soft underbelly before him and:

'From Costas Stein to Morrie Friesman, bozo.' and fires.

The bang itself is so huge that they are all thrown paces back. And before the smoke has even nearly cleared, the Judge has landed back in Fifi's lap in the pool, the women are screaming and the uniform cops have long bolted for the door. Flash G. blows the smoke from the starting pistol and bows ceremoniously towards the front door:

'Do go first, Steiny-weiney, you white bozo.'

And Frank Stein and Flash G. stroll out with that peculiar contentment that can only come, so the word of mouth goes, from a good flush-out at the Club Finesse when you're in town.

It is a minute to midnight. They are not to know that Friesman's money collectors have arrived early.

Halfway up the path, Stein and Flash G. stop to look at the three men in civvies there in the Imperial Rome garden, but they do not start. Unfashionable contentment has them by the balls. This is the time of all the time in the world.

They merely glance as if normal at two of them sitting with their backs to the wall very much like pierrots during coffee break at a doll's hospital, looking a very broken pair. They, too, merely beam smiles at the Chinaman standing casually beside these two. Mere coincidence, on a beautiful night like this. And so as natural as apple pie:

'Good evening, Chow.' Stein.

'G'day, Chow.' Flash G. Not an eyelid batted between the two of them that he should be cavalry come to save them again, before strolling on. At the gate, at a joint instinct for something yet still to have to happen that they don't really want to think about, they stop again, leaning casually against those plaster pillars. Time for a casual chat, while hastily clothed and still clothing figures dash past them back to the safety of good ole comfy affluence, even the wife:

'You owe me a hundred smackeroos. I didn't even have to use this forged search warrant you conned me into paying for.' Stein.

'What do you want for a rare copy, you bozo?' Flash G.

'I hope your three mates don't return the hired traffic warden uniforms on time and you have to pay extra rental.' Stein.

'Up yours, too.' Flash G., yawning with a wide grin. A sparkling sight in a dark night. The last of the flitting clientele has not paused one moment to admire it. It is the Judge. His glasses are at least dry.

Chow comes back out to them. Under one arm he carries the mordacious form of Milly, hiccoughing more than she is now burping or giggling, and in the other hand her false teeth. He places her upright against the bulk of Flash G. Nods them goodnight and leaves them again.]

'Goodnight, Chow.' Stein.

'Night, Chow, buddy'n'pal.' Flash G.

'Shnight, shlant-eyshes.' Milly, not in the race, Hunt.

The Gang confers again. Leastways the conference starts with Stein waking up first again, and again from a nightmare in which his father drags his bloody and torn and emaciated body .through the charnel-house that is as it was Changi Prison POW hospital, past the body of a large Chinese that Costas has just injected with kerosene with the intention of experimenting with the flammability of the human body. He groans. Again. From a moaner I've become a groaner. It must be-the wisdom of getting ancient and knowing what every day will bring. Frank En Stein. Groan. If I was a horse, they'd shoot me. If it wasn't for the jabbing ache in his neck and his whole body crying filthy foul, Stein would extra groan for the dull-ache piercing of the television still on with a loud crazy nothing. He has fallen asleep on the couch and only his body, in a sorry triumph of matter over mind, can hint at how he got there.

It is nothing later than five-thirty. The day, which promises to him already to get worse, already looks more grey than the crazy loud and crackling nothing greyness of the television fucking screen.

This is no way for an ex-athlete like me, piss off Father, I was, to try to get out of bed. Some part of the body should move; I am commanding. God protect little children. I hope the only stones that bitch wife of mine gets is in her gall bladder. I hope fucking Friesman dies today. May the good Lord strike him dead even if I lie, as I lie. Here's a groan for us all.

Finally, Stein manages to make the machine follow the ghost in the machine. He stands on feet that carry a decrepitude that no biological engineer would instantly recognise or admit to as possible. Then hounds down the snores.

The Gang begins conferring again when Stein, feeling sour enough for a monstrous little joke since in reality he is feeling lonely and rejected, flings off the doona that is covering the single considerable lump of Milly well below e rim of her cups the night before. He is chuckling to think Flash G. has piked out of his turn for the dragon's pit.

177

Yet, when it is revealed that the single lump is a plastic moulding of both Flash G. and the woman (their sleepy woofings in a syncopation continuous), jealousy brings a certain joie de joints back into his joints. Better than acupuncture needles.

'Get out, you dog.' Stein.

'Don't talk to me like that.' Milly.

'I mean him.'

'Jealousy, jealousy.' Her.

'I'm going to the cops.' Stein.

'Silly cunt.' Her, in frump.

'No more of this fucking around, Milly.'

'I'll say, he put the hard word on me, Officer. Broke into my flat. Never seen the silly cunt of a bugger before in my life, Officer. Barges in here raving about his brother given The Big Push.'

'Open your rotten and corrupt eyes when you talk to me, Milly. You left me lying out there on that lounge all night.'

'I want breakfast.' The She of the Gang, stretching, 'And while you're getting it for us, jot down "Laying here, I realised my two men fastened the curlicues of reality tighter around Mr Bigs's neck", whatever that means, before I forget it, 'kay?'

'Isn't Gurton going to say anything?' Stein, pointing to a bit of Flash G. he can see beneath her.

'Leave him alone. He's too busy munching.'

Stein returns to the cold shower of the cartoons on telly, during which he watches alone King Arthur's Gang in a right round conferring.

It is hard to find where Murphy's is at one-thirty in the morning, especially from directions given by the She of The Gang at ten o'clock before she leaves before them less stoked perhaps than normal at that hour but still mightily so. Stein and Flash G. know it is somewhere in one of these back lanes in Darlinghurst but, having failed to find it as it has been first slurred to them by her, they find passers-by are precious few, let alone those who might know the directions to the most famous illegal gambling joint for the hobnobs which, for ten years at least, the police have denied existed. Even after the regular firsthand reports of it existing in the Sunday rags. Journos with fertile imaginations and sour grapes at losing a few lousy bucks.

Fortunately, Stein and swarthy companion make a passing acquaintance with a ten-or-eleven-year-old, snowyheaded (every mum's son) lad who, at first, declares no way two at a time with him unless it's back to their place and fifty bucks extra. Who then corrects himself to tell them longsufferingly precisely where Murphy's is, around the corner and under the sign saying Murphy's, where fucking else? Who then kindly advises them (he is only a lad who needs a whelping hand) to look out for the roulette table, like it's real spongy. Who then calls after them to inform them hey batman and robin your bank-robber balaclavas are slipping.

So Stein and Flash Gurton arrive at Murphy's twenty minutes later than their best laid plans planned them to. Since they were only wearing their bank-robber balaclavas because nervousness had made them cold, they now remove them and step through the hatch-type door in the rough wooden fence there and noddingly pass a shadowy Murphy's sentry in their tuxedos. For anyone who might know them, weight they seem to have put on. Flash G. is feeling good. In his tux, bow-tied and barrel-chested above the

179

cummerbund and weightier, he feels in the flush of his high pug days again, when people let him pass. For white. So he used to feel offended by people who let him pass. Again his anger is rising. Flash G. feels good, yes. As he climbs the wooden stairs pushily in front of Stein. They bank on the door.

With a permanent security of place a grille on the other side slides back. Stein's metabolism is racing now. This is all a midsummer's night's dream; I see a voice.

'Yeah?' Gruff and rough. It is not a ladies' bridge night behind there, for sure.

'Morrie sent us.' Stein.

'Morrie the fuck who?'

'Morrie Friesman, who the fuck else.' Flash G. sparring and ready to take them all on, as if the voice could see.

'Never heard of him.'

'He runs the joint!' Stein, desperately.

'Ssh. Kiss and tell, kiss and tell.' The voice suddenly sibilant.

Stein might even see the giggle if the door does not swing open on a darkening at first filled with only human shapes to the unaccustomed eye. The smoke in the air in there swirling arabesque in the spotlighting above each of the six tables. Stein has the impression of a frozen moment in time, a muffing of sound. The whirrings and the click-clacks and the urgent human murmurs all dulled to a cathedral hymning.

In this time he could flee, run out on Costas, but Flash G. before him has already started up and is now bolting inside yelling something about a hold-up, a stick-it-up yers, a any dogbastard dares to move. Whatever it is it jolts Stein as much as any in there.

The sounds of illegal gambling reality return unmiffed by near-dawn's own strange soft presence. Besides he has his foot in the door and it is a very heavy door. Costas! He flings himself in after Flash at the top of his voice and with feet back on the ground; Clattering iconoclastic in this altar of specie sin.

The effect holds, if not waxes lyrical. Before there is so much as an untoward movement or an incontinent caterwaul of protest from even one of the losers, Stein and Flash G. have admirably smoothly, save a snag here and there, removed their sawn-off shotguns from where they were carrying them down their sides, whacked on their balaclavas on the run and have the floor of involuntary attention. The Gang akimbo and on top of things. Only faces in chiaroscuro staring at them from across the spotlights. Models. The Night Watch. I am Rembrandt of the Beagle Boys. Some of these geezers look relieved to be stopped. Doing them a favour. Call me Robin Hood. I'm Morrie Friesman's floor-show, free. Blow your faces out for Costas. Stein suddenly exalted with the excitement infected by Flash G., and now equally as lippy but forming real words:

'This is a hold-up, no shit. Everybody up against the wall!'

'Nobody fucking move, this is a...'

'Let them move!' Stein in hiss to him.

'Against the wall, bastards and bastardesses. This is a real shotgun I've got levied.'

'Levelled.' But a rebuke happy in the exhilaration of it all. Who said crime doesn't pay.

And even the doormen join the others humbly against the wall. Easy. Easy. There are some twenty patrons who, if they were there to lose their shirts or blouses, were dressed to ensure that if they lost they would lose only the most expensive silk ones. By the time they have doubled up against the wall there they are fidgety with boredom to get this damn nuisance over with. What's going wrong

181

with damn Morrie's hospitality these days. Nothing sacred? It doesn't occur to them that these jokers are here for anything but the house's takings until Lady Luck really cashes in on them for they are hearing the short 'levelled not levied' guy say:

'Ladies and gentlemen, a little *jeu d'esprit*. Turn out your pockets, hand over dem jewels, don't mind my coarse mate, and *faites vos jeux*, eh?' There are pleas and shouts and half-motions of revolt, but there is also supreme Bugsy Stein naturally above them: 'Now, come on. Be good gentlemans and ladies or become shattered bits of them.'

'I know him, I know him!' This Sibyl screech comes from the back row, coming as it does from a high-heeler who might be Bill Gates's sister but she looks like his mother and he's long dead; perhaps gaud goes with gash and makes living femme fatale dead. 'I know him. Don't let the bum escape!'

The few there that can see her clearly realise now why the lighting is low.

'We'll start with the mouthy broad first.' A Stein nod from out the gangland manual sends Flash G. towards her and:

'Okay, Steiny-weiny.'

'No names, dumbcluck!'

'I told you, I told you, I knew him!' as she is dragged forward to the very lonely centre of attention, protesting very passably: 'Lemme go, you black ox!' When there, spotlit before them, she shrugs Flash G. off with a backhand swipe that would lay low a whole rugby front row, then conjures up greater moments of Sibylline amphitheatrics -- and it is as terrible as how terrible her dress doesn't seem to fit over parts best not fit for male eyes -- by quaking a bone-atop, blub-beneath arm towards Stein and:

'It's Costas Stein!'

'*Frank*, you smartarse.' Stein having to resort to the hiss again.

'Shut the fly chomper, lady.' Flash, now Bugsy.

'They don't scare me. This is Frank Stein and he's taking it out on us just because Morrie Friesman, our host... our *host*, right? ... just because Morrie's done in that stinko brother of his!'

'Okay, so I'm,' Stein on the Mugsy Malones now, 'Frank Stein and your Mr Bigs fed my little brother to da fishes. You mugs ain't ever gonna forget it either!'

A Cagney nod is good as a cue to Flash G. With one arm he gets a neck hold on the broad (she will punch his throat over breakfast tomorrow morning in a brief flirtatious fallout of The Gang over the sauce to be spilt) and lowers her to the floor. With a diabolical laugh so all-round admirable, Stein pulls out wire cutters, drags off one of her shoes and, without reeling olfactorily too much:

'Tell Friesman this. Twenty years ago the Toe Cutters Gang cut off my little brother's real father's toes with wire cutters, and this broad gets the same for Mr Bigs who's got it coming to him for murdering my brother.'

With that, she screams and thrashes and there is such a melee of arms and legs and the snapping of incisor steel jaws that none there hears anything but agony that even an old crone of way-off prophesy should not endure, nor sees, when the threesome parts, anything but blood gushing from somewhere. The broad slivers off, a cruel mess and more now that this has happened to her, out of the door presumably to die in lonely pain in some outside gutter. It is such torture that they have never seen outside of television. From one of the lines somewhere, one cries 'Bastards!' and then another and then another. Soon the lines threaten to revolt against this pernicious and illegal show of rare violence in Morrie Friesman's Murphys of all places.

Stein and Flash G. step back quickly. The spotlight picks up that their eyes roll within their heads within their balaclavas. The patrons sense their sudden fright and the front row, pushed by the back row admittedly, moves a few paces menacingly forward. Moral indignation guides their steps, as ever hesitatingly, even though The Gang raise their unloaded shotguns as if they want to prod cattle. Then they stop. The suspended instant before the charge.

At the same moment as Flash G. pulls off his balaclava and smiles silly-old-yous, Stein pulls off his balaclava and smiles silly-old-yous. They get no silly-old-yous back, only what Stein seems to see as massed steam rising. I'm gonna be broiled, Father.

And at almost that same moment, as quick as a Flash isn't right then, a giant of a man in formshape roughly pushes his way through from the back and charges. He comes with a shrill war cry that could have been perfected for sheer chill by Genghis Khan, wrests with one single motion both shotguns from the hands of Bugsy and Mugsy, lifts them bodily at least to the near pinnacle of his Everestesque height (a mad reverential twinkle into their eyes as they snap glance into his, plus a dying of sheer relief), before he shakes them like puppy dogs of the smaller Mongolian kind, cracks their heads together (they go cripes) and flings them bodily like light sacks of grain against the wall. There can be only bone-crunchings to come. Behind him begins the beginning of a cheer of the patrons still as well-heeled as they were after Murphys was just starting to go through them.

The cheer does not go far. Given their collective luck at the roulette table, it is just their luck that this giant hero of a man, this great Chinese in a lesser tuxedo, has just missed the bloody wall and just sent them sailing out into the night through the bloody door.

Escape's number's come up. What rotten luck.

Arid with a huge grunt of. self-reproach, the giant of an oriental Khan chases after them.

184

Funny, though, Chow doesn't come back, either.

The Gang confers once more. Leastways, Stein creaks his sorry way up off the couch, that paramedical inducement to human bone distortions, pissed off again that he has been left dead drunk and contortionistic upon it when it's his turn in the sack, that lovely stretchy space, with Milly, which, by comparison to the couch, is what he was most looking forward to. So much said for the couch. They haven't even switched off the television again, so. that his head feels as jagged as the crazy glockenspieling pattern over there.

It is a monument to traction that Tie makes it so indignantly to the foot of Milly Hunt bed. Do I really have this sense of deja vu, or do I just have a sense of deja vu? It is with a very distinct sense of deja vu that Stein now stands at the foot of Milly Hunt's bed and confronts the contented, nay comfortable, duomorphic lump between the outsized comforters of doona and sheets there. It's bad enough having to stand here with about as much dignity as a tennis ball that's got a hole in it, let alone knowing what I've got to look at while talking to Madame Slackguts in there while black Face-acre snores and snuggles on, the dirty beast. To put the fact of wallowing in slop mildly.

Stein deja-vus a heave-off of the doona to find, as with the morning before, nothing that one should have to sight in the morning. This time he is determined to confront Flash G. and viciously prods what should only be a gnarled male extremity:

'What are ya, some sexual unspeakable?' Stein.

Yet the disturbed gnarled extremity still turns out to be Milly; it's difficult to tell how else the difference. She is not in a conferring mood, it must be confessed:

'Fuck off.'

185

'Pardon piggy, for Christ's sake. What about my turn? I might luv ya.' Stein.

'You join the queue.' Milly.

'I want to know who Chow really is.' Stein, wanting to confer.

'Never seen him before in my young life.' Her.

'Bullshit. I could've got killed last night if he wasn't there.' Stein.

'Wouldn't have a clue who he is. Listen, Steiny-weiny, just grab a pen and paper and jot down a few things for me, will ya?'

'No! I ain't publishing any crap of yours! Who promised? I might feel suicidal, but I don't feel that suicidal. Wake up Deadhead there. I've got a bone to pick with him.'

'Don't you touch his bone. His bone's mine.'

'Aw, Milly, Milly. I ache. I'm a wretched rejected human being. Move over. Comfort.'

'Silly cunt.'

'Right, I'm going to the cops.'

'Suit yourself, but you're gonna miss out on Juliana's tonight.'

'Okay, I'll bite. Aren't I Frank Ern Stein?'

'Juliana's Morrie's biggest-deal escort agency. More, bozo...'

'Don't call me bozo.'

'Yeah, bozo.' Flash G. in a very clear mumble.

'You suckhole out of turn. It was my turn in the cot.' Stein petulant.

'Doesn't he do it well, but.' Her face diving back into the duomorphic blob again. But Stein waits patiently. Juliana's. For Costas. I am a living martyr. Until she finally comes back with a purring mumble:

'Juliana's. It's known as Off Ya Face. There ain't one there that's not always tripping. You jiggy-jig in Juliana's and ten to one you've got a heroin habit a few months later to wall-paper over what you might have caught. They're Morrie best bagmen broads, is Juliana's. Where're you been all your life.' then, 'Honey?'

Flash G., licking milk lips: 'Hmmmm?'

'Isn't he a silly old cunt?'

'I'd leave out the old but then again I'd leave it in.'

Juliana's afloat. Joan, the manageress, Anita, Sara, Jean, Gloria, Soo Lee, Annette, Maria, Tony and Chuck, all that night's staff, regular, of Juliana's Escort Club (The Tops From the Bottoms Up -- Mate a Meet a Make) are wondering how they got to be on this launch drifting in the middle of the night now at least three kilometres off the Sydney Harbour Heads, with a police helicopter hovering overhead and police and rescue launches spearing their ways towards them. Sirens blaring and spotlights going. Right now it seems further than, say, six kilometres as any lucky freewheeling crow would freewheel it from their rooms in Highfield Street, Kings Cross. As if since they were loaded aboard four hours ago it hasn't already been a night of enough heave-ups.

They blame Joan, and she blames Morrie F. and the cops are going to blame them all when they get on board and see what's there.

They blame Joan because she was the one who took the booking for 5000 dollars from a man who described himself as Luck Sin over the phone to book the whole shebang for a night on the enchanted waters of Sydney Harbour for himself and his two oppos. Honestly, you do get some freakos in this game, but what's a good manageress chasing cash flow to say?

They, the staff of Juliana's, have all been called in, driven to the harbourside and loaded on to what the most seafaring one of them recognised as a hired 34-footer, introduced to Mr Luck Sin who looked about as much Chinese as the darkie with him looked like Errol Flynn as he was introduced as. Or about as much rich as the sort with him looked like Lady Winipher Horton-James.as she was introduced as. At least swarthy old Errol Flynn, when he got going, looked like he could drive the beast of a thing.

Anyway, a night on the water with all those Harbour lights, even if it means closing up the whole shop for the night... well, what's a gal and guy in the game for if it's not for romance?

And Joan the Manageress has been paid the 5000 greenies in real folding money and presumably she's counted it, since you couldn't get a bunch of fives past her beady eyes. And if the freakies have paid in one dollar bills shoved into a plastic carry bag, well what's a gal or guy in the game for if it's not for a bit of fun. On fucking Joan.

They have chugged up the Harbour and they have been playing their parts of feeding those two freakie male slobs grapes while they lay on these two deck chairs being fanned with these stupid branches from a gum tree and burping on the cheap grog and yakking so a gal couldn't get the business end over with so she could turn the tables on these two freakies and enjoy the starry night and all that crap. Tony and Chuck having the worst of it. No grapes and fans and Roman candles for them. Down in the for'ard hatch, they had to go at it all night with Lady Haw-Haw (no laugh, either, poor things) and Tony said one time he actually fell in. So much for the tightness around the wad of British aristocracy.

That's been all very well, but to keep having to listen to these two freakos going on and on big-timing about all that loot from old mate

Morrie for knocking over some writer or something some weeks ago like it was a broken record and we have to get the needle, like who gives a stuff, was just the living end, shag it. And that ugly old broad up front telling Tony and Chuck they'd better keep their ends up cos they're being paid with Mr Bigs's own murder money. Well, what's a guy or gal in the game for if it's not for the rumble of doing the boss's freakie mates a favour now and again. Get your pecker up so I can put my tongue down they said she kept saying.

Okay, but when that tribal kind of Brad Pitt gone-to-putty jumps up and drives us out to sea in the middle of the night, you begin to wonder, especially when he's fooling around look no hands. He was lucky Tony and Chuck couldn't raise their nose out of that Hairy Mary, like mating with a buffalo, otherwise they would have sorted him out, wouldn't you, boys? Sure would. Couldn't see daylight from nothing down there with that rhino. That wasn't no lady.

Then they get out this rubber ducky sort of thing with one of those outboard whatsit and the three of them just pile in and leave us out here, just like that. Didn't old Joan get on to them. We thought it was funny when they called back to us, couldn't even see them in the dark out here by then, that it's okay you old fart, they left the boodle on board in the carry bag and anyway they'd set the SOS radio thing going before they left. Big deal. Freakies.

And when these cops come on board, we're going to tell them we thought it a bit funny at the time. Aren't we? They saying that Morrie Friesman had done in some wog journalist or other. Big mouth freakies. Some mates. Wait until stinking Joan gets into Morrie's ear. We could all catch salt overdose out here. Here the fucking bulls come. Hooray, the conquering heroes.

On board, the Flying Drug Squad, just flown across the water on the tip-off they received and just beating the rescue-bent Harbour Police by a canvas, find what they are looking for. The haul of counterfeit notes in 5000 single bills and arrest all of the staff of Morrie Friesman's prized Juliana's. Juliana's never really got off the

189

ground again, and Morrie Friesman wasn't all that pleased from the top of his head to the bottom of his sea-legs either.

Meanwhile, The Gang disembarks at Mosman, the flagon stashed in the rubber dinghy already three-parts gone. Into Milly's guts. Three high old jolly rogers. She particularly content with the rogering she's had. Those two, Tony and Chuck, took a lot of guts. Content that the counterfeit bills will go back to where they were loaned from by the few friendly cops who still care about Costas. My Costas. Dear god, dear man. Jesus, the night's black. Why is it so black? As they disembark to the sand of Mosman Beach. Jesus, isn't it ever pitch black.

Pitching, Stein faints flat on his face in the sand. All black, except for white lightning bolts of pain. Now black, full pitch.

The Gang further confers. Leastways this time Stein doesn't wake up from a dream, but dwells within it. I know I'm not really here, but am I here? Hello out there. I know I'm thinking. Slinking thinking. Sinking. Costas. Hello, Costas. The Costas with the mostas. My Costas. We swim with da fishes. Father, we have the sharks. Swimming with you, Father, across the rice field, swaying. We are Criado Liyi and Sergeant Mario Flocco by your side. Charging enfilading. It is bright and cold up here in the Timor mountains. It's cold and bulleting in these Timor mountains. Vicious little wasps zing the bullets, Father. Mean pingy air rushes all round. Wait. Father! The ache, the burning in my chest. Sleep, Father. The black river. The black bright river. Why am I being beaten from this hospital bed to wash the bamboo floor. They won't understand that the bright dark river, the dark bright river and my chest is burning. What is this place? These thin soldiers in all these wooden beds, planks. They say I am to die of dysentery. They say I am to die of malaria. They say I am to die of this weak heart, but I will give lectures at the University of Changi. I am talking of Cambridge and Rhodes. They don't stop beating me. They keep striking me across my mouth, across the wound in my chest; it

190

won't stop weeping. I am not going to die in this bed. This Korean guard isn't Japanese, he wants to speak. I cannot speak. He is not Japanese. These men aren't Chinese. Liyi. Live Liyi, please live. I cannot carry these stones to this railway line. I think I will die here and let my chest burn and my legs throb, the black bright river. Has it been all this time since my rice field? They are trying to tell me it's been two years. This Captain is trying to tell me a year ago back in Timor they have taken my Liyi and shot him. They move him against a tree. He does not take a blindfold. His black eyes are burning at Sergeant Flocco. They are trying to tell me my Criado Liyi told the Japanese to wait across the rice field. Flocco is telling them so. Father! They are shooting me! I am you and you. I think we should sleep now.

So The Gang confers by Stein's hospital bedside. He comes awake with a low moan of loss. There is a sense that he has lost a fabulous sum of money in the deep mourning hearts of people he knows but has never met. All that he recognises at first is the right and sore awake timing of the grey dawn light. He looks for the television, but the walls are bland green. He can remember the beach, stepping off onto the cold and damp sand, a feeling of it gloving his face. This is a hospital room.

Stein turns his head and looks at the sleeping lump in the next bed. Whoever is there must be in here to have about ten stone shaved off, the size of it. What am I doing here? If this is some monstrous joke, my name ain't Frank Ern Stein. Stein drifts off again, a new life in the dawning.

He wakes again when he hears gruntings from the other bed and this time he wants to confer:

'What are you doing here, what am I doing here?'

'You fell over, you,' she pushes her head above the blankets, quite unashamed at the shock it might give a sick man, 'silly old cunt you.' then, as though talking to her own body in there: 'Didn't he?'

191

Flash G. raises the second of the heads of the large beast in that small bed, just as unashamed at the final shock the sight of it might give a sick man: 'Conked right out, like St George Illawarra in last year's semis.'

'What are you two doing here?'

'We're looking after you.' Milly, pained to her quicks which she is noticing need new nail polish.

'What are you two doing here?' Stein, disjointed.

'He doesn't believe us.' Her.

'Yeah, well what would you reckon.' Flash G.

Stein thinks he is dozing again. He has never felt so warm. This is where I wanted to go at the top of that cliff. Finally he can hear himself saying:

'Didn't I say what am I doing here?'

'You just got a revolting erection when that nurse was washing you. Didn't he?'

'Milly darls, let a bloke sleep now.'

Stein: 'I don't want to sleep. Wanna confer.'

'I'm talking about me, bozo,' Flash G., and, 'Jesus, ain't hospitals noisy these days.'

'What am I doing here?'

'Here, here,' Her woman's kindly heart beating a little faster and, as she climbs out of bed to go to him, the all-over, the crumpled sight of her really a great shock to a sick man; I am going to be inflicted with the Passion of Saint Wafts, 'you're only in here for a few tests.

Anyway, you've got to; stay here a few days, you silly old cunt. Morrie's got the apartment staked out and we've gotta have somewhere to stay. We've booked you in the best private hospital in town and they don't mind. You're paying for it. Meet brother and sister; We refuse to leave your side, so they've given us a double private.'

'I can't afford to pay for this.' Stein.

'Mean, man. A double's only two hundred a day more than a single.'

'Tell him to go to a bank and get a personal loan.' Flash G. on the turn-over.

'Steiny-weiney, you need the peace and quiet. I can really write here.'

'Tm not ill!'

'I've told you not to worry. I've been slipping you a few pills to keep your blood pressure up, so they won't find out you're not ill. That's right. You just keep groaning like that and they can give you all the injections in the world, but they won't twig. Now lie back, have a good long rest. Don't wake us, we'll wake you.'

The Gang has conferred. Bathing in luxury coming out of Stein's pocket, Milly dives back into the wet spots alongside of Flash G. Two-thirds of The Gang is a single entity again. It's amazing how restful a little conferring can be.

If Morrie Friesman is reputed to have a fleet of businesses in the fantasies industry, then Les Naughty Girls Nightclub is certainly his vox populis flagship, as it is said. He has denied this. I only own the building, he has said. I only go there occasionally to enjoy myself with the real people, he has said. My bodyguards have been seen there only because I guess they have the same tastes in good healthy fun as I have, he has said. Witnessed counting the takings, Morrie Friesman has said that he was only helping out a casual acquaintance who couldn't come out that night because he had a tummy upset and couldn't get his corset on. That is another one of Morrie's genial jokes. He is known to be very proud of the naughty but nice reputation Les Naughty Girls gives him.

If you're smart, you book for the nine o'clock sitting for dinner, catch the two main floorshows, get terribly cut, meet all the epicenes you can meet and get out before the real drunks come in and the female impersonators start to get a bit scratchy and the fondling begins in earnest with Ena and Co. On their ways to getting cut, ladies get office-party cut prices. This is good clean fun. Morrie's fagship.

A whole houseful is smart on this Saturday night, when the meal is served by these buxomy men, all fresh olive-oiled even as yet. There is not a cane-cutter or a sailor on leave who is drunk and in sight. This is ordinary decent Australia curling its toes at play. The dollars don't count. Behind the bar already the dollars are being counted. Backstage the gails are turning themselves into guys; the guys are turning themselves into gails. Regalings. Half an hour to go, ladies and ladies. You can hear the waiters, the little duckies, clunking down plates out there. Wears the sequins, don't it? Where's the tape; oh my, aren't my bollocks getting weary of its worn, aren't they ever.

Above the hi-gang announcements and the suturing brassy rock warming up their souls, almost, is the slurping of the soup. It could be eyes down for bingo. Someone must have rung the dinner bell. Those who haven't been there before are frenzied into feeding by those who have been there before; if you don't get into it pronto the donto, they'll whip the plate away before your very eyes, and if you don't keep them peepers open they'll flash past you with the next included course. It's the bib and slurp time, a time of hard work for the staff. Nobody's taking a blind bit of notice of them wriggling

194

their bums on past. Makes you wonder why we keep practising. Must be for the glory of the quince. The meat in the mince. Cows.

Morrie Friesman is not in the nightclub. It is just as well. He might get very upset at the loudmouth on two tables back. The soups have hardly had their sweet corns spilled when there is a hey!, then a louder hey!, then a louder than loud fucking hey you!, which makes all the waiters dressed as waitresses instinctively dive for cover and all the waitresses dressed as waitresses roll up their sleeves to bare their biceps. What mouthy bugger?

It is a he, of all things, up on his red-faced feet. He might have come in a raincoat but that white dress he's got on is as coarse as a hospital gown, bloody thing. If it ever isn't one, I go 'he'. He is now -- he must be a he or a rampant feminist escaped from a pregnancy ward -- up on his feet and actually shouting. For a waiter. There are no waiters here, only waitresses. He must be blind or blind rotten drunk: And, finally, there is not a slurp of the sweet corn soup that is loud enough to cover the loud kerfuffle of him:

'What's a cockroach doing in my soup?! Where the fuck's the cook?'

This minor human being is actually standing on his feet and gesticulating. He is not of large size yet all around him on the same-type and adjoining tables seem to have shrunk, as they're trying to do. Perhaps their heads are closer to their soup plates for to see if there are any cockroaches in their soups. They float, you know, like the devil's breezes. They can swim a mile in tumble-turn laps before a spoon ever touches them, and then don't they shit themselves.

'What's this cockroach doing in my soup?!'

Ha, ha, haven't we heard it all before. If being like you've just fallen off an operating table and looking like some monstrous joke in drag, then being in drag has come down a number.

He stands red-faced alone.

195

When no one comes to tear him apart there, the diners start to take courage that it might be part of the show. From the first moment when the black man from the table three right from the front stands up yelling at this creature from two back, most of Morrie's guests out for a giggle think that it must be the floor show, part of, until the exchanges come too raw'n'rude:

'Shaddup and sit down, idjit!'

'I'm asking what's this cockroach doing in my soup?!'

'Fucking breast-stroking, what else? What a dickhead.' Someone else joining in the shouting match as well, sounding strangely familiar. Obviously cockroaches there have friends.

'Yeah, you'd work for Morrie Friesman, too.' One other than Morrie F. is now shouting across the room's sea of averted faces. 'Everybody knows bloody Friesman's a butcher. The bastard what runs this joint murdered my brother, now he's trying to poison the water by impugning a cockroach who was minding its business with a little splash and taking about poison in his soup!'

From the shadows they emerge to shift this bum in the nick of time. The bouncers. Most of them believing they have to clear this mental case out before other cockroaches are found more than anything else. But before the circle can tightened its noose around Stein's sickly head, they have to swing to the attention of an even greater emergency (one of those nights). A woman screams. A real woman. This is serious.

She is on five right back and in this panelling light she just looks passably a woman. She has screamed and she has swung her handbag across the table at the innocent man-like creature sitting opposite to her and, when it has missed, she has launched herself bodily across the table for to tear him to pieces, possibly. Even now she is in midair and almost upon him. If her dress wasn't up around her waist because of flight dynamics, it is obvious that she has metaphorically had her dress torn off. She falls upon him like a harpy she is not known then to be and rolls and rolls amongst the tables, over-spilling many a plate of soup and releasing many a cornered cockroach.

By the time they have rescued her from this pervert, she has gained so much of an upper hand upon him by way of fingernail grooves in the poor victim's face that she has regained her composure enough to stand, straighten her dress while they see how far his arms will go back without breaking, hold still for a moment while the more disbelieving of the bouncers (those that thought they'd seen it all) inspect her more closely to see if she's a real woman (she'd just pass a muster of sheep; no wonder most guys want to be gay), and huffs her way out of there, going:

'Nobody's gonna come on top of me when I'm out dining. I don't have to pay good money to be propositioned. I ain't no silly cunt!'

All of which has allowed Stein and Flash G. to slip out just before Milly Hunt unhinges the door on her own outraged way out.

Morrie Friesman will hear of this. The staff is aware of that as they try to restore calm by throwing the innocent unknown out on his ear. He escapes for a brief moment to cry out to his invisible friends making-up back stage: 'Underneath I thought she was a guy, honest I did!'

At the same time, another who has had soup spilt all over her new organzine by Milly's diversion, has herself gone after the culprits and shouts down the stairwell: 'Stop those people!', especially as she can just see the legs of The Gang slip out into the street below. She realises that the only person capable on those stairs there of stopping them is a grinning Chinese of a large type (she knows he is grinning because when you've seen one Chink in the face you've seen them all) leaning against the wall of that stairwell. Between him and that wall are two struggling men of the Caucasoid breed in the Friesman-employed mould, but right now in the Chinese squeeze. They too are of the large type but evidently not as large as he.

The upshot is that this innocent lady returns to her table and enjoys the show, wondering as a member of all the public there who Morrie Friesman murdered because it's different from all the nice things she's read in the papers about him, but having to destroy her organzine next week due to the dry cleaner's ability to cope with soup but not with the dyestuff got from crushed cockroaches.

'There's some hardnut at the door from Friesman's lawyers. He wants to give you a writ.' Flash G.

'Tell him to piss off. I'm trying to write.'

Yelling: 'She said piss off. She's trying to writ.'

Such turgidity to a poor bailiff at the door just doing his job.

The Gang is about to confer amore, about amour. Leastways, they are back in the apartment after the Friesman stake-out has been lifted. It might have been because a person of oriental extraction was seen slashing all the tyres of the Friesman stake-out car while its occupants caught forty winks. The henchies inside it caught more from Morrie Friesman via The American when he heard.

So The Gang is back home and are about to confer amore, about amour in a leastways sort of talking way. This time Stein does not wake up by his own steam in his OWQ lather, but is prodded awake so rudely he could be sleeping in the path of a pilgrim's pursuit of excellence. He is so stiff from sleeping on the couch that even his eyelids have trouble with articulation. What they see is a sight that could unhinge them too.

Milly and Flash G. stand before him in that again-conferring grey-dawn light. They are stark naked in a way that no textbook has ever shown to a medical student. What's even more indecent is that they

198

are holding hands. It makes Stein's morning glory of an erection pull its woolly head in quick smart, to think that sex could lead to that. Is nothing naked sacred? And if that's not enough, they are truly indignant that he should be lying there like that:

'Cover yourself up, bozo.' Flash.

'Cover yourselves up yourselves. I'm shocked.' Stein.

'We don't have to, you silly cunt. That's what we've come to tell you. We have decided we're in love.'

'What?' Stein.

'True love's won out over trial and adversity, bozo.'

'You wanna turn me off eating forever?' Stein.

'Is that all you're gonna say?' She turns on him. Stein thinks she looks just as atrocious from the other side. Turn off.

'No. Where's breakfast, whose turn?'

'Come on, Flash honey. He's a dead mullet.'

They wheel away in high gudgeon with some parts of their anatomies following them but most parts seeming to wait much longer.

'No, wait up.' Stein trying desperately to gather his wits. Is this still a nightmare I haven't woken up in or am I really awake and it's just visually a nightmare?, and: 'What happened?'

'If you must know he kissed me in the morning.'

Stein: 'It could've been worse. It could've been in the box.'

'Don't talk to my fiancée like that.' Flash G., his swaining showing.

199

Stein: 'Oh no, fiancée. Not that, Flash. Take antibiotics, it's sure to come right, whatever it is.'

'He will hold my family jewels and I will hold his.'

If there were more teeth in her mouth than missing friends, she might truly be prettily in flush.

'Okay, congratulations. Now, please, please, can you put some clothes on?'

'Not on your nelly.' Flash.

'Oh, you can on mine, honey.' The Her of the Gang. 'Sweetie pie.'

'Lamb's fry.'

'God.' Stein rolls over to go back to sleep hoping for at least a bad dream if he can't forget reality with a nightmare, hopefully.

Later The Gang gets down to serious conferrings again, but not amore about amour.

'Chow was there again last night. At Les Naughty Girls. Did you see him on the stairs going out?'

'Isn't he the ants pants? Have any of you two guys ever tried a foursome?'

'I ain't going to,' Flash G., asserting his moral droit du seigneur as the betrothed, 'jump into the pit with a Chinese who'd make the Incredible Hulk look like a sock.'

'They're supposed to have small willies, the Chinese.'

'I don't care how small his dick is.'

'Listen, let's not have a,' Stein, mandarin, eyes rolling towards the great improbable heaven, 'lover's tiff over Chow.'

But she is not to be put aside a large path by such a small prod. 'It was just something that would be good for my book. And don't forget what we're doing this for first of all.'

'We're doing this for Costas, you dud.' Stein instantly ready to punch her because he already knows her reply:

'Piss off, we are. First up, we're doing it for my book, you silly cunt. If you're lucky, you might get Friesman and I might cut you in on the promotions of the film of the book. Tell him, Flash.'

'Tell him what?'

'You're as big a silly cunt as he is.'

'We're getting hitched because of your book?'

'Well, you've got to have a bit of,' her pout actually resembling one, 'romance somewhere in it, don't you?'

'I don't believe this.' Stein.

'You don't have to believe it. You've only got one more opportunity and that's your lot, mate. You can't nail Morrie after this, that's your problem.'

'What one more opportunity?'

'Busting up his regular drug run, silly cunt, what else?' 'Now you must be joking.'

'Take it or leave it. It's your last chance. You ain't flushed him out yet, matey Steiny-weiny, smart alec. I gotta have some plot guts in the plot. You're so useless you're ruining my story.'

'Friesman has a regular drug run and you know about it?'

'All my jewels didn't come from where my good looks came from. Once a month a ship comes from one of them places up there where Chow comes from and drops a bag overboard with this buoy thing attached. Somewhere up around Torres Strait wherever that is. Then different cronies so-called out fishing come along in different hired boats, pick it up and run it down to or up to, who cares?, some joint called The Entrance. He then has this hired truck or van or car, he's even had a hearse, drives it down to or up to Sydney. It goes into those places in Darlinghurst where they pack those Asian refugees into and comes out on the street. Simple.' She takes their silence and reads their minds, perhaps because Stein already has his hand on the phone. 'No cops, or no info. I can't do press interviews for my million dollar best-seller in the boob.'

'Some boobs, too.' Flash G. in genuine admiration of the weight of her affront.

'Aw, you're just biased, you swarthy dark and handsome stranger, you.' She is all modesty. It must be the Modess time of month.

By rights it should make a difference, but in fact it's the converse.

Stein stands on the top of the hospital steps the day before The Gang's drug bust heist and, yes, gazes at the day through the silkine veil of his eyelashes. If his heart could sing, his heart would sing. He has just come out from getting the results of his tests. He has felt limicolous in there. That is not cool, quiet reason in there. That is a rain forest where the sun never warms its hearth. That is squelching along the slippery corridors of the undergrowth. Their voices are hidrotic, helminthic. Sluggies, all. The day is so beautiful out here. I have never felt the sun seethe into me like this. I have never felt the earth so hetherwards before. I am a part of this. I am of all things sharp and stunning-edged that are turning towards the sun. My body is dancing. It wants to walk. It thrills me I just have to move to rejoin the great flow. There is so much light of whites and blues that I feel I might sunburst. This joy, this vibrant joy, I have never

202

experienced before, never. This must be love. This must be the start of it all. The eternal elation. The latria. The world that I am in is beautiful and it is beautiful that I am in it. I remember once how the water cuddled me. It was so blue, as blue as this. It must have been a pool, still, a pond, still, swaying reflection on the bottom; I didn't need breath. Oh my, oh my. It is so good to be alive.

Stein in ecstasy.

When he moves he does so very slowly at first as though he is taking his first steps. By the time he has reached the near corner, Stein is laughing aloud and has started to sprint. He is not looking behind him.

But his radiance is going before.

The one, the doctor, nothing much older than any intern could be, has sat Frank N. Stein down, that once monstrous joke, and talked down to him while sitting level with him, knee to knee as any other situation might have it, his hand resting on Stein's outer thigh lightly (as any other situation might misconstrue it) and his voice so avuncular that it has made him sound thirty years older than he really is, as it would have to make him to be Stein's uncle.

Stein has said only one word before getting up and coming out to exalt in the sun of his very being. That word was 'No'. That Uncle Doctor has softly explained that they have the results of the tests back and there wasn't any need to call him, Stein, back in for further tests because given the chip off the old block of the lump in his groin as well as the lump in his armpit as well as the melanoma on his back as well as the X-rays showing the growth in his kidneys which, taken altogether, really is a medical impossibility since cancer, if it was cancer, would normally have been thought to lodge first in one place, so in effect Stein gosh you sir are some kind of medical freak, yes I suppose you could say if you wanted to some kind of monstrous joke yes so the first thing I'd like to tell you is that I plan to write this up in Lancet if you wouldn't object too much, although ethically one could write it up anyway without one's permission, but one wouldn't really like to do that without asking you first. Of course.

The second thing he did want to tell Stein is that it is cancer and taking all those incredible lumps and things together really incredible cancer, obvious you don't do things by half measure, ha ha, it's cancer at a very advanced Stage. I wouldn't ever want to use the term terminal, I'd prefer if you don't mind to say it's on the fast lane with all the hydraulic fluid to the brakes leaked out.

One knows what you want to ask next, Mr Stein, and 'you wouldn't want me to kid you about operating on the kidney, it's called a nephrotomy with a probable nephrectomy on the unavoidance in case you're wondering what I'm talking .about when you read Lancet when it comes out hopefully soon. No, I wouldn't kid you, Mr Stein, without the operation I would say you'd have left to you as likely as .not probably around give or take approximately as much as anyone can ever say a shrewd guess six months. With the operation we could put it at a rough stab, a pin in the old donkey's tail, a working hypothesis, a sort of empirical inkling, a jab in the dark, a pretty sophisticated guestimate, that you might have nine months. Of course it would take you roughly three or four months to be able to get on pretty shaky legs again after the operation, so you'd be sort of kinda be back to square one anyway, but they're life's little decisions, I suppose. Coming operation, or not, ha ha.

It is then that Stein has said his one word 'No' before getting up to walk out to exalt in the sun of his very being.

He has not heard the young man, that doctor, say after him how much it has filled him with scopophilia to see him in that condition. Just as elated as Stein is to come to be out on the top step of the steps to the hospital.

I am in you, Costas, now. I can understand, Father, now. I can feel the pain, the ache lift from me. I am at One. And I can feel it now. It is beautiful. It is a miracle. I have shared it with you. It is no monstrous joke now because it is a monstrous joke now. And it's

204

good. I feel so good. I am in the world. The world has lifted from me.

At everlast.

As the cabin cruiser edged a shaky way towards the wharf, The American shifted uneasily in the back seat of the car. If only that dumb guy knew how much that load was worth he wouldn't be coming alongside down tide, the fucking moose, and he wouldn't have those brats hanging over the side like that. One of them falls overboard and we're all in the stool.

He is sitting with two other Friesmanmen, henchies, in the white Merc across the harbour where he can watch the proceedings without being seen or, if identified, can claim unhappy coincidence if something goes wrong, it better not. Just come up from Sydney for a little fresh air, full of saltspray as the gimpies might say. On time, though, good day for it. Augurs well. The American feels so good he could bash a few heads. I'd like to start with these two dummies I've got in this car.

He watches the cruiser defy wind and tide and (relatively) safely berth, then the three families aboard with millions of kids (don't they have to breed, these Aussies!) pile off in waves of tumble, making for the ice-cream van standing so conveniently nearby on the wharf there that The American winces again. Raving sonabitches amateurs. Rank. The American's man s last off the boat. He waves his seemingly bitching wife and certainly moaning kids on before to follow the others while he tiddlies around, sorts out the cabin cruiser hire office with the final inspection and the handover'n'back, then struggles with the three remaining duffle bags back onto the shore proper.

It is not exactly a perfectly proportioned sleight of hand, either, that is used by the man to fling the three duffle bags into the selling window of the ice-cream van. For one thing it happens that he has to pitch each one over the heads of two unknown kids who have suddenly appeared at a hot pace, hotter than his and certainly faster than his inbuilt reaction time, at the window there with legal coin of the realm in their grubby little mitts, and demanding actual ice-cream service. For another thing, he missed the window opening twice, each time making those tiny unwelcome visitors duck quickly because of falling bags from a henny-penny sky and beginning to bawl. But the little cunts still won't go away, iccies being better than real injury. And isn't The American now itching for throats. From away over there on the other side, to him it looks for all the world as if the ice-cream van itself is gulping down, rejecting, gulping down, rejecting, gulping down the precious cargo.

And as soon as the last bag does down the hatch, The American sees the shutter clamp down on that black mouth of a window-hole and an agonizing thirty seconds later the van takes off at not exactly breakneck speed, given the obvious five or so attempts to start it and the kangaroo-hopping that followed. Now suddenly relieved to languid, The American watches the ice-cream van chuff away for its drive back to Sydney, those hundred kilos or so, fucking better make it or I'll kill the real owner I hoicked it from.

He muses a tiny moment on the figures of the two tiny tots still standing there with their money still held high in their grubby little mitts in a frozen form of disbelief that ice-cream man has gone from us. Not even Atari can make things disappear like that.

The American knocks three times with his index knuckle on the head of the shamus sitting behind the wheel in front of him in the signal to move on slowly as she goes. Five minutes behind the van all the way'll do nicely. A gesture that was a monument to the scale of economy of the language of communication.

The American wasn't the only one watching the two brats.

206

A few kilometres before Newcastle, where he would have to drive through the thickest shopping maul at that time of day, the driver of the ice-cream van couldn't believe the luck he could see through his two ice-cream cones. Even in the distance he could see she was blonde and that is only talking about her knickers partial to her crutch there on the side of his road. She is sitting on a suitcase, never mind the suitcase, and she has her legs wide open (oh, the stars that can twinkle in those heavenly vaults!) and her hard calves on those high heels are all that a man could dram on. Her pink sweater and her purple velvet mini swim like a mirage into his thirsting mind. No vestal virgin cocks her finger like that.

It is thoughts of being on the job that makes him pull over, not a thought that he is on an important job. Even the ice-cream van shudders to a halt beside her.

What makes him not rev up and drive away, having halted by her, is the shock of the face above that bodily al- and il-lusion of a heaven-sent nymphomaniacal opportunity sort of kind. And the unfortunate fact that a face which looks like a pasty as yet not even met with a decent oven has his foot unleverable from the brake out of the shocking distortions that the distant eye can induce. It flashes to him that she might be death warmed up or something alive out of one of those Navy films about what sexual excesses can do to a bod.

Still his right foot won't move from the brake, despite his left gunning the accelerator.

Milly Hunt is at the window, her bright red lips a painter's last mad slashing protest. His eyes are bulging with what he might have done by stopping:

'What?'

'I said give's a lift to Brissie, big boy.'

'Brissie?'

'You mad impetuous gypsie, you, move over for the time of your life.'

When the time of day dawns through the panic, he almost cries out with so much relief that he calls out with so much of a relief:

'It's back thataway, Brissie is. You're standing on the wrong side of the pissing road.'

'Well, turn around.'

'It's a thousand kilos or something.'

'So what?'

'Well, if you want to really know, lady, one kilometre'd be too much.'

'Don't call me a "lady" like that, you silly cunt. I'm someone's daughter, you know.'

'You'd be someone's great-grandmother, too.'

By then, the ice-cream van has mercifully regained the kinetic charge of the road and, even more mercifully, he is tanked up inside it. He doesn't look back and it takes him another twenty minutes before he dares to. By then he can believe his lucky stars that it was just another one of those near things.

Going through all that Saturday morning shopping traffic and all those mums and dads and kiddies and nuns and priests and church wardens and bowling-club matrons, yes, all of those, who like any other human being the world over love to watch the ice-cream vans go by, helped him take his mind off her arid back onto business. It's good to be an ice-cream man for a day when everybody wants to watch you go by and point. Hi, all you folks. I've got enough stuff in here to blow you all right off your boring faces.

He would never know, and The American would not know until he catches up with the van on the other side of town, that an exceedingly clear-writ and wittingly large cloth banner -- not there before he stopped before Milly Gladrags -- has appeared hooked to the back of his van. And on it the wording there reads: SEXUALLY ABUSE ALL LITTLE CHILDREN AND UP GOD, TOO!

And that all the curiosities in town were turned to scandalised outrage followed by fingers pointing. Followed by a run of complaints on the local constabulary switchboard. Interspersed with phone-in complaints by constabularies on feet. Precedent to two highway patrols hot on his hammer on the other side of town.

What The American does realise when he comes upon that scene on that other side of town, of the ice-cream driver lying in a pool of blood in the middle of the road (the first patrol car has gunned him down so fast on the highway that he leapt from the van blazing away) and cops crawling all over the precious white stuff stashed inside those duffle bags, is that the vaguely familiar faces he saw in a Mini they passed a while back were those of the three creeps giving Morrie so much trouble lately. He does not need to put two and one together. Bloody madness makes him rap viciously with his five knuckles on the back of the head of his driver.

The white Merc careers through a U-turn and belts back the way it has just come. Out of eye- and earshot of the cops now back there, there is another gunning along the road.

He sees it coming the other way, and for a moment can't work it out. When the white Merc flashes by him going the other way to that in which he has been following it at an enpaced distance, Chow has already worked it out and is swinging his Toyota in as sharp a semicircle as the wheel-turn will allow. Even before he has completed it, his foot is down, his head is down and his urge for more power out of the four cylinders mightily up. The white Merc is

209

already lost to him by the time he straightens up and he knows that he might as well be going backwards.

In his frustration, his great hands begin to bend the steering wheel out of skew. And in his great and awful premonition his great hands are bending it back again. Askew, true, askew, true. As much as fast as the Toyota, comparative to the fading white Merc, is going forward, is the steering wheel putty in the palm of these Chinese's hands.

After a longer time than he wants to remember, Chow sees up ahead what clearly is a commotion involving the white Merc and the Mini he knows contains The Gang. Though it is a commotion that might turn a few heads, it is not stopping any cars riling on past there (back where the ice-cream van is, it has even taken three squelches across the driver's body and the subsequent police road block to partially stem the mad holiday rush back home, so shows you). The white Merc has obviously forced the Mini off the road. Chow switches on his lights full beam and clamps his bonecrusher on the horn. If he could step on it any more he would be steeped in chassis up to the knee. It's all he can do. The speed is all the Toyota can do. It is all he can do not to burst out screaming. The whine in the ageing diff would drown in it anyway.

But at least he can be seen to be forthcoming.

Doing so, seeing and perceiving, The American coolly nods to his reluctant companions, who at that time are enjoying rapping heads rather than being rapped on their own, and they leave off Stein and Flash G. and return to the car. They need, though, no second invitation. That The American is dragging, with as much exertion as if she was a paltry rag doll, really, rather than just looking like one knocked up by an unimaginative granny, that horse-arsed she-who-must-chase-cars-and-bite-tyres broad (all over and very) along the otherwise good earth and into the car means that the Yank means skedaddle, like time to shoot through. Since there has been never in their joint lives that they have, Morrie Friesman's two companion henchmen don't ask questions. So they don't. They merely shut the doors behind The American and Milly and cruise on past at least twice the speed (even at cruising speed) Chow's Toyota is coming on the bushido charge.

Chow does not even bother to try to swerve to cut them off. He doesn't see much of them going on past him, but rather senses it, just as he senses the warrior challenge in The American's glare the instant the two cars pass. Instead, Chow does his best to stop the Toyota by Stein and Flash G. and does so fairly passably, given that it seems as reluctant to stop as it was to get up and go. All the other world continues to sail pass.

Stein and Flash G. hang over the bonnet of the Mini in a dual marvel to anti-gravity. They are not too waded-into considering. The American has back-chopped with speed and ineffable grace Stein's adam's-apple then Flash G.'s adam's-apple (that coffee costard) in one fell and quite singular swoop before, even, his two schmupk companions can get as much as a toecap of a boot in. Which they proceeded thereupon to do anyway and were just beginning to settle down to a real enjoyment when The American noticed Chow's charge-on and decided this is not the time, oh soon, nor the place, oh soon, for a showdown with our Chinese mystery man coming.

Chow lifts this Stein then this Flash G. into the shades of side-by-side trees on the verge there. They could be pieces of Chinese rice paper, he handles them so gently. The Mini there in the ditch, he lifts as though he was teaching a trifle to swim above a two-arm support and swings it around to point the right way on the right side of the road. He picks up, too, Milly's headscarf (the scurf drops like mourning snow as dolefully as it might have once been like sludge) and puts it reverently on the back seat; this could be Gargantua poking around into a little folk's place. Then does Chow return to stand over Stein and Flash G. He allows them time to be able to recover enough to look balefully up at him. They have this pain and he has that pain and they have this other pain and he has that other pain. It is not the first time that Milly Hunt has been called this and that.

The pain of this and that for Chow is crossing his face forming of it a mask of the Monkey King where the mouth is the opening of the Heavenly Gate and the tongue is the lolling of gliffing fate and the ears are the rebellow of life on the long river and the face is the puff of the proudman's grief and the eyes. Above all, the eyes! Above Stein. Above Flash G. Are leaking this tear and that. This pain and that. Above them both. And his head is slowly shaking. Delicate for a huge man. So this is what he looks like in real light. Chow. She's right, Chow. It's all right, Chow, I understand. Stein cannot speak as yet to talk to the Chinaman to say it's all right Chow I understand. He doesn't know how ashamed the man is anyway. The shaking of his lamaist head and the surprising euphonic, mostly, English at last:

'Sorrie, sorrie.'

and a bow. Before he turns and leaves. Each step towards the Toyota an enveloping shame; the driving off solemn and determined.

Stein is just about getting out a calling after him it's all right mate, if we didn't think she was worth it we wouldn't have tried our all either, when Flash G. has found his voice as a betrothed, as a found-wanter, as a prize fighter on which the towel has neatly and shroudly landed:

'Whatever happened to my left hook...?'

Whatever happened to the great manus indeed.

But Stein is more worried ('sorrie, sorrie') about what might happen to Chow. The American's back-chop to his adam's-apple might make him feel that he's left the whole of his neck back there where Chow put him, but he is already moving what he hopes is the rest of his bodily possessions back to the Mini. He senses that it might be their turn to help Chow. And How So Why Not.

2.

They've kidnapped her and for the life of me I don't know why I haven't gone to the cops with my amateur tail between my legs. I don't care what they do to me. It'd be safer with them than fooling around with gutrot Friesman. So what? It doesn't matter now. I'd rather go for her, go for old Chowsie baby, try to gut Friesman myself. That's life. A glorious thing as long as you're dying. But what I want to know is: what the hell am I doing out here. Poor old Flash, you great wonderful no-hoper, you don't know either, do you. You think I know. I don't know. You sit there beside me, we've been here for hours, waiting for Chow to come out and, you great wonderful darkie you, you think I know what we're doing. Nooo.

Stein is getting agitated for action. The dusk, that time of that day in which they have arrived outside this terrace house in Darlinghurst (they didn't get the name of the street) by following Chow (but not inside like he leadening dragged himself inside), the dusk has long ago turned past the last dog's hour. Chow has been inside those peeling walls for two hours, while Asians have come arid gone. Stein and Flash G. are under no illusions about what the place probably is, yet it still amazes their journalistic minds that all of this can be so open. That doesn't matter, too. What matters is that they know their Chow has gone in as a customer. You don't go back to base so seemingly broken of spirit like that; you go to a soothing ground. Let's say a pub.

This ain't as .sure as hell a pub. They look at each other peculiarly attuned. There is no need to say I'm going in there, but not at the same time, and get out of the Mini. They have jointly relief more than a sense of danger. Inside that Mini there has been no automobile designer's dimensions for the ideal stake-out.

To get inside the house requires little more than great cheek of pushing the front door gently. That sweet capnic hall. Stein and Flash G. stand for a moment inside the hallway there until an embroidered robe clad, embroidered slippered, Mandarin capped,

Mandarin sleeved, waxed moustachio'd, sleeved arms folded gent who comes like Charlie Chan's look-alike shuffles tremendously out of the dim interior towards them. At first they think he is making a break for it until he jerks to a halt in front of them with an inquisitive lift of manicured eyebrows as much as ever an inscrutable lift of manicured eyebrows could be inquisitive. He could be accosting them for their next auction bid. And Flash G., the world traveller:

'We likee in. See Number One Matey.'

'You want to look around, look around, fellahs. Have a good time. A bit of Asian pastime,' this relic from the Ming Dynasty has already turned from them and is proceeding back down the hall, must have a winning streak in mahjong going, accompanied by the back waving of long manicured fingernails stuck on the joint, 'never hurt anyone.'

With nowhere else to go except back out in a metre-wide hallway, the nonkidnapped members of The Gang follow what is presumably their host into the business part of the house. Laid back, Stein is thinking, opium must do that to you. A marvellous virtue for the Old deaths. At the part at which they are just about to pass the bottom of the stairs and the Venerable is about to disappear through the door at the end of the hallway, the Venerable half turns and, with as kindly a smile as inscrutability can bring, points an aged claw towards the heavens that lie on past upstairs.

Without missing a beat of their otherwise cakewalk of sorts, they detour to move up the stairs, both in thought-sync not of any danger but whether smoke from the Big O pipes rises or falls. Thickest on tap or thunkest on the blow-out?

But their minds really on Chow about the way he can mysteriously know all things. We want our Milly, Chow. She might be a dog, but this ain't The Year of the Dog as far as I know and no dog pounder like Friesman's going to keep her. She's our buddy, our oppo, our mate, our companion in yarns. She's my writer and if I've got time left I'm going to publish that million dollar best-seller rubbish full of morbid sentiments and that phonetic spelling of hers, and she's this poor sap's fiancée, Chow. You can't lay down on us now, whoever you are.

But Chow has laid down. And so ashamed at letting Milly be taken from under his nose like a third-world reject, he has laid down deliberately on them. On the cot in the corner they can see just so vaguely, over past those other cots they can see too clearly, Chow is spread-eagled upon his back. His great lungs wheeze resonantly above all the rest. The pipe dangles in shadowform from his dangling hand. The cot seems so small it seems to be a mere support of his back and buttocks. He remains as dead to the world as he does to his strange grief, but so essentially peaceful there that Stein and Flash G. back out. They can only wait and wait outside.

And that's all right. They have nowhere else to go. For the time being.

That being in time within a neo-Mini capsule outside lasts for another two hours, during which time Stein takes up Flash G.'s cigarette habit simply because at his time of life in state of health, why not indulge in every deadly vice. There's a few others around that I'd like to get around to, too. Father, where art thou, safe and vegetable-like in thy wheelchair. Let's spin whoopee around the block. Let's shed skin and do it in a dead heat. Because I think I am coming to love you, Father. Your joke at the beginning of my life is an impeccable prophesy of all that is possible at the end of my life. You were trying to tell it like it really is. I've got to say that like they say it. Father, Costas and now Milly. I can't even talk to Flash over there. In that time of waiting for another two hours, Flash G. also sits in a hopeless reverie, of pain, yes, and of ineffectuality, yes, and cannot speak to Stein sitting over there.

They wait for those two hours, the one smoking, the other taking up smoking, turning the Mini into a space like an opium den out of China, and their unalternative patience is just enough to let them be there when the white Merc bursts explosively onto that street calm

215

there, where it does not ennoblingly jolt to a halt outside the terrace house and when there is nothing noble about the ugly way The American they recognise very well now heaves himself out and marches up to and through the front door. This certainly is another Friesman's house. This certainly is not just a regular call by The American.

'Fuck!'

Flash G. has spoken upon legs that have him already out of the Mini and just behind Stein dashing in front of him. He lets him go ahead when he sees the driver of the white Merc see Stein and grinningly grapple with the front seat door to get out and win prizes from Boss Friesman.

As part of the fighter squadron he now is, Flash G. peels off from Stein's slipstream and needs only two felled swoops -- one for to drag the henchie out of the Merc by way of a gnarlish helping hand in what the gentleman was intending anyway; the other for to discover that whatever happened to his once all right left hook was that it really hasn't deserted him. The man must have a glass jaw, straight up. And straight down to a receiving road surface.

Even, then, Flash G. is only a few seconds behind Stein in crashing through the front door and making the top of the stairs.

He arrives by Stein to be part of the instant frieze of Stein by the door and The American frozen with surprise at being caught, about to cut the throat below him. Chow looks like a sacrificial in bliss down there. His neck thrust upwards, his head thrust backwards, his voice thrust open in rictus of gimme the charitable bejesus. This Flash G. sees at the moment The American could go either way, but he is too flushed with the rediscovery of the lost left hook now to be the brunt of the blunt end of the royal prawn or the sharp end of a sluicing knife. He shouts. It is all or nothing, yet it rings and it so punches at The American in its primal challenge of howl that The American is shrugged backwards from his purpose, is storped and, thus unfriezed, realises it.

The American falls away from his intended gutting, swings back onto the charge. They see his face flush and his blond hair crash with annoyance and his bulk breaking towards them. At that instance, Flash G.'s resolve dissolves into the suffering-witness fright of Stein beside him. This sight is fearsome.

But when The American comes on, he just slams past them. They a spray, a puddle he has to get through, and then is gone.

Friesman!

They have found the hotel key in Chow's pocket. Fifty dollars got them out of there, with even the needed assistance of the Mandarin, who has reacted like a little contretemps in the joint now and again merely underlines the whole purpose of the joint anyway. He hasn't helped all that much. One of the great feet of Chow. But for fifty bucks, it's what you get. They have stowed Chow into the Toyota like a university comic who's going to live through life filling up small aerospaces with elephantine humour (the foot over Flash G.'s right shoulder in the front there looking like a block on the old chip; if ever proud Gurton's shoulders have sagged...), and have wielded the car since it seems so reluctant to the private hotel where it would appear to be quite normal to watch one white and one black ergates workerlike in dash for the elevator beneath a great Chinese trunk as though they have just returned from some adjoining estate having exercised their common of estovers. They have tested the capacities of their hearts in the lugging of Chow and have found thankfully that bigness has just beaten burst by the shortest of half head. They have stretched Chow out on the faded red vinyl lounge that would have seen better viewing days before the black-and-white TVs come and gone. Sitting there across from him as he snores on, they realise he looks so outlandish over-proportioned there too that they could have left him snoring on the cot back there in the opium den and saved themselves the distinct possibility of cardiac arrest. Each of theirs. In fits, they have dozed and awakened, dozed and awakened through the rest of that night and most of the rest of that next

217

morning. And each time one of them has stirred and looked anxiously over at Chow he has been almost overwhelmed with the great relief of seeing Chow unmoved and still snoring. Stein and Flash G. have realised during that night and the next morning how much they need the Chinaman.

And Stein is hurting. He is not showing it. He thinks he is not showing it. Carrying the great lug must have jolted the little carcinous nasties to start new excavations at different parts of my vital organs; grind away you little buggers, I've got another lode you're never gonna touch. Yet when he is moaning in his sleep, Flash G. has woken and wondered why he should be so grey and sweating, so unyeasty. Father. Chapter One: My Father was... Images of his father ho more than bone lying uncovered in thick black mud and chattering malarially. I will not die.

These things Stein and Flash G. have been through. In this late morning now, they still have not moved much. There is too much now a bit beyond them in the world to move much. It has become frightening. And Chow first moves, his great snorings jerking out of rhythm then seeming to settle back into him, muffled into a buzz show now. Flash G. talks first for the first time in a long time:

'Who do you reckon he really is, bozo?'

It is a cue for Stein to talk down the pain at and to Chow as though the Chinaman and he have arrived at the same place through the same causes:

'Aspirin. Are there any? I think that little shithead of a doctor was wrong. I don't think it's going to be six months. Who do I reckon you really are, Chow? You'd have to be really off your planet to want to take the silly old cunt and come on top of her and yet you looked to me like you were really ashamed at letting them get away with her. What's it got to do with you, chinky Chow? They blew the dust out of my Costas's head. What's happened since has been sort of funny, you know?, but I feel like I've come to share something with my Costas and my father that I never could while Costas was kicking. Around. Me. I loved him. But you. Why do I think you feel ashamed?'

'What's wrong with you, you ponce?' Flash G., as sensitive as a wounded bull when some other cows are coming home without him. Yet sensitive enough to stiffen when he sees Stein stiffen. He looks across and is as jokingly transfixed as Stein is by the one black and bland eye that Chow has open and unwaveringly upon them. There is nothing ashamed in it and there is nothing of a welcome in it. It surveys them as being there and that's all, and they dare not move while within the scrutiny.

When he does finally open the other eye and move his great head, he merely lifts it to then survey his own body. He could be Gulliver just twigged onto what we Lilliputians have done to him. Then, with a loud fart and a singularly impressive hawking of the throat and a remarkably accurate gorbying that seems to bullseye upon the opposite wall, Chow swings to his feet with a singularly impressive and remarkable accurate agility. His gaze moves slowly around the room. It searchlights across them as though they were not there. He moves into the bedroom with what seems league-boot strides and checks that all is as it was in there, and still Stein and Flash G. have not dared to move, except to glance at each other with some amazement that they have not once thought for all those hours about there having been a bedroom off there.

As Chow emerges again, Flash G. starts to rise to his feet but the Chinaman has already moved to be standing above him before he has got halfway up or before his mind can begin to ponder on the sparks in the quirks of oriental extrasenual perception.

'Sit.'

The voice of Chow explodes shockingly intelligibly to their ears. This is a threat. This is a tone that you do not challenge. Flash G. has re-sat even as his locomotive parts have got the message from its central and very nervous system to for fuck's sake drop back and lie doggo, and only dares to flick a very jaundiced eye upon Stein as much as to say ashamed my arse, you really are a great ponce, you ponce.

Funnily, Stein seems to be hurting inside and bearing it well.

Flash G. is all confused and all angry and all frightened again.

What goes? I'm sitting here between fucking Stein who looks like he's hurting inside and bearing it well and that great bullocky son of a pigtail over there, still staring at us as: though daring us to lift a little finger that's all, and laying; back there with those fucking great meat maulers under his head. What's he waiting for? What are we doing here? Bugger that, what am I doing here? Milly, even the thought of you is rising my tom doodle. Like to slosh it around in you. Give a man a great sense of freedom, like space walking, you great universe of soft smells, you. Come back, my little rich bankroll. What's a little handout or two? Hand in's the thing. What are we waiting for? Shit, that bloke could beat the seven bells of hell out of me. Stein, you ponce, you're looking like Death warmed up, bozo.

In the new nightfall, no electric light yet. In all those hours hardly a movement. They sense the great displacement of Chow swinging himself off the lounge, hear its wooden legs lose something more out of a long life. He could be a ghost before them and they choirboys before its apparition. The next a miracle of the spoken word:

'Do not call me Chow now. Name is Liyi.'

Criado. The word springs associatively into Stein's mind. Jumbles. Rolls. Criado. He tries to cope with it, to bring it to book. Chapter One: The day after my assassination of him, my father was... Stein can feel himself falling backwards. Is this it then? But his body is not tumbled. He is on his feet only. Why? Lightnings of pain jag through his head. He only hears:

220

'You, Frank Stein the young one, come.'

The young one. Yes, Father. Yes, Criado Liyi. Is this a joke? Has something become of monstrous proportions again. The lightnings, stab, jag. Yet he is walking. He hears Flash G. whisper something of urgent inquiry to him. But he is walking. He is shaking his head, no you stay, at Flash G. He feels this. He knows this. He knows you tread alone among the seedings of the past. Whose past, what?

Stein has followed the Chinaman Liyi out of the room. On certain nights, probably nearer dawn in most, my father would have picked up his rifle, rolled away from the dankish groundsheet very weary and very scared too. He would have nodded to his Sergeant Mario Flocco, let's go, think of your wife back home but let's go. Perhaps my father might have thought of me to come, not as just some monstrous joke, just for that moment. Let's go. He would have nodded to the men. They would not have spoken. Only killing is planned in the early hours of the mornings. The animals, the scrub around, .the jungles all further around there, all quite quiet at this hour of the morning, of the finished night. Man plans the kill. This spur of night. And then my father would have moved on before Mario Flocco and on before his men. He would lead them on after his Criado Liyi to the some one place of ambush, trusting him completely. Knowing that at that place they will kill that day.

Stein is following Criado Liyi.

They do not even speak to one another when Liyi accelerates the Toyota at the Friesman iron gates instead of bringing it to a halt. Bringing them to a state of imminent and powerful collision with them. It is inexorable. At the last moment he pulls mortified Stein down with him, drags him down to seat level. Bringing him down. Bringing the gates down. Bringing them just powerfully enough to get through. Stein has never heard such an appalling noise, never had such a metal rendering all around him. Such a silence after.

He feels himself being pulled across the driver's seat by Liyi, heaved out of the door that can open. I'm all right, Liyi, I feel fine. I

221

feel calm. 'Salright. Have we ever made a mess of fucking Friesman's gates. Stein stands beside the Chinaman Liyi, his feet at last on the Friesman manor, knowing that they have come at last to wreck. They stand there quietly, waiting. I am Frank Stein. Costas. I feel how deep down this man beside me is silent at his core.

It is when they come hiving out of the front door that Liyi suddenly moves. He bolts straight at the two men leading The American out. It is a huge rush that hits them even before they can comprehend what is going on. He has clamped them and has half-crushed them together like a working crane, has swept them up and is charging on forward with them as his shield, his battering ram.

The American throws himself away from the path of this phalanx as best he can but, intended for him as it is, it swerves to side-swipe him in midair. He is flung against the wall of the house as his legs are taken away from him. He feels his feet crash against brick, something crack, perhaps an ankle, but keeps rolling, turning, twisting until he can claw his way to his feet. Something is wrong. He feels lopsided. But he stands and hops to swing around to face the Chinese. His face is set with brutality, with the bliss of the instinct to kill. He waits. But is aware of hurting. He seems to have to be hopping to stay upright. It is suddenly too dark. He feels the body come at him first before he can chop down on it. It hits him with all the force of free flight and he cannot stop himself from flying backwards with it.

Even as he realises it is one of his own people, he feels this body of his pulled backwards, something like wire around his throat and something like a knee in his back. The American is still in the feeling of bliss of the instinct to kill as he begins to gag, his head forced backwards as though his neck would surely snap, his mouth erupting, his tongue stretching for air, such an icy wind. He feels his arms thrashing and the bliss reside and the hardness of something too solid under his chin.

Liyi moves one hand from the wire around The American's neck. He shifts slightly his knee in the middle of The American's back.

He continues to force The American's neck back into the low garden brick wall and his chin upon it. With his free hand on top of The American's head he slowly forces the man's jaws shut upon his lolling tongue. The struggling is decreasing and, when he knows it is right to, he releases the wire and bangs down hugely on the top of The American's head with all his great weight. At least an inch of the tongue flies off guillotined. The scream turns Stein sheerly cold.

Turns to a gurgle, but the thrashing frantic, a rictus, for a renewed time. For Liyi is now keeping his great weight upon the top of The American's head so that the jaw can't open and the head can't move. He is now choking The American in his own blood spurting out from the severed tongue.

Stein and Morrie Friesman now standing almost side-by-side. They cannot know what is happening, but both know they are watching something indescribably cruel that they could never come near to. Even when Liyi releases the man, they cannot move. They see The American slump and begin to crawl away. Blood burbles from his mouth and lines his trail.

The American can't see. He can't feel or hear. But instinct makes him crawl away towards the gates.

Now Liyi turns and looks straight at Friesman and nods a silent command. He walks past Friesman and into the house. Morrie Friesman smiles sickly at him as he passes.

His blond wave kicks as he shrugs before moving up the steps behind the Chinaman. In the doorway he turns back to Stein who is still standing there mesmerised with watching The American crawl past the Toyota and the gates to seemingly be lost to the world outside:

'You going to stand there? She's inside upstairs, you arsehole,'

I wonder where he's going, if he's going to die? I don't care. They killed you, Costas, and I'm going to die. Will I be able to crawl away like that. I think there must be some lair we all want to go to. Did you? Would've you crawl back home to me? You see, I'm here. I made it. Chow, Liyi, I can't think of him as Liyi, some son or nephew or something of our Criado. Chow finally brought me here to get Milly, I think. I don't know if he knows I'm going to kill Friesman. Do you? Costas, do you know if you can bring the rage to me when I need it now? It should be. We shouldn't always be so weak, all of us always.

Yet there is a heaviness inside him that is almost unbearable. He feels as though he should drop to all fours and follow the blood trail of The American. Not even the thought that The American may have been at Milly can spur him on to anything other than to plod his way of pursuit of Friesman. Christ.

He stands in the hallway upon the Italian black-and-white marble tiles and for a moment imagines himself a chess piece, the last one on the board, a solitary pawn, and meat if he moves right or wrong for the falling chandelier up there. He listens for a short pawn's time to vaguely infuriating conversational tones of the voices of Liyi and Friesman in the room off to his right and two down (pawn could move to L14) before moving, with the true stunted progress of a pawn, up the stairs. The first steps are hard, but the next better and the next better still. Stein feels his blood begin to pump hard back into body with each step. I am really in here, a step, I am here, a step, and I am moving.

Stein feels his body once more and jumps alive. He pumps it up the rest of the stairs. Here is the rage, it's coming, it's come. I'm here and by Christ I'm pumping. Milly! Stein is running skywards. He hears her answering cry. He calls her name again but doesn't slow down even at all at her second answering cry. He has known she would call out for him again and his senses will radar in upon. There is no unsharpened question of it.

He swerves into the bathroom, claws involuntarily at the steam. God, they have rammed her into one of those 1940s steam bath boxes and turned up the steam. Stein pulls his way into that vast damp hot steam-dripping area. Her head will be the fattest thing of her.

'Milly!'

'Over here, you silly cunt!'

Fog-bound, Stein makes it into the very far corner of the torture chamber. The drifting damp mist, like scales, clear from his eyes, his momentary panic of asphyxiating subsiding, his next cry for her to hang on. Milly for God's sake.

Milly sits back in the bubble bath that has overflowed the sunken pink bath like salt-spray puffs on a surf-won beach. Her toes are wriggling and her head bobbing. All else is fluff and pink bubbles in the air. All around her looks like an unguentarium, even the erythrites to match the colour of her radiant complexion, even those impossible to imagine to match her natural complexion. And Stein so in shock at this turn-up that, yes, he slips on a cake of soap in the shape of a poodle that she has on a string lead and winds up by dint of slide and slather a static measurer of his own length upon those black tiles at the bath's edge, literally only centimetres away from being eyeball to eyeball with her. That I should live to see such ruddy tracks in life.

And Milly leaning easily across ever so pertly to kiss him on the end of his nose as her toes wriggle in the greater luxury of being appreciated to being in a state of luxury:

'Steiny-weiny darls, I should never have left home. Do be careful of the grouting, dear.'

Damp and very damply, Stein makes his way back to the fog and goes downstairs. Fucking Friesman's beat me again.

He finds them silent and steps into the room. I could be in a merchant banker's boardroom. The lines of bookcases. The panelling of walnut. The cabriole desk that Friesman is sitting

225

thoughtfully behind, without shocking injuries, only slightly cut back as if he was on the wrong side of the best option of a deal having to be swallowed not too hardly. Liyi, that great man, suddenly looking like Chief of Corporate Affairs standing statuesquely with the phone in his hand like he is waiting confidently to be told it's up on the ole tickertapes tonite. I never realised he wore a suit. And being beckoned in by fucking Friesman like it was the quiet and secretive after-hours and me the cleaner to do a quick whip-around. Get in, lower thing, do your quick flick-around and be gone, you won't understand anyway. Men's talk. Stein, quite admiring his own cleaner's presumption, hears himself shouting:

'Friesman!'

meaning I've come to get you, Friesman. I'm here. The cops couldn't do it. All the silk brigade wouldn't do it. All the loners and the paupers and the suckers and the shysters and the hooked-upped and the down-turned and the victims and the run-downs and the in-up-to-their-necks and all the good guys and all the God's-in-His-heavens have never dared to do it. All these years, you've got away with it, fucking Friesman. Those years of the con. Puppeteering people like you've got a license to make human beings assets. But we're here now, Costas and me. My father, Costas and me, we're here now and you might be the dentist, Friesman, but I'm the patient with your balls right in the middle of my hand, you nothing.

'Friesman, you,' and the beauty of it is, fucking Friesman, you, 'you stink filth!' is that I am in rage and it's sweet at last.

And the amazing thing is that Friesman does not fall to his supplicating knees, nor does the Chinaman Chow-Liyi pull away from the single crushing of this low-life, but both put their fingers up to their lips, oh do be quiet, can't you see we're on the phone? And the other amazing thing is that Stein finds that he has not moved at all from that doorway there after all and that he has actually rebuked himself for making a sound that might have disturbed some far-flung operator's sensibilities. Satellites have

226

ears. And the yet more amazing thing is that Liyi is now talking into the phone piece as though he really was in the boardroom of BHP after a willing apprenticeship following a degree from Sydney Uni in corporate affairs after a scholarship from Singapore or somewhere suitable for an upstanding and upcoming lad. Stein, the cleaner, doesn't understand anyway, and stands reverently with metaphoric duster in one hand and the metaphoric trolley of the waste bin trailing in the other, while international affairs he could not possibly understand take place over the phone at the very moment he has stumbled into the boardroom of BHP at the very wrong moment. Chow the boardroom exec, speaking chow, and then going:

'... Father, I speak English now. Mr Friesman must understand all the choices. What? Ha, yes,' looking across at Friesman, 'no choice. That is right. Mr Friesman? He is ready to talk to you now, Father. He has apologised for having been impolite to you.'

Stein watches his once mute, poor-bruiser, thick-brained Chinese (the world I've got wrong; the wax is gonna wan me) literally demote this Friesman to a messenger boy with a holding out of the phone towards Friesman and one of those nods that Stein has come to know as undeniable in the corridors of power on a cleaner's circuit. And even his rage has dived back into its cage for the fascination of watching Friesman get wearily up off his chair and actually stand almost to attention to take the call with Hong Kong.

'Morrie Friesman. Yes, Father Liyi. Yes, I agree. Fifty per cent and your right to territory. Okay, let our lawyers agree and have a nice day in Honkers.'

Returns the phone, returns to his desk, returns the bland look of Liyi. It says, even to the Stein eye, we've got a deal. This smugness is all too much. I am Stein. What the shag has this to do with anything?

'Friesman!'

But suddenly it's all Friesman, not he, who is in rage:

'Shut up, you piece of turd. Punk. Worm. Fucking dope. When I want you to talk, I'll lift the dunny seat. You're lucky to be alive, you punk.' I am not listening to this. I am listening to this. Costas. 'You turd. You cement drop in the ocean, Stein. You think you idiots can rabbit around town and drop Morrie Friesman right in it? You shitheads. Maggots. You're lucky, punk. Take slackguts up there and wonder off free, but don't you ever show your punk heads in any of my places ever again.'

'Mr Stein,' Liyi, a great blockage come hoven between Stein and Friesman, corporate and executive now, 'take advice. You go now with the lady.'

'No, Chow.'

'Not Chow. Liyi; Criado Liyi. You're something to do with my father, I know you are.'

Now Friesman, the shrug of the Chinaman taking him away from being between them: 'Your father. That dummy. Lay off with your brother Costas, punk, or I squash you underfoot without laying a heel on you. I never touched your brother and none of mine did. Look under your own rock. Now beat it, you Stein slag.'

Oh, the rage. Stein doesn't feel it come. It just comes. He is already three parts across the room flying at Friesman before he even realises he has moved to kill Friesman by some grace of fixed tearing. He has a moment of exhilaration then Friesman is before him. But on his feet already before him, and somehow upsetting some sort of applecart of procedure, of how it all should be. Stein feels some sort of pain, I shouldn't be here. He tries to stop this crazy momentum of suddenly the other way to the way he should be Friesman going. He feels his back thump against the sharp edge of the desk, he thinks, has the dust of the carpet assaulting his nose. He feels the weight on his back, has the vague pounding on the back of

228

his head. There are sounds of Friesman above him. He's killing me. How can that be? I should be hearing all this better. What?

Stein lies there in a sudden silence. The weight is lifted from his back. There are no more sounds that he can't figure out. He cries out, tries to scream. Tries to thrash his way upwards and out of this. Costas. But there is a pressure on his back, but this time more gentle and soothing words are coming at him from above there. There is not yet a moving. The more gentle pressure is just as irresistible. He realises he is hearing the voice of Liyi sibilating just behind his ear, commanding but in slow-down. But in steady now steady. And it is saying:

'Mr Stein, you go now. Mr Friesman and I are good friends now. No more Americans now. I come and see you later.'

Then there is Milly at the door. It is odd, Stein is thinking as he is somehow being carried past her, that the silly bitch is chewing gum like that, what is it about eating and getting gut cramps while you're swimming or having bubble baths? She is patting him on the cheek and I'm sure I can feel the silly bitch laying a big lipstick one right on that bald patch I've got up there. Bloody cheek. I do believe I'm being carried out bodily. That warm and sweet and ricey breath of Chow, no Liyi. Criado. Father, Friends, he and Friesman. Fucking Friesman, I'm going to kill you. Bastard. Friends? It is odd, too, Stein is thinking how the night feels so cool out there. The crunching of the great Liyi clodhoppers on the gravel beneath me, they could be my feet, those great legs my legs. Life. Like life. I go into fucking Friesman's pad wet behind the ears and come out carried like a baby. Get off.

'Get off.'

He is put on, first the bonnet of the car. This is this Toyota, I think that is me reflected in that windscreen. He ; is put in, next gently, he can feel it gently as gently as it is, into the front seat. The womb I've recently come out of, going back in. Stein thinks he has shouted get off to Criado Liyi or Chow or whoever he is, but nobody's taken any notice of me. Monstrous joke. Frank Err Stein. Yep, that's me. Get off, all of you. I can hear that engine going. I know that this car is going. I know I'm going. Friesman, friend? Chow said he would see me later. I think I'm going to throw up.

As Milly Hunt grinds the Toyota backwards out of its metal crush with what's left of the gates and convinces it to grind towards home, or what's left of home, with what is just mechanically left to it automechanically, what is left to Stein to stop him from throwing up just then and there beside her is the invidious fascination he has of her gaudy red high heels on the pedals topped with nothing but her fairly considerable mountains of naked flesh. Driving on the naked highway like that before my own naked eyes. A man could throw up. How can she chew gum like that in a state like that? Disgusting.

The Gang confers again. They seem to be realising that it is for the last time and, leastways, they are sitting silently around Milly's living room. Neither one seems to be willing to break that silence, and that's not just because they and Stein know and knows he is still hurting (looking ringwormy like that he reminds Flash G. of former glorious bush-tucker times, but that's not to be said at this time either). They each feel the wash-up. No more heists against Friesman. They each don't know why, nor why they really began it all in the first place.

They sit there with nothing really changed. A few laughs. But nothing accomplished. Friesman still up and away. More unknown to them than when they began. Milly Hunt feeling the taking of bubble baths a truer destiny for a classy dame she can yet be easier than trying to write for a million dollar royalty take; Flash G. feeling the taking of a rich white bitch wife a truer destiny for a true gentleman of the ethnic ring than fireballing it any longer with Caucasian and Mongolian gents of shady connections. And almost as safe when you think about it.

230

Stein feeling the truer destiny is to give up gracefully to the final destiny of every human being. It's not so much after all what's happened to you and yours while you're *in*; it's how you cope with getting *out*. The last laugh. The butt of the monstrous joke turning out to be me who laugheth lasteth, and that would be nice. Costas, I feel you are settling in your grave and wouldn't feel too bad against me now. I would like to see Lorna and the kids again. Just once would be enough. Let them at last give me the long farewell with tears in their eyes and hanging around my neck. Poison phials probably. We're going to remember you, Father. I could get one last boot into Lorna's slackguts. A barrel close-ranged. My head aches deep inside. I guess the cancer cells are multiplying even quicker now.

For a conference, The Gang sits in silence for a long, long time. It is the soup of twilight all round.

'Nobody blow a fuse talking,' Flash G., suddenly pugnacious in wanting to get on with the marriage vows and the swapping of cheques with invoices. But apparently catching Milly on the uphand of a harddoneby thought:

'How could anybody write anything interesting about you two deadheads anyway?'

'Come off it, gal.'

But when hot, Milly is really hot:

'Don't silly cunt old Milly Hunt. I had a million dollars staring me in the sweet puss, and you two blew it, didn't you what. Trouble with you two is who'd want to read about you two? Where's your oomphf, you silly cunts? A girl needs inspiration to bring out the best in a promising writing career. Pin-stripes, and drunken polish. Hard-boozing. *Womanising*, for buggery's sake! What'd I get for trying to stick with you? Not even proper *womanizing*! Hey, I wouldn't have you for my publisher. I reckon you tried to come on top of me, making me think you were a publisher. I wouldn't let you publish my book because you'd be too much of a dill to publish it.'

'So there, bozo.' Flash, flashily at Stein and springing to her almost married side.

'You leave him alone. You're just as bad.' She leaping to Stein's hurting kidney side.

The Gang is conferring. They sit in silence again. Until Stein can look up to her. He looks so ashen that, in a fit of compassion for him she cannot understand, she almost wishes she could bite her biting tongue; just as well it instantly passes:

'Milly, have I ever told you that when you're nude, you're sure as hell nude.' Stein.

'Never mind me.' Her.

'I don't mind. We got in there and tried. But, Milly, what you've got to do now is just go to the cops.'

'What for?' All round-eyed innocence.

'About Costas, and whatever. Whoever. Tell them now. Don't let Friesman, all the Friesmans get away with it. Say it.'

'I don't know what you mean.'

'What you know, darls.' Flash G., thinking with relief that they probably haven't got around as yet to allow conjugal visits for female prisoners. Don't worry about anything; I'll look after the money angle outside. Just sign here.

'What about Costas? I don't know anything about Friesman doing over anybody. Morrie wouldn't do that, not for real.'

'Fucking hell, wouldn't he?' Flash, flushing.

'Am I hearing right?' Stein, his voice as weary as he looks now.

'Morrie's a big cream puff.'

'What about the set-ups you gave us?'

'What about them? I know them, but I knew they wouldn't really lead anywhere. You wanted the places you could get at Morrie. I gave 'em. I had to have some local colour for the book. Don't call me a silly cunt.'

'I see.' Stein lies back on the couch. He is feeling better, though more tired. Somehow it is good for it to have all petered out this way. 'Do you mind if I wait here for Chow? I think he'll be coming to see me.'

'You all right, bozo?'

'Yeah. I was just wondering what we're all going to do.' He closes his eyes.

'Me,' she, reaching metaphorically already for her cosmetic case, 'I'm going to take up Morrie's offer.' .

'Whatdya mean?' Flash G.

'He said I still had it, the sweetie. Come on back home, he said, be my housekeeper. A bubble bath a day keeps the rectum open. I'm going to be the classiest matron of a tart in this town.'

'What about us getting hitched?' Flash G. on the gosh.

'I'll organise his business conventions and all that stuff.'

'You white nontribal, what about these tears you're bringing to my eyes?'

'Not all over the nice, clean carpet, dear boy.'

Pause.

'You couldn't.' Flash G. oh-welling at her, 'tide a bloke over with a few bob?'

Stein continues to wait for Liyi. He snoozes alone without the light on. Flash G. has left to restore his faith in sporting ' mankind by kicking a few cub reporters (Cubs O, Gurton 5 off the right boot). Milly has left to restore her face about this Morrie Friesman town.;

Stein waits, and dares to know that it is not yet quite finished.

Liyi seems to be part of a dream sitting across the room there. Has he just come or has he always really been there? He sits like a visitor at my bedside. Even if I could make him out, I would know that he has been coming here for a very long time. That long horizon over my shoulder ever since that day on Timor when my Father turned to me and us as we watched the 45th Division of the Jap Army land down below us and he said, 'Bugger them. Let's get on with the job.' A lot of killing. That long horizon over my shoulder. Criado.

'Criado.'

'Yes, Mr Stein.'

Liyi is carrying a rifle. Even in this light across over there I can see it's a rifle leaning up against the seat by him. Stein waves a hand at it in order to ask why but he finds he is already listening to the why and the whys and they are no surprise. Hospital beds of hard bamboo at Changi and the right to know the whys, not surprising. The soft and sweet and ricey breath of Liyi, yes. He keeps looking at the rifle, that drowsy form, and he hears the voice of Liyi whispering to him through the jungle ferns of our ambush, toning above the rumble of the Jap trucks coming up the trail of how they are coming and how he has come. It is all no, no, surprise. I am come, the voice says, because it is owed to you, because your father associated with one of our cousins during the great war on the island of Timor a long time ago, because of the murder of your brother, because you think that our present associate the man Friesman did that to your brother. Look at the rifle; I have brought it here. I am looking at the rifle and I know it is the .22 that killed my Costas. It is the rifle that has killed your brother Costas Stein who we know was not really your brother but the son of Sergeant Mario Flocco, who was also with our cousin Liyi during the great war on the island of Timor. Your father adopted him and Costas hurt so much when your father told him so cruelly. This rifle is not of anything to do with our present associate, the man Friesman. Listen. I am listening. You are owed this explanation... In the great war on the island of Timor our cousin the Criado of your father and Flocco asked them for help when the war is over to ship a great haul of a certain drug back to Shanghai where our family was once strong. I am listening. Our family had paid very much money to Portuguese officials to buy this certain store of drugs before the Japanese had come. It was ours and our cousin Liyi had it buried in a cave in the mountains. I am listening: in the mountains where my father won his VC. Listen, this one Mario Flocco betrayed your father and he was shot and then he betrayed our cousin Liyi as the one who did that and our cousin Liyi was shot too. After the war this one Mario Flocco returned to that island of Timor for our family's property and brought it back to Australia where he set up many operations here. It is said our property was worth five million pounds to him and his American friends down here. I am listening and I know it was heroin. But it belonged to our family, our Tong, so it became the way of rightness when we had to move to Hong Kong from Shanghai to have our associate down here, the man Friesman, deal with the thief Flocco and to take over the empire that was and is rightfully ours. I am telling you this because you are owed. I am listening. We were glad when your father the Commissioner adopted the young boy Flocco. Costas, listening. It was good that the children of our cousin Liyi's friends should prosper we thought but we did not know then why the boy was adopted. 'Why', what do you mean 'why'? Then our own Mr Friesman began to prosper so well too that he fell under the influence of the Americans too and began to consider that his empire was not rightfully ours. So I was trained, Mr Stein, and I have come to this new country and our family will come too when the Communists take back Hong Kong when the Treaty is finished. We will take up what is rightfully ours as you have heard the man Friesman agree to. Are you listening, Mr Stein? I am listening, Criado Liyi, are they coming, how far do you think? Our family has protected you and your two friends because we do not want trouble. We are sorry that I let you down with the lady that one time. Nonetheless the man Friesman did not kill your half-brother, you must understand that now. I understand. Nor did the Americans, do you understand? I understand. Above all these reasons, you are owed an explanation for two main reasons, Mr Stein. I am listening. The first is that when he thought he too could take alone what is rightfully ours, the man Friesman was at first protected by your own police at the time your father was Commissioner, do you understand? No. The second reason, Mr Stein, is our family does not know but I know, my new friend, you are dying. Yes. I understand..

You will feel better soon, Mr Stein.

Yes, I understand you have drugged me, Chow.

'You have been nodding, Mr Stein, so I think you have been listening and understanding what I have told you. My family does not know I am doing this, but I am taking you now to the house where this rifle that killed your brother came from. I wish you well. I have enjoyed our meeting...'

There was no light in the house, except the small globe on the front corner of the eaves he knows so well. There are the house lights down the end of the driveway where Luce might be home and little kid Kevvie would be screaming. The pines along the driveway still the dark threats they have always boyhood been for him. My father

236

might be dead. How long has it been since I have since stepped down here? All these miles backwards and forwards, up and down here, and always with the same foreboding that I have now somehow. I am not surprised to be walking back.

Stein walks down the driveway of his father's house. He is still feeling more the great, gentle, sweet and ricey pressure of the Chinaman Liyi squeezing his arm before he has stepped out of the Toyota. He is aware most of all of himself swinging the rifle in a casual way that should not be, coming to the possie along the trail. Where the ambush that's always been. There was a time, too, when my father rode a bicycle into a Japanese camp firing an Owen gun as he went. Unharmed he went pedalling out of the other side of the camp. They found eleven Japanese dead in their huts there. He had pedalled towards a VC...

I understand.

Now. I think.

I must be understanding now. Waking up to where and what I am now. I have not said a word to Liyi in all that way that he has driven me back to this place, this my own father's place, and yet he did nod to me in that sweet, warm and ricey way to what he knew I was thinking of understanding, so I must be understanding now, and that's a fact. This gravel crunching beneath me is the same crunch of mine and Costas's and my father's and it is the sounding shell that is taking me back through all of time. It might as well be. Should I say that I have come to this? I have to ask is this what it's all come to. Back here. Step. One. Step. Two. Step. Three. I used to do this when I was coming back down here from kindergarten, would you believe. I am doing it now. This is my signal and I'm on my shunt line, ever shunt line. Yes, and so this is it.

Stein is momentarily standing beneath the pale globe under the eaves of his coming home. There is for sure no brass band welcoming me. It is as it always was. He moves the few paces to stand on the front doorstep and tries to breathe regularly when he realises his heart is thumping. I might be too late. Perhaps I should just lie here on my father's doorstep. Stein stands there on his father's doorstep, and waits, and it is very dark.

When the doorway light goes on above him, he seems to stagger back a pace but steadies to hold his ground. It floods him. The bright eye of God, but glaring. Stein sets himself to stay when his instinct is to run, as he seems to have been doing from this door all his life. I still fear you, father, don't I, but it's all right this time. Just the centre of the stage. Let the door be open now.

It is, with a suddenness that is rude. He sees his father's face coming at him sneeringly as it ever was before it dissolves into the form of old Cowcher standing there. Cowcher stands blocking the way in. This is my threshold. Stein senses rather than sees the custodian of his father shift his eyes from Stein to the rifle, notices the old form stiffen and then relax as though some air from it has escaped.

'Cowcher, I've come to see my father.'

Cowcher steps forward to him then. Stein has never noticed before what a hard man he really is. This crusty and wiry old man of some faded regiment and an eternal fierce loyalty. And the veins upon his head and forearms. Those black striving grafts. He lets Cowcher take the rifle from him and turn back into the house. Their eyes have met just very briefly but it has been enough to make Stein wait a polite moment before following the old man. Stein has seen tears there. You are old, old man.

Inside, there are only a few candles. My house lies underground. Stein does not turn towards the front room where he guesses his father lies dead, but moves down the catacomb to Cowcher's room. The air is dank and fetid down here. I have come to our burial place. The restless spirits, we will wander in the shades. But Costas, I feel you are still. I feel you have gone from this Stein vault at last and are still. I never meant us to hurt you.

238

By the time Stein reaches Cowcher's room, Cowcher has all but finished packing his one suitcase. Stein leans against the doorframe watching him like I used to do when I was a boy, this man who had the way in to my father, and is as silently reverent now as he ever and always was. The rifle lies on the bed. Placed neatly there, as though a final act of careful duty.

Cowcher stands up and topples but rights himself with the help of the wardrobe. I am old, young man. He picks up the suitcase and nods once at Stein.

'I have been waiting for you to come back, young Stein.'

He walks. He walks past Stein. He walks down the cold passageway, his movement disturbing the candles, the lamps of the underground passages. Cowcher walks out of the front door of the tombs of Stein. He moves away to his own somewhere dark corner.

This, my father. This VC. This Rhodes Scholar. This hero. This Commissioner of Police. This great man.

This insanity.

This me.

Stein stands above his father wondering why he has never noticed the animation still left in that face. He realises it has always seemed dead to him until now. I am seeing my father alive for the first time ever. I saw him wince when I switched on the lights. I have never noticed how his eyes are dead. How his hands still twitch beneath the rug. How. you won't, die, will you, because there is still too much amusing. Those green blurs of eyes are not so cataract bound.

Stein senior sits below Stein. The nerve in his neck Js leaping. He smells of urine. He smells of cold sweat. Food stains, the front of his gown. The stubble on his chin. You are mummy, Daddy.

239

Cowcher has left you unkempt of later Stein doesn't know whether his father can hear:

'I don't know whether you can hear. I can only guess. I've always guessed about you, haven't I? I've never known, and it's still the same. See, I'm here, old man. Your monstrous joke. I've come back to tell you I understand. How it must have been. Those years in Changi, those hospital beds. When you heard they had Criado Liyi shot and Flocco had got back to take over the haul you knew Liyi had; stashed, I guess you realised what Flocco had done to you. So you used your authority to get at Friesman... remember Friesman?... and have Flocco kidnapped by him. And tortured by him. And killed by him. While you were supposed to be running the investigation. So you backed Friesman into the big time, didn't you? My father, Commissioner of Police, murderer, thief and racketeer. Yet that revenge still wasn't enough, was it? That bullet, those years in Changi, those hospital beds, Criado Liyi and that fortune mostly lost. I can only guess. There had to be more against the line of Flocco. So you adopted my brother, that man who I loved, and you waited until he was a grown man with a family because to pay out on a boy wasn't enough pay out on his father. You had to see the line grow first, didn't you? You had to change the name Flocco first and then you had to cut the line. You held my Costas under sentence of death all those years and you would have contracted Cowcher to do it for all that time. Your monstrous joke. I thought it was me. Costas all the time. Raising him and praising him and playing proud father and savouring the pay out to Flocco all that time. My father. This living monument to hate. This insanity. I guess you might have always even been mad. The irony is that I might die before you. I don't mind if I do. I am so programmed by you that I can't even look down on you at a time like this. But if there's nothing beyond here I would like to think I could be there to tell you there's nothing and if there's something beyond here I like to think I'll be there to pay witness against you. I hope so. Oh, I hope so, old man. But then...'

(Stein leaves him alone in a very bright lighting.)

'… you see. I've only ever been able to guess and you know that.'

In the house of Frank Ern Stein, they finally just had to discover the by-then monstrous forms of Stein Senior and Stein Junior in their separate chambers.

In the Frank E. R. R. Stein chamber of the House of Stein, the police found a .22 rifle by the body. But it was obvious that it was no killing weapon. It was taped upright against the old typewriter there. As if a flag pole. As if a flag, part of a sheet tied to the forward gun sight. As if an ensign, that flag had an emblem drawn upon it.

It was a large and square head and it seemed to have slant eyes like a Chinese and what could have been a large bolt sticking out on either side of its neck maybe to attach olden electrical lugs to. On the head looked to be a lot of stitches.

The Detective-Sergeant who was first there was anxious to get out of the room because it was smelling quite a bit by now. But he stopped to puzzle over the flag at the end of the rifle. Then he called his offsider in and, holding the flag out as perhaps for some last proud ceremonial flutter, asked him:

'What do you reckon this is? Some kind of joke?'